THE CUNNING
OF THE DOVE

The Cunning of the Dove

Alfred Duggan

NEW ENGLISH LIBRARY
TIMES MIRROR

First published in Great Britain by Faber & Faber Ltd., 1960

© Alfred Duggan, 1960

*

FIRST NEL PAPERBACK EDITION JULY 1974

*

NEL Books are published by
New English Library Limited from Barnard's Inn, Holborn, London E.C.1.
Made and printed in Great Britain by Hunt Barnard Printing Ltd., Aylesbury, Bucks.

45001822 9

Contents

ENGLAND
in 1043
~ 11 ~

SCOTLAND. Tweed. Holy Island

Solway Firth

IRISH
DANES

EARLDOM OF NORTHUMBRIA

Ribble Ilkley Humber

DANISH

MERCIA

EAST
ANGLIA

WALES

ENGLISH MERCIA

WATLING STREET

Severn

COTSWOLD

London
Thames

KENT
Canterbury

Glastonbury
Athelney

WESSEX

Winchester

SUSSEX

Prologue

It was said by the wise men of old: 'Call no man happy until he is dead.' I am still alive, but in the nature of things I cannot expect many more years; and I am happy at present, in a household where I am held in honour. I cannot be accused of boasting when I say my life has been happy, and I can look for it to be happy right up to the end. A castle is a queer sort of place to live in; I work among foreigners and serve a foreign lord. But as chamberlain to the Count I am a local personage, and I shall end my days within a mile of the house where I was born, surrounded by the grandsons of boys who played with me when I was a boy. That is always best, to come home at the end to the scene of the beginning, to be buried in the church of one's baptism.

If I had been no more than a happy man there would be little to tell. But for much of my life I filled a humble post in the intimate service of the great. I was never an actor in great events, no one ever followed my advice or depended on my help; but because I was insignificant, and I suppose because I was also easy to get on with and a good listener, I heard what went on behind the scenes. Sometimes I talk at supper-time of the stirring days of my youth, and of the holy King who was once my master. The other officers of the Count are always interested in my stories, and whenever a great man visits us I am called to the high table to answer questions. So when one of the Count's chaplains offered to write down what I should tell him I thought it would be absurdly modest to refuse. Of course I have to tell my story in French, and he writes it in Latin; that means that I can't break into verse to mark a crisis, or rattle off a jingle of alliterations when things seem dull. That is how good writers keep alive the interest of their readers, but then I am only a chamberlain. Peter the chaplain says he must write in Latin, because no one has settled how French ought to be spelled and there are so many different ways of pronouncing it; and if I told him my tale in English he would interrupt every minute to ask the meaning of some unusual word. He understands English well, for a foreigner; but it is a difficult language, full of compound words and poetical metaphors. Even my holy master sometimes stumbled in it, though it had been the tongue of his infancy; when he had to say something important, which must be accurately understood by his hearers, he would sometimes drop into French without noticing it. I have seen great Earls very angry at being addressed in a foreign language which they could not understand; and they would be even more angry when my master switched to Latin, the best language for real accuracy.

But there it is. The curse of Babel was especially a curse on the great. A humble ploughman may live and die believing that all the sons of Adam speak as he speaks; a burgess of the great city of Winchester knows that in Christendom there are hundreds of languages, and that men who deal with the world at large must be patient of clumsy translation. I think in English and speak in French; Master Peter thinks in French and writes in Latin. I shout through the fog as clearly as I can. But the reader must do his share of the work; for undoubtedly a great fog lies between us, the fog of vanished manners and a dying language.

CHAPTER I

The Lady Emma

I was born in the year 1027. That was the year when the great Canute, the King of the North, was received honourably in Rome by the Pope and the Emperor. It was a good time to be born, for there was peace and prosperity in England, and especially in Winchester, the home of Kings. I was the eldest son of my father, and so I was christened by his name, Edgar. I grew up among a crowd of younger brothers and sisters, but they do not come into this story. Indeed my father scarcely comes into it, for we were not important folk; but it is important that my father was the best cordwainer in Winchester.

When rude urchins want to insult a cordwainer they shout after him: 'Stinking cobbler!' But making shoes is the least part of his skill. The real art is in the dressing and dyeing of the leather, to make it smooth and supple, to colour it a bright and even red or green or blue; above all, to tan it with as little offensive smell as possible, and then perhaps to fix a pleasant scent throughout the fabric. Anyone who can do that, as my father could, will find it easy to sew pieces of soft leather into fine shoes for the nobility.

The King and his court were often in Winchester, more often than in any other city of England. There were plenty of rich folk to buy our shoes, and as a child I was always well fed and well dressed. When the great King of the North died I was eight years of age. Canute's peace died with him, and for the next seven years there was constant war throughout England. But we in Winchester were protected from the worst of these troubles, for our noble city is the traditional dowry of the Lady of England. The widowed Lady Emma came to live permanently among us. She had a great hall of her own, quite distinct from the King's hall; and there she stayed all the year round, protected by a bodyguard of the mighty housecarles who had fought for King Canute, and served with the splendour that was the due of the widow of two Kings (though King Ethelred her first husband was almost forgotten, and she was always spoken of as the widow of King Canute).

The axebearers of her bodyguard kept the peace in Winchester, even while the rest of England was ravaged by the wars between the sons of Canute. Not quite so many rich nobles came to buy my father's shoes; but the family still lived well, and so did all the city.

In my fourteenth year my father had to decide how I was to earn a living, for soon after my fourteenth birthday I must be bound apprentice. I was not the heir to my father's business, for we English burgesses follow a custom which must always be explained to incredulous foreigners: the heir to a craftsman is his youngest son, not his eldest. That is fair, when you come to think of it; a man's eldest son will be settled in life by the time his father dies, it is the baby in the nursery who must live on the stock in the family shop until he is old enough to support himself.

The trouble was that I could not abide leatherwork, especially the stink of it. I have always been in love with cleanliness, and perhaps more nice and dainty than is fitting for a common burgess. In childhood, if I dirtied my hands by accident I would run sobbing to my mother and beg to be washed, and I was always bothering her to give me a clean shirt when she thought the old one would do for another two or three days. Tanbark revolts me; the stench of undressed hides is even worse; even the pungent but not unwholesome smell that comes from the bubbling dyevats is more than I can bear.

Three friends of my father in the same line of business refused to take me as apprentice, when they noticed how I wrinkled my nose at the smell of their workshops. After the third refusal my father brought me home in anger, and stormed at my mother for encouraging my ridiculous love of cleanliness. 'The boy's too dainty for this fallen world,' he shouted. 'He'll never eat bread in the sweat of his brow. If he were a savage Dane we could send him off to be a viking, but that's no life for a civilised Englishman. The minister won't look at him; monks preach that too much washing is evil luxury. He's fit for nothing but to carry basins of scented water for some fat old woman to wash her hands in.'

'Then that's just what he'll do,' answered my mother with spirit. (Her father had farmed his own land until he was ruined by ravaging Danes, and she thought she had come down in the world by marrying a cordwainer.) 'There's a fat old woman at the end of the street, and I hear she has vacancies in her household.'

'That's no way to speak of the Lady of England, the King's mother,' said my father severely. 'All the same, it's an idea. I must go to her hall in a day or two, as soon as I have finished that pair of purple slippers. I know a chamberlain slightly, and I shall ask if he has room for a clean young page. Would that suit you, little Edgar? There's no future in a job like that, and you will never be your own master. But you will live softly, if you do as you are told. Someone has to carry wine for these great lords, though it's not really honest work. But then you turn up your nose at honest work.'

I had never before thought of such a calling, but as soon as it was mentioned I saw it was exactly what I wanted. I am not lazy. I would not be in charge of all the menservants in a large castle if I could not be trusted to keep them up to their work. But I like to do my work in pleasant surroundings, particularly in surroundings that smell sweet. There are always a few stinks about, even in a prosperous castle; but now it is my job to get them cleared away as quickly as possible, and I do it willingly. 'I like living in a crowd, for people amuse me; every man in the world is quite different from every other man, when you get to know him, and it is my delight to know people and revel in their difference. I am always willing to obey orders, or to give them if that is my duty. I consider that a mark of civilisation. Only heathen Danes try to live on a little patch of land, paying no taxes and obeying no lord; Christians must remember that we are all members of one another, and that nothing worthwhile can be accomplished unless one man directs and many obey him.

A few days later I left home for ever to live in quite a different world, though it was only a furlong away from the little house where I had been born. I had expected to wear different clothes, to eat different food, to keep different hours; it was a shock to

11

discover that I must also learn a different language.

While the under-steward was fitting me out in my livery, a handsome red tunic and leggings of white linen crossed by garters of narrow red cloth, he informed me of this.

'You will begin by standing about in the anteroom to the Lady's chamber. She likes to be served by boys and young men. In the anteroom there are always housecarles who decide which visitors should be admitted, and women to help the Lady when she needs them. But when she rings her little bell for someone to run an errand you will answer it; she calls her women by name. The only trouble is that she may give you her orders in French. It's her native tongue, and at home she prefers to speak it. If you don't understand what she says to you, ask her to repeat it in Danish. She doesn't mind doing that. But she gets very angry with servants who are too shy to ask for a translation, especially if they then guess what she wants, and guess wrong.'

When he saw my look of dismay he added kindly: 'It won't be long before you understand French, though it's a tricky language to speak correctly. There are a great many Frenchmen in this hall, and the rest of us can manage it fairly well; so you will hear it spoken all round you. In any case, the Lady won't be conversing with you. She will only tell you to fetch something. Learn the French words for comb and wine and a basin of water and a few other things, and you will soon be as useful to her as if you had been born and bred in Rouen as she was.'

The under-steward was quite right. A great many of the upper servants in the Lady's hall were French-born, including nearly all the women in her bedchamber. She liked to be surrounded by people who understood French, though it was enough if they understood it; she would rather be answered in fluent Danish or English than in stammering French. In a few weeks I had picked up the ordinary forms of French politeness, and the few necessary names of the things I might be asked to fetch. I was determined to be slow rather than make a mistake, and if I did not grasp what was wanted I always asked to have the order repeated in Danish. That language sounds like English with a broad northern accent; any Winchester man can understand it.

In those days the Lady Emma was a splendid figure, worthy to be the wife and mother of Kings. Her hair was white, and her figure certainly on the plump side; but she wore her girdle tight round her waist, so that she bulged above and below it as a woman should. The skin of her hands and face was smooth and very clear; she was tall, and held herself erect. It was the first time I had seen an elderly woman who was obviously in perfect health, without rheumatism or gout or any other crippling infirmity; her stately walk and good eyesight seemed to me almost supernatural attributes. But then, unlike all the other old women I had met, the Lady Emma had never once been cold or wet or hungry since she was born.

She was considerate to her servants, and at the beginning made allowances for my shyness. She gave her commands in clear distinct French, though when she chattered with her Norman women she slurred her consonants in the Norman manner; and if she saw that I did not comprehend she repeated what she had said in careful Danish with a French accent. She could never have been mistaken for a native Englishwoman, but her foreignness was not the most striking thing about her.

I was not as frightened of her as a stranger would have been, for though she was the Lady of England and I was merely the son of a burgess she had a good reputation in Winchester. We knew that she was mild, and very generous to the Church; and if some said that she was niggardly to the lay poor – well, hardworking burgesses never like beggars.

My duties were light and pleasant. For a few hours every day I waited in the Lady's anteroom, taking my turn with the other pages. I had to be clean and well-dressed and graceful in my movements, but that came easily to me. For the rest of the day I made myself useful in the wardrobe, caring for fine robes or polishing beautiful jewels of silver and gold; I am in love with fine craftsmanship, and it was a pleasure to clean those glorious cups and splendid brooches. The under-steward quickly saw that I enjoyed my work and did it thoroughly, and he seldom had occasion to rebuke me.

When I first came to live in the Lady's hall I was a little bothered by giggling girls. I was a new face, a well-set-up youth on the threshold of manhood; and in any large household love-affairs occupy most of the time of under-worked servants. Half a dozen young sewing-maids competed to catch me, not because they loved me for myself but because they wanted another trophy. Young women would creep up and tickle me as I sat dozing on a bench by the fire. But when they saw I was not interested they gave it up. I may as well confess now, for it will make the rest of my story easier to follow, that I am not attracted to young women. I find handsome boys more enticing, and if I had been born a heathen Dane perhaps I might have sinned with them. But that is one of the sins that Christians just may not commit, and it is all the easier to resist temptation because the public opinion of everyday England happens to be on the side of virtue. I have never yielded to my private inclination, perhaps because the fear of God was reinforced by the fear of the neighbours. In a way I have been born lucky. Some men are inclined to drunkenness or murder, and no one helps them to resist those temptations; at Christmas it is difficult to keep sober, and anyone who inherits a blood-feud is incited by all his friends to go out and slay. But no Englishman makes it easy for his comrade to be a sodomite.

I have never married, yet in a large household of men and women I have always behaved with decorum. But that is enough on such a subject. I am not yet making my deathbed confession.

I had hardly grown used to wearing my handsome red tunic when the court went into mourning and I had to change it for a grey one. News came that King Hardicanute, son of the Lady of England, had died suddenly in the prime of his youth. His end was very terrible; as he stood to drink the health of the bride at a wedding feast God struck him down without warning. He went to Judgement unshriven.

On the next day came further news, which meant that the Lady, my mistress, was still mother to the King of the English. We heard that the great men of the Council had chosen as successor to Hardicanute his half-brother, Edward. This Edward had long been recognised as the destined heir, but no one can be sure about the succession of the crown of the English until the new King is proclaimed. In this particular case the election of Edward as successor was by no means a foregone conclusion, for it entailed a change of dynasty. So much has happened since, including many greater changes, that I had better explain the position as it was in the year 1042.

As a girl the Lady Emma had come from Normandy to

marry Ethelred, King of the English and, as you would suppose, an Englishman. She bore him two sons, Alfred and Edward. Presently Sweyn, chief of the heathen Danes, conquered England from Ethelred, only to be struck down in the hour of victory by the miraculous spear of St Edmund, the martyred King of the East Angles (on a peaceful journey Sweyn fell from his horse, crying that St Edmund had run him through). He was succeeded by his son Canute, who accepted baptism and ruled as a good Christian. This Canute married the Lady Emma as soon as she was widowed, and by her he had a son, Hardicanute. But in the manner of his heathen countrymen Canute fathered other sons on various concubines; and when he also died suddenly and young (for a King of the English rarely sees old age) his bastard Harold seized the Kingdom. This Harold reigned for a year or two and found time to murder Alfred the son of Ethelred; when he also died in the flower of his youth he was succeeded by his half-brother Hardicanute, son of Emma the Lady. Now Hardicanute was dead, young and childless, and no one was left to carry on the line of Canute; though in Denmark and the north there were young men of his kindred, descended from his ancestors, who had some claim to be considered hereditary chieftains of all the Danes in Denmark and England.

Thus the succession of Edward meant a return to the dynasty discredited by the incompetence of Ethelred, and a setback to all the Danes settled in eastern England. It meant also a return to the old dynasty of Cerdic, who founded the Kingdom of Wessex more than five hundred years ago; so that it was popular in Winchester, the cradle of Wessex. But in upstart London and the Danish north-east some great men were not pleased.

Strangely enough, the Lady also was not pleased. Naturally, she did not express her opinion on important political questions while I was in the room, but even a fourteen-year-old page could see that she was dissatisfied. The housecarles of her bodyguard made no secret of their views. They were Danes, who had served the great Canute; they said quite openly, as they drank the Lady's ale by her fire, within the special peace of her household, that if any Danish or Norwegian claimant tried to upset the decision of the English Council he might count on their axes to help him to the throne. I heard one of the Lady's Norman tirewomen remind them that of the great men who had given the crown to Edward the greatest, Earl Siward, was a Dane; and the second, Earl Godwin, though a South Saxon by birth, was married to a Danish wife and had been a trusted servant of Canute. A King who was good enough for Danish Earls ought to be good enough for common Danish axemen.

Then of course the fat was in the fire. No man would dare to call a royal housecarle a common Danish axeman; and even among the women only a Norman would have the courage. The housecarles protested that all of them had been the trusted companions of King Canute, and that the great Earl Godwin had no prouder title. I believe that in Danish eyes their position was in fact most honourable; though to Normans and English they seemed ordinary hired soldiers. I listened eagerly to the beginnning of the dispute, because I like hearing foreigners expound a foreign point of view. Presently I saw that the housecarles were so angry that they longed to pick a quarrel with any man, even a half-grown boy; and I went away before one of them should sink his axe into my head.

We wore mourning until the autumn, which seemed right when the Lady had lost a young and beloved son; though some people thought it a queer way to welcome another son to the throne of England. Anyway, our mourning did not mean that the Lady retired into seclusion. During all that time we were kept very busy as great men came and went, or came to stay.

They were not at first the very greatest men in England, not Earls of the front rank; but rather substantial landowners from the eastern parts, Danes who had risen under Canute and remained faithful to the widow of their lord. The most prominent among them was the Bishop of the East Angles, who about that time came to settle in Winchester and act more or less as chaplain to the Lady, though he did not lodge in her hall. That is, if he was indeed the Bishop of the East Angles; for throughout his long life there was always something dubious about the ecclesiastical position of Stigand.

We servants were commanded to kneel for his blessing, and in every way to receive him with the respect due to a Bishop. But of course we thought it odd that a Bishop with a fine minster at Elmham among the East Angles should come to live permanently at Winchester among the West Saxons.

Two explanations were current in the hall, and to this day I am not sure which was the right one. According to one story he had been consecrated Bishop, and then expelled from his See by King Harold or King Hardicanute; according to the other version one of these Kings had granted him the lands and revenues of Elmham, but could find no Archbishop willing to consecrate him. Whatever was his trouble, I am sure the root of it was political. Stigand was a man of more or less regular life, or at least not so obviously debauched that an Archbishop would refuse him consecration. But he was a very busy and partisan politician. I remember him in those days as an urgent, thin, haggard man always in a hurry, always with a bundle of writings under his arm. He was affable to servants, but we did not like him. We could see that he was not quite a gentleman, but not holy enough for ordinary men to overlook his humble birth; and he was such a typical Dane of the Danelaw that his speech and manners grated on every West Saxon.

During that autumn and winter nearly everybody of importance came to Winchester, except the King. That was odd, because in those days the Old Minster at Winchester was the shrine where a King of the English must be crowned; and until he had been crowned and anointed Edward would not be completely King. The official explanation for the delay was that Edward, as acknowledged heir to the Kingdom of Hardicanute, had already received the oaths of all the magnates and himself sworn the customary promise to do justice and protect the Church; so that only the religious rites remained to be performed, and they might as well await the convenience of the busy Archbishops. I believe the real reason was that the Danelaw was restive; the King and the great Earls dared not come so far west as Winchester.

It was amusing to listen to all this gossip about the troubles of the great, and to pick up half-understood scraps of the plans of intriguing politicians. We felt that we were on the inside, hearing secrets that would never be known to the vulgar; and we were quite sure that whatever happened to the crown of the English we would not be affected. The Lady Emma, widow of two Kings, mother of two Kings, would live peacefully in Winchester and protect her household.

At last the date of the coronation was announced, Easter Day, the 3rd of April 1043. My mistress had a place of honour in the Old Minster, for so long as her son was unmarried she was still the Lady of England. But there was not room, even in that great church, for all her servants; I saw what I could from an upper window of her hall. During the week of festivity I saw all the great men of England ride below me, and thought how well they portrayed the characters that popular gossip had bestowed on them. I saw the mighty Siward, a heavy load even for his magnificent horse; his bushy red beard, tinged with grey, covered all his breast; on his back was a round Danish shield ornamented with silver and enamel; his great doubleheaded axe, hanging from his saddlebow, was damascened with gold; on his head was a winged Danish helmet. Here was obviously a great chieftain of the pirates.

I saw Earl Leofric, of the ancient Mercian line. He was fair and slight and elegant and very splendidly dressed. It was pleasant to know that at least one noble of high English blood had a place among the greatest magnates, even after the Danish conquest of England.

I saw Earl Godwin, who as Earl of the West Saxons might be considered almost my own lord. But in Winchester we served the Lady of England, and there were few cheers from the crowd for this renegade Englishman who had risen by the favour of Danish Kings. Some of his Danish sons rode behind him, fierce pirates by the look of them. But Godwin himself, a short dark man, looked affable and almost cringing. We were told that in his youth he had won victories far away on the shores of the Baltic, but he had not the air of a warrior. He smiled uneasily to placate the sullen crowd, and his slack mobile lips were those of an orator rather than a doer.

Last of all I saw the King. Or rather, I did not see King Edward, for I could see nothing but his robes of state. He was tall, and he sat his horse well; so that he looked a mighty war-leader, a true son of Cerdic and of Woden the devil of the heathen. We cheered in frenzy, longing for the day when he would lead us against our Danish oppressors.

Besides the great men of England, envoys came from all Christendom to congratulate the new King, bringing him splendid presents. King Sweyn sent an embassy from Denmark whose coming delighted the burgesses of Winchester; for it showed that the Danes oversea acquiesced in the restoration of the old English line. All our merchants had been afraid of

18

war with Denmark, for that would have unloosed the vikings and closed the seas to peaceful commerce. Magnus of the Norwegians sent a message of defiance, claiming to be heir to King Canute in all his dominions; but that was not at the time a serious threat, for Magnus was fighting for his little realm of Norway against a coalition of powerful enemies.

The most costly gift offered to the King came not from a foreign ruler but from one of his own subjects. Earl Godwin gave him a warship, complete with its crew of professional Danish warriors. The ship was displayed at Southampton, and I heard from those who went to see it that it was a magnificent affair, adorned with gilding and costly red paint. The crew were armed with fine new axes, and Earl Godwin had paid their wages for a year. A ship is about the most expensive thing that can be bought with money, and it must have cost the Earl a fortune. But he could hardly avoid giving it, for he had set himself a troublesome precedent; he had given a similar ship to King Hardicanute at the last coronation less than three years before, and he felt that he must repeat the gift lest the new King should doubt his loyalty.

The coronation was a great event for the burgesses of Winchester, but we of the Lady's household took little part in the festivities. There could be no doubt that the accession of King Edward was a slight on the memory of King Canute; the Lady's housecarles, and all her upper servants, had been devoted followers of the great King of the North. To some of us juniors it seemed odd that the Lady should show so little joy when her son was made King; but we were too young, and too lowly, to understand the mind of one so elderly and great.

There followed a summer of peace, bright with the optimism which always brings in a new reign. The King ruled in peace, no extra taxes were imposed, veteran Earls who had been trained under the great Canute kept order in the countryside. The weather was appalling, drenching rain with cold blighting winds; but that did not worry the servants of the Lady, snug in her warm hall. In the middle of a crowded city we were hardly aware of what was happening to the fields, so that the disaster of that autumn took us by surprise.

The harvest failed utterly, all over England. Even the

peasants had not expected such a miserable yield; right up to the end they brewed barley into ale, and they had stored up very little of the old harvest. Immediately there was a panic, as burgesses saw supplies grow scarce in the market. Men with money, but no land of their own (my father among them), rode through the villages buying corn at any price; until it was said that the cost of grain reached as high as 50 pennies the sack.

It was not quite so bad as the devastation of a Danish army. Peasants went hungry, but country folk can usually live through a single bad season by eating roots and nuts and vegetables and the small animals of the waste. Of course they would not part with their land, and if they had been willing to sell there was no one to buy it. The people who were ruined were the burgesses. My father kept his family alive by buying bread in the open market, by begging at the doors of religious houses, by cooking all my mother's laying hens, and by other shifts honest and not so honest. I stole for him what I could from the thriftless kitchen of the Lady's hall; but the other servants were doing the same thing, and in my humble post I had few opportunities. When plenty returned with the excellent harvest of 1044 few men had died of actual starvation and the peasants soon grew fat again; but practically every craftsman in Winchester had sold his stock and his tools to buy corn, and must start again as a penniless journeyman.

In the midst of this frightful distress, with the streets full of whimpering beggar children, quite another disaster befell the household of the Lady. Dusk was gathering on a gloomy November evening, and I was on duty in the anteroom; in her chamber the Lady sat by a good fire, listening to one of her Norman chaplains who was reading from a new poem. Suddenly we heard a tremendous trampling of hoofs, as though a great company had ridden up to the outer palisade at full gallop. The two housecarles who guarded the chamber door straightened themselves and caught up their axes, but the feet we heard pounding towards us were those of the commander of the bodyguard; of course they allowed him to run on into the chamber without challenge.

I could hear all that followed, in the sudden hush of amazement before fugitives began to scurry through all the passages of the rambling hall. 'My Lady,' gasped out the Danish captain, 'an army of Englishmen has ridden against us. Shall I bar the hall? We can perhaps hold it for a short time, long enough to smuggle you out in the dark.'

'What do you mean?' the Lady answered. 'The English are not at war with us. My husband, the great Canute, conquered them and made peace with them. Throw open the gate, send out ale to the common soldiers, and ask the leaders to wait on me here in my chamber.'

Though the Lady answered in Danish I could follow all she said. It was a revealing answer. I saw that she thought of herself as a Dane, even as a Danish conqueror of England; an odd point of view for the Norman widow of King Ethelred. But then I suppose a woman who had been married to the mighty Canute would forget any lesser husband.

The captain of the bodyguard had promised more than his men were willing to perform. As he left the chamber I could hear a throng of soldiers pressing through the gate into the courtyard. Ordinary housecarles dared not defend this timber hall against an army.

The chaplain also bustled out of the chamber, and when I looked round the two axemen who should have guarded its door had vanished. At the time I blamed them for cowardice; but cowardice is seldom a failing of housecarles, and now I know better. They were experienced veterans, taking a wise precaution. When a hall or a town is taken by storm it is the custom to kill all the men in it but to spare the women; yet a warrior who has begun to kill finds it hard to stop, and if he comes on men and women together he may kill the women also. The best chance for their safety is to leave them alone with no men near them.

In my ignorance I thought I alone had stayed to guard the Lady, and though I was unarmed I determined to keep my post to the last. Above the noise of increasing confusion I could hear the march of armed men; they came steadily nearer, but there seemed to be only a few of them, and they were not shouting warcries.

Then four warriors crowded into the anteroom together. They wore mailshirts and helmets, but they were not prepared for immediate massacre; their shields hung on their backs, and their axes dangled by thongs from their wrists. With amazement I recognised men whom I had seen at the coronation.

21

They were the four most powerful men in England: the King and the three great Earls, Siward, Leofric, and Godwin.

Nevertheless, my duty was still plain before me. I stood in their path and appealed to them to halt. 'My lords, this is the private chamber of the Lady of England. It is the custom that all visitors wait here until the Lady signifies that she is ready to receive them.'

Earl Siward grasped his axe, but before he could raise it the King checked him. 'Don't harm the boy. I am glad to see that one of my mother's servants is still faithful to his duty. Boy, announce to the Lady that the King and his Council have urgent affairs to discuss with her; she would be wise to admit us without delay. Come back with her answer, and then leave us. You had better go to the kitchen, where you will find the other servants under guard.'

I did no more than put my head through the door-curtain, for I was so frightened that I could hardly walk. I saw the Lady seated in a tall chair, with her frightened women clustered round her; but she looked stately and composed, more angry than afraid. She heard my message with an unmoved countenance, and told me to admit her visitors. I pulled back the door-curtains and scuttled away to the kitchen.

There I found the household siting gloomily on benches, too scared to discuss this surprising adventure in tones louder than a whisper. Axemen clustered at the doors and peered through the windows; most were strangers of the King's following, but among them I recognised some of the Lady's housecarles.

That is characteristic of the behaviour of housecarles in a tight place. They are honourable men, and take pride in their honour; they boast, with truth, that if they are beaten they would rather die than flee; but they like it better still if they can arrange to join the winning side in the moment of victory.

As darkness fell outside we sat on. Torches were lit, for it was long past supper-time. But no food was served, and even the leather jacks standing on the tables were left empty of ale. No one dared to drink while those axemen watched us; they would have seized a share of the ale, and if they managed to get drunk they might have slaughtered the lot of us.

Presently, after a stir among our guards, the King stood in a doorway, black against the flaring torches behind him. He addressed us all, in a loud carrying voice.

'You are within the special peace of the King, and not one of you will be harmed in any way. Tonight you must stay here. Tomorrow there will be a great deal of work for you, packing all the treasures of this hall. After that I suppose some of you will have to seek another mistress, though the Lady will still maintain a household befitting the mother of the King. Now be quiet and try to get some sleep.'

Then he went on in another tone, as though talking to himself. I was close by, and could overhear him. 'I haven't a servant nearer than Gloucester. I could get a soldier to prepare my bed and disarm me, but I don't like soldiers in my chamber. Otherwise there will be only my mother's women, and that would never do. A woman summoned to the King's chamber would expect the worst, and be disappointed when it didn't happen to her. But the young men here are all greasy scullions.'

'I can prepare your bed and disarm you, my lord,' I called, too excited to realise my temerity.

'I remember your face. You are the page who stayed at your post when the housecarles fled,' the King answered with a smile. 'You shall prepare my bed tonight.'

I knelt to kiss the King's hand, and a housecarle with an axe on his shoulder led me to the little room in which the King would sleep.

I had never before prepared a bedchamber, for of course in the Lady's household such work was the province of her women. I sat down to think what a King would want when he retired for the night, and then I decided that any sensible King would want what I would have wanted myself if I could have had my own way in everything; that is, very clean bedclothes and plenty of them, and before going to bed scented warm water for washing and clean warm towels for drying. Every cupboard in the hall was at my disposal, for the upper servants were penned in the kitchen. I helped myself to a new copper cauldron and filled it with clean water from the drinking-well. I raided the empty bedchamber of the mistress of the robes for linen and towels, and there I found a jar of sweet-smelling paste which I decided must be soap. I tried a little on my hands (for never before had I seen soap) and it seemed to work. I took a fine glowing brazier from a deserted guardroom, and set my clean water to heat by the furnace in the brewhouse. An hour later, when the King came in with two housecarles to guard him, the room looked cheerful and inviting.

The King dismissed his guards and sank down on a stool. I had never before handled a mailshirt, but he showed me the fastenings most affably, and told me how to take off his shoes and hose. The nightshirt I had already warming by the brazier turned out to be a feminine garment, with a great deal of frivolous embroidery; but he put it on, roaring with laughter, and said cheerfully: 'Well, everything in this hall now belongs to me, and I suppose that includes the nightshirt of the mistress of the robes. I see her furred bedgown over there. Help me into it, and then hold the basin while I wash my hands and feet. This campaigning is great fun. It doesn't matter what I look like so long as I am warm and comfortable. The housecarles can't see me, and no one will be the wiser.'

Even in women's clothes he looked imposing and regal. In fact, now that I had leisure to inspect him closely, I saw that he was a striking figure of a man. In those days King Edward was not quite forty years old, but already his abundant hair had turned white. He wore his beard long, after the Danish fashion; but because it was also white, and trimmed to a neat point instead of spreading all over his breast, it made him look more like a holy image in a church than a savage viking. But he was a benignant image, not a prophet of doom; his clean smooth skin was pink and glowing, and his mouth stretched into a happy smile. For the rest, he had the slender well-balanced figure of a good horseman. But the most striking thing about him, except for his benevolent face, was the grace of his long white hands, the tapering fingers so fine that the torchlight shone through them. He was proud of those beautiful hands, and of his beautiful hair; he took a long time to clean them and get them ready for the night.

When he had finished washing he went over to his armour and fumbled about looking for something. He would not let me help him. Presently from inside his mailshirt he fished out a little image of St Peter, and set it up on a stool. In after years I learned that he did not like anyone else to touch this image, which he always carried with him. When it was balanced upright to his satisfaction (the manikin of ivory was less than three inches high) he prostrated himself before it, spread his arms wide in the form of a cross, and began to mutter his prayers.

I knelt upright in a corner, where I could keep my eye on him, and said my own prayers under my breath; because that seemed what good manners demanded of me. But he went on for very much longer than I had expected, and by the time he had finished I was dozing on my knees.

At last he climbed into bed. When I saw he was settled I walked quietly to the door. But I was still ignorant of the etiquette of the royal bedchamber. He called after me, in a pleasant voice:

'Don't go away, my boy. Let me see, what's your name? Ah, Edgar, of course. A King must remember names, it's most important. But a King may never sleep alone, either. Someone might creep in here and cut my throat, and then my whole following would be under suspicion. I haven't been a King very long, you know, and I must keep the rules laid down by my predecessors. You will sleep on the floor of my chamber, to raise the alarm if anyone intrudes or to fetch me anything I may want in the night. Go and collect some sheepskins to sleep on; you will find them scattered all over the place. Make yourself comfortable on the floor, but don't undress in case I should want you to go out on an errand.'

With a couple of sheepskins I made myself a couch at the foot of the King's bed. After the day's excitement I was very tired; but I could not go to sleep, for the King would not stop talking.

He was not talking to me, but rather to the world in general. This, I discovered later, was a habit of his. He often spoke his thoughts aloud, not caring who might overhear them; especially at night he would run over the events of the past day. I suppose this was how he examined his conscience.

Now he seemed to be arguing with himself, or rather accusing himself.

'Crowned seven months ago, and the first time I ride in arms it is to plunder my own mother. That will look bad, whatever the dress my Councillors put on it. But then it is misleading to think in cut-and-dried categories; every case is a special case. The Lady of England is not an ordinary mother. In fact she is scarcely my mother at all; she is so busy being the widow of King Canute that she has no time to think of her children. And I am her son by the husband she despised – the husband who had the bad manners to run away after he was beaten, instead

25

of dying like the gentleman on a lost field. All Normans despise failure, and a failure who can plausibly be accused of cowardice is best forgotten by any Norman princess.'

After a pause he went on again. 'For twenty-five years she forgot me. I was a fugitive in Normandy, going in daily terror of Danish assassins, whilst she lived softly as the wife of the Danish pirate who had conquered England. I must not think of her as my mother. I must think of what the King should do for the welfare of his people. . . . Yes, that's all very well. A King must sometimes do discreditable deeds for the good of his country. In that case a virtuous man should not consent to be made King. But I didn't want to be King, and when the time came I took a deal of persuading. . . . No, that won't do. When I came to my brother's court I knew that Hardicanute intended to make me his heir. Unless I was willing to be King of the English I should have stayed in Normandy. But if I had stayed as a private man in Normandy sooner or later the Danes would have murdered me. Any Danish King would see me as a menace. It's nice to know that now I am safe.'

I was afraid to listen to these secrets of state. I coughed, to remind the King that I could overhear him.

There was silence for a moment, but before I could get to sleep the voice began again.

'When I accepted the crown I did no wrong, that's certain; though a really virtuous man would have refused it. But that's not the point. As King, am I justified in seizing the treasures of my mother? On the whole, I think I am justified. She didn't want me to be King, and I can't blame her for that. But once I had been chosen she should have respected the decision of the Council. I suppose she genuinely loved Canute, and hoped to carry out his wishes even after his death. Again, there's nothing wrong in that. She can't be blamed for disliking the memory of my father; everyone is agreed on the incompetence of King Ethelred. So if I punish her I do wrong. . . . But to take from her the treasure of King Canute is not to punish her; that treasure belongs to the King now reigning, myself, Canute's heir. I'm pretty sure she was using the money to help my rivals, Sweyn or Magnus or perhaps both of them. If I let things slide, a time will come when I have to wage open war against her. So what I have done today is really the best solution. I have her money. No one has been accused of plotting, but the plots will

26

cease. Very well. Now I can sleep.'

I myself slept fitfully and uneasily. Probably the King had forgotten that there was anyone in the room to overhear his soliloquy. When he saw me in the morning he might decide that the easiest way to keep his secrets would be to have me killed at once. Kings are very terrible folk.

But if I were spared I would not betray his confidence. I felt no scruple about leaving the service of the Lady. I believed what the King had said to himself: the Lady was planning to bring back the Danish Kings, even after the extinction of the direct line of Canute. There were men in England who would welcome the return of Danish rule, but Danish pirates had ruined my grandfather.

Very early in the morning the King woke, and ordered me to put him in a warm bedgown so that he could go along the passage to hear his first Mass. I knew that later in the day he would attend High Mass in the Old Minster, for that is what every great lord does when he comes to Winchester. Until then I did not know that King Edward always heard a short Mass in private before beginning the work of the day. He said nothing to me about his spoken meditations of the night, and of course I did not remind him of them. When he came back from Mass I dressed him in the armour he had worn when he first arrived, and he went off to meet his Earls. After tidying the little chamber I wandered off to the kitchen, for I had eaten nothing since dinner on the previous day.

I did not know what would become of me. The Lady's household would be dispersed, and anyway I did not care to continue in the service of a mistress who had plotted to bring back the Danish Kings. My father was now so poor that there would be nothing for me at home. I wondered whether some minster might take me in as a servant; I have no vocation for the hard life of religion, but I feel at ease in the company of monks and among them I would not be bothered by women. On that gloomy November morning the kitchen was full of frightened servants; everyone was wondering what to do next, and in the confusion it was impossible to make sensible plans.

About midday the army prepared to ride, and to my great surprise the King sent for me. He was already mounted when a housecarle fetched me to stand before his horse. In his mail he looked very stern, sitting his tall stallion in the warlike foreign fashion; for he had been trained to fight on horseback as Frenchmen do. But I could see a friendly smile lurking in the bushy white beard.

'Hallo, young Edgar,' he said pleasantly. 'You didn't gossip in the kitchen about what I said to myself as I was going to sleep last night. My men were near you, and I know that for a fact. I am looking for a young man of your stamp. Not long ago a page of mine was killed out boarhunting, and his place is still vacant. Would you like to come to court, and take your turn in the bedchamber with the others? In the daytime you would help to look after my robes, under the orders of the head chamberlain. In case there's anyone depending on you I shall give you a year's wages in advance. But you must make up your mind quickly, for we leave now.'

So it was that in my seventeenth year I entered the service of Edward, King of the English; and I remained at his court, always close to his person, until he died.

placed King Edward on the throne, Godwin Wulfnothsson, was married to a Danish woman of high birth and had first distinguished himself in fighting for the Danes against the savage Wends of the Baltic. Godwin was descended from a noble family among the South Saxons; but he had been trained in administration under Canute, so that he spoke his wife's tongue more often than his father's. In any reckoning of the Danish and English parties he must be counted as a Dane.

Yet after King Hardicanute had died childless even Godwin, the Anglo-Dane, had preferred the old English line. There is something special about the descendants of Cerdic. They have been Kings here in Wessex for five hundred years and more; and though the founder of the family boasted himself to be only three generations away from a devil who passed himself off as the heathen god Woden, there have been pious and mighty rulers among them. Canute was a great man, but he stood alone; his sons were as wicked and barbarous as his father.

Of course, while they enjoyed the support of a strong party in England, the pirates must make a try to conquer the land. In the spring of 1044 word came that Magnus of the Norwegians was preparing to invade us. But in those days the English had a mighty fleet, which was gathered at Sandwich to defend our coasts. These were the ships that had once belonged to the great Canute, and though their crews were professional Danish pirates they were loyal by long habit to their English paymasters.

All summer the fleet remained at Sandwich, which was very expensive. But Magnus never came after all, for he was busy fighting rebels at home. By October we knew that there could be no invasion that year, and the ships were laid up for the winter.

In that year my lord did not visit Sandwich to take command of his fleet; the sailors were accustomed to taking orders from Earl Godwin, and the great Earl might have been offended if he had been ousted from command. Besides, the King was not interested in fighting. He left problems of defence to the experienced servants of Canute who advised him on such matters; while he himself managed the affairs of the Church, which he understood better than they.

Even in ecclesiastical affairs Earl Godwin might not be

ignored. It seemed almost as though he were the King's partner in the government of the realm; whenever the King got his way in some matter that displeased the Earl some other appointment must be found for a follower of the house of Godwin. For example, in this very year there was need to appoint a new Bishop of London. I remember King Edward talking about it as we undressed him in the evening. He was so excited by his new plan that he fairly bubbled over with it, and did not care who might overhear him.

'I have found the very man to be Bishop of London, and what's even more remarkable is that he's willing to take on the job. He is a monk, and a devout one; but for the sake of our old friendship he will return to the secular world. As it happens, he is a foreigner, and I'm not sure that he can speak English. But what does that matter? The clergy ought to speak and write in Latin; there has been too much of this writing in the vernacular since my great ancestor King Alfred set the bad example. It's outlandish and provincial. England is part of the civilised world, and the civilised world thinks in Latin. I'm glad to have the chance to promote a foreigner. It will remind those Danish pirates that learning and true piety come from the south.'

'Who is this paragon of piety and learning, my lord?' I asked, just to prove that I had been paying attention.

'I don't suppose you have seen him. He was my friend in the days of my exile. He's a Norman called Robert, at present Abbot of Jumièges. Our friendship doesn't matter, though I am glad to help an old friend. The principle is the important thing, the principle that the King may search through all Christendom to find worthy rulers for the Church in England.'

'I suppose some Englishman had been expecting this splendid promotion,' I said in an expressionless voice. There must have been trouble over the appointment, or the King would not be so pleased at getting his own way.

'I don't know about Englishmen,' the King answered carelessly. 'Of course Godwin wanted it for one of his Danes. But since he wants everything it's impossible to satisfy him. For the moment we have done a deal. He agrees that my Robert may have London, on condition that his Stigand is restored to his Bishopric among the East Angles.'

'*His* Stigand? I thought he was the trusted adviser of the

34

Lady. When I served in her household he was always running in and out.'

It may seem odd that a young page should talk so to the King his master; but in private my lord liked to hear the frank opinion of his servants.

'You forget, boy, or perhaps you are too young to remember. There was a time when my mother was the ally of Earl Godwin. Together they put my brother on his throne; it's only since Hardicanute's death that they have disagreed. Anyway, Stigand is a Dane, and he got his first preferment from King Canute. So naturally Godwin favours him.'

'I see, my lord. But though it sounds like a compromise the gain is really yours. Robert of Jumièges is advanced from Abbot to Bishop, but for years Stigand has been Bishop among the East Angles. You arrested him because he gave the Lady bad advice, but no layman can deprive him of his Bishopric.'

'A very good answer, young Edgar. I'm glad to see you so firmly grounded in the fundamentals of church discipline. Stigand is a Bishop, to all eternity. If he happens to go to Hell he will be a Bishop there, and I am sure the Devil will be proud to meet him. Yes, my unfortunate brother made him a Bishop. But then my brother was not always well advised. We are not a very bright family. Once I had another brother, who ought to be King in my place at this moment. Poor Alfred was my companion in Normandy, and it was always agreed between us that when our chance came he would be King so that I might go into a monastery. He would have been a very good King.'

I tried to comfort my master, who would sometimes pass a restless and wakeful night if he went to bed thinking of Alfred.

'My lord, the Danes killed him. That is a bereavement we must all endure. Is there an Englishman now living who does not mourn some kinsman slaughtered by those pirates? We owe a duty to the living, and your duty in particular is to keep the Danes out of England. Anyway, it happened a long time ago.'

'A long time ago to a boy like you. To a man in his forties it seems like yesterday. Yes, my brother was tortured by the Danes until he died of it; and that, as you say, is a fate that has befallen many Englishmen. But how did those pirates get their hands on him? It's pretty evident that he was betrayed by some Englishman. I should like to get to the bottom of the puzzle one day, but I don't suppose I shall. In a question of that kind those who know the sordid truth will lie on oath, and it is impossible to find out what really happened. Hardicanute inquired into it, and so did I when I first came to the throne.'

I went off to fetch a basin of hot water. I had heard rumours about the fate of the atheling Alfred, but I feared to pass on to the King the suspicion believed by every burgess of Winchester.

My good lord, King Edward, was undisputed King of the English. But during the summer of 1044 everyone could see that the real ruler of the country was Earl Godwin. This was not solely because he had a great force of oath-bound dependants, so that in an emergency as many thanes would follow him as could be found under the royal standard of England. That had something to do with it, of course. But though Godwin was the greatest lord in England he was not greater than all the other lords combined. Siward and Leofric disliked him, and most of the lesser folk would follow the anointed King against any rebel.

No, it was rather that the King would not bother about matters which he himself considered unimportant; while to Godwin, a busy politician, everything was important. King Edward chose his Bishops, and took continual care for the good order of the Church; he preserved the peace of his realm, against dangerous threats from the northern pirates and the merely tiresome but bloody raids of the Welsh. When he had done that he went to his hunting, or to his prayers. But a great many lesser matters came before the Council. In every shire there must be an Earl or his deputy to preside in the law-court and lead the free men to battle; every landowner who broke the peace must forfeit his land, and this land must then be granted to someone else. All this was the sphere of Earl Godwin. He was a fine speaker, always in control of a naturally easy temper. As a rule he could persuade the Council, and he had a wonderful knack of recognising really stubborn opposition and giving way to it before he had made a determined enemy. When forfeited land must find a new owner, when minor benefices must be distributed among the lesser clergy, Godwin's friends prospered; month after month the number of his friends increased.

The King did not seem to care; though he never disguised from his intimates that he disliked Godwin as a man. When he really set his mind on anything he could be sure of getting his own way; where he had no strong views Godwin's energy saved him a great deal of trouble. The King and his greatest subject were not rivals, neither were they ruler and minister; rather were they partners in the business of government. There seemed to be no reason why this partnership should not endure until dissolved by death.

All the same, Godwin already had as much power as any subject should enjoy; and, as I have said, the King disliked him personally. Therefore we were all very surprised when in Advent the King made it known that after Christmas he would marry Godwin's daughter.

It was always easy to get the King to talk freely while he undressed for bed. The next time I attended him in his bed-chamber I made some tentative remark about coming changes; soon, I supposed, the waiting-women of the new Lady would take charge of the royal bedchamber, and if my lord wished to be attended by pages he would have to use a dressing-room. The King answered, with an enigmatic smile:

'Perhaps my marriage will not make so much difference as you suppose. I don't like to see women round me when I prepare for sleep. Don't be afraid that you will lose your post in my household. I shall keep on all my pages. I want you in particular to stay by me. My senior chamberlain is getting old. I inherited him from King Canute, and after such long service I can't ask him to leave until he is ready. But one of these days he will want to retire, and then I should like you to take his place. You handle my beautiful robes as though you appreciate their worth (and indeed they are very beautiful; English embroidery is the best in the world). I don't sleep if my nerves are jangled just before I go to bed, and you never jangle them.'

We all knew that the King had lived completely chaste for forty years, and the manner in which he discussed his future brought an odd suspicion into my mind. To find out how the land lay I answered, perhaps with more freedom than a page should use.

'I am glad to know that I do not upset you, my lord. But after your wedding mine will not be the last face you see before you go to sleep.'

'Don't be too sure of that. Years ago, in Normandy, when I was in peril of death and very miserable, I made a private

37

vow of complete continence. God accepted my offering, and in return I have been given safety and prosperity. So of course I must keep my vow for the rest of my life.'

'But you are going to marry, my lord!' I said in surprise.

'Well, what of it? Clerks say that a married man may enjoy his wife in all chastity. Bishop Stigand has explained it with a great many quotations from the Fathers and instances from canon law; I can trust his theology, even though I deplore his politics. But that wasn't what I meant when I bound myself by my vow. I offered complete continence, and God has requited me. I wish I could have taken the full vows of a monk, for the life of the cloister appeals to me. But as my father's heir I have a part to play in the world, and that refuge is forbidden to me. I would have been a contented monk. Do you think I would have been a holy one?' he added with a smile.

It crossed my mind that a monk would not be able to spend six hours every day hunting or pottering about with hounds and hawks. There are a few abbots who behave so, but they are denounced by all earnest reformers. If he could have given up the pleasures of the chase the King would have made a very good monk indeed, and I said so. Since he seemed in the mood to discuss his private affairs I went on to ask: 'Is your bride aware of your resolve my lord? It will be hard on her if she is trapped into a virgin marriage without knowing what kind of life she will lead.'

'I have explained everything to little Edith. She doesn't mind. She is a nice little girl, young enough to be my daughter. Her only faults are ambition and pride, and you can't expect her father's daughter to be humble. She wants to be Lady of England, so that she can go through doors in front of all the other girls who were her school-fellows at Wilton convent. She doesn't want a white-haired middle-aged bedfellow. She won't miss my company at night, and she is honourable enough to behave as my wife should behave. It will work out very well, depend on it, and after I am married my Councillors can't pester me by choosing rows of suitable young women for me to marry.'

'Does Earl Godwin know your intentions?' I asked with interest. Like most Englishmen, I disliked that imitation Dane. I hoped that the King was planning to make a fool of him in public as a preliminary to stripping him of his lands and honours; nothing weakens a great man so much as ridicule.

'I haven't told him, but perhaps Edith has. I didn't ask her to keep it a secret. Soon all the court will know. Whether he knows now or not, when the time comes he will take it peacefully. He is not making plans for the future of England after he is dead. He wants to keep power while he lives. He also wants to see his children provided for in his lifetime. Now a daughter of his will be Lady, which means that she will be rich until she dies; and I can't be seduced into marriage with someone else, perhaps a supporter of a rival house. At the wedding feast I shall promote his sons and kindred; it would look odd if I didn't. If he longs for grandchildren his sons will provide them. In fact, though they are still bachelors, I believe they have already done so.'

The King climbed into bed, and as usual continued his discourse.

'Nobody likes Godwin, and certainly I don't. But that doesn't mean that I am plotting to destroy him. I am not responsible for him. When I was made King I found him here, the greatest man in England, jutting out above the other Earls like a high mountain. He is a feature of the landscape, and I must accept him just as I accept the river Severn. That river is a nuisance, making it hard to reinforce the garrisons on the Welsh border. Godwin also is a nuisance, but I must never forget to take him into account. If he should choose to make war on me it would be an even fight. I might win or I might lose. But so long as I let him have what he wants he will be loyal, and luckily what he wants I do not. He wants a great deal of land and a great deal of money; in England there is enough for us both. Even if I took Godwin's wealth from him I would not be able to keep it for myself. What he has is the rightful emolument of an Earl, though his Earldom is much too big. If I gave his offices to others they would need the land also. No, Godwin may remain my chief minister, so long as he is willing to serve me as King. In the meantime I shall promote each of his sons as they grow old enough to hold power. That will please him. But in the long run it will weaken him. That family is too numerous, and too wicked, to remain united after all the sons are great men.'

The King's muttering died into silence as he fell asleep.

In January 1045 the marriage between Edward the King and

Edith the daughter of Earl Godwin was celebrated with great splendour. The new Lady received the city of Exeter as her morning-gift, and it was understood that she would succeed to all the other customary endowments of the Lady of England when the Old Lady, Emma the King's mother, should come to die. In addition her kin received many favours. Her eldest brother, Sweyn, was already an Earl; during the marriage feast the same dignity was conferred on her second brother, Harold, and on her cousin Beorn. You could hardly move in the hall without stumbling over a Godwinsson; all that numerous family hung round the source of royal bounty.

Godwin and his Danish wife had produced six sons, and another daughter besides Edith the Lady. You could pick them out in any crowd, for they had the dashing, careless, pleasant air of young people who have been born to greatness and know that no stroke of fate can harm them. They were so certain of their superiority to the rest of the human race that they could afford to be cordial to their inferiors. But both in body and mind they differed greatly from one another.

Sweyn was pure Danish pirate, all the more dangerous because he possessed such a great measure of the family ease and charm. He was not bloodthirsty or actively cruel; but you could sense that he was utterly ruthless, and would kill men by thousands if their death would increase his comfort in the slightest degree. He was said to be a competent warrior, which was why he had been given an Earldom on the frontier of the unsubdued Welsh; but though he prided himself on his skill in war he was even more proud of his record as a seducer of virtuous women. In spite of his faults there was something attractive about him; you guessed that underneath he had some greatness of soul, and that if he would only serve some worthy cause he might die for it heroically.

You all know about Harold, the second son. In those days he was perhaps the least remarkable of the brothers. He was efficient and well-mannered, and even in youth he had gained a reputation as an eloquent speaker. He was very handsome: tall, with masses of fair hair and a fine moustache which stuck out so fiercely that you could see it as plainly from behind as from in front. But he seemed slow and cautious, at least when compared with the other members of his fiery family; a wily politician and a clever administrator like his father, not a stark hero like the brothers on each side of him. At this feast he was given the great post of Earl over the East Angles. The Danes of those parts were pleased to be governed by such a competent ruler, and he proved to be as strenuous and just as had been expected of him.

Tostig, the third brother, had the most vivid personality in the family. As yet he was too young to be granted an Earldom, but he was old enough to sit at the high table during the marriage feast. He was as dark as Harold was fair, but in other respects just as handsome: tall and strong, with the figure of a warrior. He talked much of the need for justice in government. Of course he was trying to prove to the King that he also was worthy of a great Earldom, but it was impossible to doubt his sincerity. He was in love with justice; but because he was a typical Godwinsson he would all his life be a stranger to mercy.

The three younger boys, Gyrth, Leofwin and Wulfnoth, were too small to sit down with grown men at the feast. They were present in the hall, so that the great men of England should get to know them; but no one would suggest that they should be made into Earls until they were very much older.

To complete the list I must mention Gunhild, the younger sister of the Lady; she was not at the wedding, being still too young for public functions. Later I saw her once or twice, but she never played any part in political affairs. She was not at all a typical member of the family, being pious and virtuous. She never married, and I believe she is at present living in a convent in Bruges, that haven of English exiles.

Young Beorn counted as a member of the family, since he was a nephew of Gytha, Godwin's wife. Though in fact he was a Dane on both sides of the family, while his cousins had only a Danish mother, by some odd chance he looked more English than they. He was a nice, shy, brave young man, who behaved honourably and expected honourable behaviour from others. It would be an absurd exaggeration to say that he was too good for this world, but perhaps he was too straightforward for English political life; later it proved to be quite easy to murder him.

All these young men were delighted to feast at the court which their elder sister ruled as Lady. But it did not take me long to observe that the Lady did not like all her kin, and that

41

the brothers themselves were an enmity. Tostig was Edith's favourite, as later he became the King's. His manners were charming, he was not so proud as other members of his house, and in addition his private life was chaste. But if Tostig was the favourite that meant that Sweyn and Harold must be jealous of their junior. Harold was more than jealous. He hated his brother.

The King was the first to observe it. He hardly knew the young men, but sometimes very good men are granted unusual insight into the souls of the wicked. While I carried another pitcher of wine to the high table I saw Harold and Tostig scuffling together, down on the floor under the benches. Harold had just been made an Earl, so that he should have behaved with decorum; but he was very young for his great position, and Tostig was still a boy. I was told they had fallen out because Tostig had grabbed some dainty which had been served to his elder brother. Perhaps their behaviour was unseemly, especially in the presence of the King; but it was not really extraordinary on the part of the two lusty youths.

The whole company were surprised when the King sternly ordered them to withdraw, and not to appear before him until they had been reconciled; it seemed to be making too much of mere highspirited foolishness. Immediately the young men apologised to the King and to one another; soon they took their places at the table again.

At last the banquet ended. It was long after dark and a great deal had been eaten, but no one had taken too much to drink. Nowadays these lengthy feasts have gone out of fashion, and I must explain that they were not crude drinking-bouts. When our modern French lords meet to discuss matters of state they gather on horseback in the open air; the English custom was to sit on benches in the hall, with the long table in the midst covered with drinking-horns. Good manners demanded the presence of plentiful wine and ale; but the lords were there to discuss important business, not to see who could empty the most flagons. It was usual for great men to go away sober, after sitting at the board for a full six hours.

When the King withdrew after the wedding feast I had already done a long day's work. But the crisis was still to come. According to custom I waited in the King's chamber, to prepare him for bed; meanwhile waiting-women escorted the bride to

42

the Lady's chamber, at the far end of a long passage. Would the wedded pair separate for the night without any public explanation? And if so would the great house of Godwin take it meekly?

All passed off quietly. No one waited to help the bride undress, or to entertain the happy couple with music. Privately the King's vow had been explained to all the Councillors, and they knew in advance how he meant to conduct his married life.

As the King got ready for bed he hardly discussed his marriage. For the first time he had seen the whole Godwin family together, and his bride was not the member of it who had made the deepest impression.

'I shall get along all right with the Lady,' he said easily. 'She's a pretty, modest little thing, and already she regards me as a father. I can't imagine how such a nice girl can come from that frightful kindred. Did you notice young Harold and that brother of his, Tostig is it, as they quarrelled in my presence tonight? Ostensibly they were squabbling over a sugarloaf. But I could see their eyes, and there was murder in them. Those brothers hate one another as Cain hated Abel. If I hadn't checked them at once there might have been blood spilled in the King's hall, and a heavy fine to pay for a breach of the King's special peace. And all the time their fool of a father looked on with an indulgent smile, pleased that his stalwart sons could wrestle so strenuously. Godwin is a clever politician; but where his own family is concerned he is blinded by affection. Well, today's marriage should have pleased him, and for the next few months he will be in a good temper.'

Tired after long ceremonial, the King soon went to sleep.

We of the household had feared the coming of the Lady; either she would displace us to make way for dependants of her own, or at least as a new broom she would make us all work harder. But the Lady Edith was a darling, and we soon grew fond of her. She fitted very well into our celibate way of life, and did not attempt tiresome innovations. She was beautiful, but in a nun-like comforting way. After all, if she had wanted a husband and children the daughter of such a powerful Earl would not have remained unmarried until she was more than twenty years old. She had a filial affection for the nominal husband who was old enough to be her father, and she was content to remain a virgin all her life. She was naturally devout, pleased to accompany the King to great ceremonies of the Church. Hunting did not amuse her, and in the afternoons she occupied herself with embroidery, in which she was expert; but whenever the King invited her to discuss affairs of state she could discuss them intelligently. She was merciful, and generous to the poor servants of God. The saying soon got about that she was the rose on the Godwin thorntree, and all the more gentle for coming from such a spiky stock.

That summer there died Bishop Britwold of Wilton, a very holy man. Soon after a story became current which did much to explain the King's vow of continence. It is not the kind of thing that anyone can prove, but I believe it because it fits in with so many other things. It seems that long ago, when Sweyn and his pirates were laying waste the country, the holy Bishop Britwold was granted a miraculous vision. He saw God enthroned in Heaven, and St Peter presenting before Him a young man who was destined to be King of the English. God had chosen him specially for this office, and he would enjoy a long and prosperous reign; but there was one condition, he must remain continent all his life. Britwold knew, by divine inspiration, that the young man was Edward son of Ethelred, then an obscure exile in Normandy. In the vision the young man accepted the condition. But of course it worried him, as it would worry any conscientious King; if he must die childless, how could he arrange a peaceful succession to his throne? St Peter answered his doubts in striking fashion. 'The Kingdom of the English is God's,' said he. 'After you are dead God will provide for Himself another King pleasing to Him.'

And thus it happened, though at that time no human prudence could have foreseen it. For when Britwold saw the vision the heathen Danes had conquered England, and Sweyn had a flourishing family to succeed him. But God blotted out the whole line of Canute. Edward, without any effort on his part, was called from poverty-stricken exile to be King, the first King within living memory who received the crown by the unanimous desire of his subjects and did not have to fight a rival for it.

At first Bishop Britwold kept this vision a secret; to mention

44

it would be to set even more Danish assassins on the trail of the exile in Normandy. But he lived to see it fulfilled, and knew it for a true revelation from God. Therefore during his last illness he told the whole story to a holy hermit, and bade him publish it abroad as soon as he was dead.

Now everyone knew that King Edward would be the last of his line, and there was great speculation about the successor whom God had promised to choose for him. I suppose at that time Earl Godwin expected that he would be able to nominate this successor, and that was why he remained faithful to the King he had set up. He was at least ten years older than Edward, but he might reasonably expect to survive him; since the days of the great Alfred very few of the house of Cerdic have lived to see fifty years. But God had promised a long reign to Edward his faithful servant.

To succeed Britwold as Bishop in Wilton the King appointed a holy man from oversea, Hermann of Lotharingia; he ruled in Wilton for many years, and reformed his church after the best Continental models. But, as usual, when the King appointed a holy man from oversea for no other reason than his piety, the magnates led by Godwin insisted that this should be balanced by the promotion of some Englishmen who could do useful service to the secular state. About the same time Aldred, a Mercian, was made Bishop of Worcester. He was a clerk of blameless life, or the King would not have granted him the Bishopric; but he was better known as a skilled diplomatist, who could reconcile warring chiefs even while they marched at the head of their armies. In later years he had plenty of scope for his peculiar talent.

CHAPTER III

Sweyn Godwinsson

In those days, when the King was active and spent long hours in the saddle every day, his court seldom stayed very long in one place. This was partly because much of the royal revenue was paid in kind, and it is easier to go to the corn and beef than to bring foodrents long miles to a distant kitchen; but even more because the King's strenuous hunting soon cleared the neighbourhood of game, and to enjoy good sport he must move to another forest.

I have never considered riding at full gallop among thorn trees a rational amusement for a grown man. Any member of the household was welcome at the royal hunt, where to drive the deer needed many willing helpers; I could have taken part if I had wished, but I did not wish. Occasionally, especially in wet weather, I would go out with a dry cloak and dry boots, so that the King should not take cold on his ride home; but that was all I saw of the royal sport. So I cannot state of my own knowledge that King Edward was a courageous and skilful horseman and a master of the intricate lore of kennel and mews; but that was the judgement of those who understood such things.

Although we travelled a great deal, we did not journey all through England. The special homeland of the house of Cerdic is Wessex; we seldom left it except to go to London, which is so populous and turbulent that any competent ruler must visit it frequently. The normal routine was for the King to wear his crown in Gloucester for Christmas, in Winchester for Easter, and in London for Pentecost. Between times we would travel slowly through the forests that border Cotswold, which the King preferred for his hunting. He never in his life went north of

46

the River Trent, and only the threat of invasion could bring him to Kent or Sussex; Wessex was his home.

There is always trouble on the northern border of England, where the King of the Scots disputes the boundary. The northwest is exposed to raids from the Danish pirates of Dublin. But the Anglo-Danes of the north are nearly as savage as their heathen cousins, and they preferred to conduct their own affairs without intervention from civilised Wessex. Earl Siward understood pirates, since he was himself of pirate stock; he could cope with his neighbours, and we left him to do so.

In Gloucester we were very near to the other hostile neighbours of England, the thieving and treacherous Welsh. They will never make a firm peace with us, because for the last five hundred years we have been driving them westward (they used to celebrate Easter on the wrong date, and tonsure their priests from ear to ear; so they deserve all the misfortunes that have befallen them). Gloucester and Hereford are outposts of civilisation very close to these barbarous cattle-thieves. The King charged himself personally with the defence of this menaced border.

In the year 1046 the Welsh were more threatening than usual. Normally these dangerous robbers fight as much among themselves as against their more civilised neighbours, so that it is possible to hire one petty chieftain to attack another. But in the spring of that year, after several complicated campaigns, all Wales was divided between two rulers only; most tiresomely, both were named Griffith, though they were not related.

King Griffith of the North had been fighting successfully against the men of Chester, who are a mixture of Mercian and Anglo-Danes and Danes from Ireland; he had conquered a part of their land, and settled his Welshmen to farm it. But King Griffith of the South had been raiding towards Hereford, and that was much more serious; for though Hereford lies in Mercia it is not far from the boundary of Wessex. So Bishop Aldred of Worcester, that cunning diplomatist, devised one of his strokes of policy. He suggested that the King of the North should be invited to visit King Edward at Gloucester; during this friendly visit he should be recognised as rightful lord of his conquests near Chester, which might just as well be held by Welshmen as by Irish-Danes only one generation removed from heathendom. In return he would recognise Edward as lord of all the lesser Kings in Britain, as many Welsh rulers had done before him; and when he had gone back to his mountains he would lead his men against the really troublesome King of the South, in alliance with an English army.

Bishop Aldred could generally persuade people to agree to his treaties, though whether these treaties were well contrived in the first place was another matter. King Griffith duly came to Gloucester and knelt at the feet of his suzerain; a small English army was gathered to co-operate with him, led by young Sweyn Godwinsson. This gave the lad a chance to prove himself in a campaign where defeat would not menace any vital English interest. Everyone was satisfied except the displaced landowners of Chester, who were of Danish descent and so did not much matter anyway.

King Edward took the opportunity of this visit by a prominent under-King to organise a grand hunt. I remember this hunt particularly well, though I was not present; for in the course of it there took place an incident which displayed more than one side of my lord's fascinating character.

The purpose of the hunt was not merely pleasure; with so many eminent guests to be fed the royal kitchen needed fresh venison. Therefore all the deer in a large wood were to be driven by hounds and beaters into an enclosure of nets; the King would have the sport of hunting his pack until the enclosure was reached, and then the great men would fall on the trapped deer with arrows and javelins. If everything worked out according to plan all the deer in that particular forest would be slain.

Everything did not work out according to plan, because a small farmer wished to preserve the game in his native woods. While no one was looking this man made a gap in the nets, so that many of the deer escaped to his land. When the King came up, blowing his horn among the hounds he loved, he saw the day spoiled and lost his temper.

I heard all about it from those who were present. The King had a very hot temper, like all the race of Cerdic; he was in a towering rage as he stormed at the miserable peasant who had wrecked his hunt. 'By God and His mother,' he shouted, 'one day I shall repay this injury – if I get the chance.'

That was the end of the episode. The frightened yokel made himself scarce, and lived happily afterwards to tell the story of his encounter with the holy King. That was the point which

48

struck me when I heard of it, as it struck King Griffith and Earl Sweyn who were present and saw the King's anger. If either of these great men had been vexed by an unimportant farmer he would have ordered his followers to put a torch to the farm buildings without a moment's hesitation; probably his men would have raped the womenfolk into the bargain. Our noble King was so eminently just that even in a moment of blinding rage he could not punish a rustic who had committed no legal crime. He did no more than warn the man that if ever he found himself before a tribunal he must expect a stern judgement. Has there ever been another absolute ruler who did not think of breaking the law of the land even when he was furious with anger?

The campaign planned by Bishop Aldred had as much success as most of these expeditions against the Welsh. King Griffith of the North and Sweyn Godwinsson his ally plundered the lands of King Griffith of the South until the latter begged for peace and offered hostages. The Welsh, who are light-armed skirmishers, cannot face an army of English axemen, and always submit when the English march against them; but they do not scruple to break their agreements, and the hostages they offer are often inconvenient royal kinsmen whom they would be glad to see dead. After South Wales had submitted the allies separated, and on his march back to Gloucester Earl Sweyn committed a frightful crime.

As I have said, he was a great breaker of hearts, and took pride in this manly accomplishment. He halted for a few days at Leominster; and when he left he took with him Edith, abbess of the local convent. Men still dispute as to whether he carried her off by force, or seduced her into following him of her own free will. It is not a question that can ever be settled and in my opinion both views are correct; Edith was persuaded to follow the handsome scoundrel, but if his men had not held the town she could not have escaped from the convent.

What was really revolting was that the faithless lover sent her back to her nuns as soon as he was tired of her. Even libertines were shocked at such callous selfishness. Of course the convent would not take her back, and I don't know what became of her in the end, though I believe she soon died. Sweyn took fright when he saw how men despised him, and put it about that he was willing to marry her. Everybody knows that an abbess cannot marry, and everybody knew that Sweyn knew it; so his offer failed to impress public opinion. Mind you, if Sweyn and Edith had been deeply in love they would have found friends to shelter them, no matter how grave their sin; ordinary men in the world make excuses for genuine love, even if it happens to be adulterous. But by sending her off Sweyn proved that he regarded her merely as a whore, a body to be enjoyed and then tidied away to make room for the next one. Even Danes are not often so faithless.

The King was very angry. For a moment it looked as though he might break with the whole house of Godwin; but he had no excuse, for the great Earl and his other sons did not attempt to defend the rascal. Harold, for one, seemed rather glad at the downfall of his elder brother. Sweyn was outlawed as soon as the Council could meet, and his great Earldom in Hereford and the midlands was divided between Harold and his cousin Beorn. Sweyn sailed off to Flanders, the refuge of every English exile.

As always after great estates have been given to new masters, there was unrest among the nobles; presumably because great men were disappointed at their share of the booty. In the middle of the Christmas feasting Osgod Clapa was suddenly outlawed. His punishment was nothing graver than exile, and nobody tried to murder him during the days of grace while he gathered his wealth and prepared to leave the country; he was a Dane, who could live as happily in his native country as in England. But his fall caused great excitement. He was a very great man, and had been great for many years (King Hardicanute had fallen dead while drinking at his daughter's wedding). No one could discover the nature of the crime imputed to him. I am still not sure whether he fell because Godwin was jealous of him, or whether the King tried to weaken Godwin by driving out another Danish Earl.

Soon after Christmas began the coldest winter ever known in England; deep snow lay without thawing from January to March. Many of the poor died of cold, though the King was generous with firewood from the royal forests. Luckily frost so early in the year does not harm the harvest, which in 1047 was up to average. The snow must have been an omen to warn us of impending trouble, but the wise men could not agree as to which peril the portent was designed to foretell.

One impending peril did not come to pass. At that time there was a great war among the Danes of Denmark, between Sweyn the nephew of Canute and a rival for his crown, Magnus of Norway. King Sweyn asked for help from the old subjects of his uncle in England; and Earl Godwin, who had risen by the favour of Canute, was eager to help the nephew of his old patron. But King Edward declared that Englishmen must not meddle in the quarrels of barbarous pirates. For the first time since this reign began Godwin was overruled in the Council. No help was sent to Sweyn of Denmark.

Soon afterwards came news that Magnus was completely victorious; he now ruled the Danes as well as the Norwegians, and laid claim to the whole inheritance of Canute. He was fitting out a mighty fleet, and would invade us before winter. At that time, Pentecost, the court was in London, and all our Earls began to fit out their ships to oppose the barbarian invasion; but our navy was spared a useless and expensive muster because God revealed to His servant Edward that the Danish expedition would never set sail.

It was the solemn crownwearing of Pentecost, and the King heard High Mass in St Peter's, the famous minster on the western outskirts of London. This was still the cramped dark church which had been built in the early days of the conversion of the English; but though dark and oldfashioned it was a place apt for miracles, since a miracle had marked its consecration. The story is well known: how the first Bishop of London went to consecrate it, and found the oil of consecration gleaming fresh on the floor; on the previous night St Peter himself had come to hallow it, carried over the river in the boat of a poor fisherman.

As the King stood in his stall during the long Mass all the monks noted that he was distracted; there was a smile on his face, as though he saw something pleasing. He was not following the chant, and at the Consecration he was late in kneeling. All this I tell as it was told to me, for of course a youth of my rank had no place in the choir; but I was standing in the crowd by the west door, and I heard what King Edward said as he left the minster.

Even in those days Westminster claimed to be exempt from the jurisdiction of the Bishop of London; and though the claim was not universally admitted Bishop Robert, to please his friend the King, had sat during the Mass in a choir-stall, not on a throne by the altar. Bishop and King walked out side by side, and Robert leaned over to speak familiarly to his old friend.

He spoke in French, I suppose assuming that no one in the crowd could understand him; but thanks to my early training in the household of the Lady Emma I could follow a simple French conversation. 'My lord,' he said in a rallying tone, 'is this the way to set an example to the uncultured English? The High Mass of Pentecost, with the King present in state; but when his subjects look at him they can see he is thinking of his hawks. Your smile showed that you were very far from Westminster, and that at the most solemn moment of the Mass.'

The King smiled to prove that he was not angered by the rebuke. 'I have been distracted from my prayers. But I believe that God, or at least one of the saints in Heaven, distracted me. No, I was not caught up into bliss – that comes to holy hermits, not to Kings who live in this wicked world. What I saw was secular enough. Yet I saw it only by miracle, and I believe that I saw the truth.'

'What was that, my lord?'

'I saw a great fleet ready to leave harbour. I knew it for the Danish fleet, though you must not ask me how I knew. In the same way I knew that the great lord whom I saw being rowed out to his flagship in a little boat was King Magnus, my enemy. He wore mail and carried a great shield; so that when he missed his footing, trying to scramble from the boat into his longship, he sank like a stone as soon as he splashed into the water.'

'My lord, indeed God has favoured you. At dinner you must tell your vision to the Council. If King Magnus is dead we need not fear invasion.'

'Of course I shall announce it to my Council. The trouble is that they may not believe me. Why should God send a miraculous vision to *me*, of all people? I am King of the English and one of the richest men in the world. Can you find me a very small camel, small enough to go through the eye of a needle?'

'God has granted you a miracle, my lord. Such things obey God's laws, not ours, and it is temerarious to try to explain them.'

The King said no more. I could see that he was genuinely

puzzled. He had absolute confidence in the truth of his vision, but in his humility he thought it strange that God should favour him.

When the Earls heard the story they also were puzzled and doubtful; but they agreed to suspend the mustering of the fleet until news should come from Denmark. Within ten days the news came, that King Magnus was indeed dead; though, oddly enough, it was said he had been killed in a riding accident, not by drowning. That is not important. However he met his death it came opportunely for England, and our holy King had miraculous foreknowledge of it.

That evening I overheard him as he argued the matter to himself, trying to get it straight in his mind before he dropped off to sleep.

'Magnus was a Christian. As a rule God does not intervene in quarrels between Christian Kings. It's not as though we had been saved from a heathen invasion. Why should God send a miracle to help *me*, Edward the son of Ethelred? My father was chased from his kingdom without anyone in Heaven lifting a finger to save him. The Cerdingas can claim no special protection from above. Perhaps God feels an affection for the English? That must be it. Come to think of it, we had a pretty creditable conversion; not a single missionary martyred, and most of the Kings baptised after a very few years. Whereas those Danes. . . . There are heathen among them to this day, and they have martyred thousands of Christians who wished them well and wanted only to convert them. The vision was granted to the King of the English, not to poor old Edward. I must avoid the sin of Pride. . . . '

All the north made peace with England after Magnus was dead. His possessions were divided, Denmark returning to Sweyn the nephew of Canute and Norway going to Harold Hardrada, uncle to Magnus. These two fought a long and bitter war, and while it continued they were too busy to molest their Christian neighbours.

There was war also on the other side of the Channel, where Count Baldwin of Flanders attacked the Emperor and sacked the old palace of Charlemagne at Aachen. But in England nothing happened that summer, except that Bishop Stigand was translated from East Anglia to the wealthy See of Winchester.

That was Godwin's doing, of course, though he could not have done it without the King's consent. I suppose the King gave way because he owed Godwin some return for his loyal service, and anyway it was hard to keep down a man like Stigand. He was a competent administrator and an effective politician; and if such men happen to be clerks it has long been the custom to reward them with wealthy bishoprics. The King had a great dislike for Stigand, because he was a Dane who had persuaded the Old Lady to favour the Danish dynasty even against the claims of her own son. But the King was determined not to allow his personal dislike to be a bar against merited promotion, and at that time there was nothing to be said against Stigand as a clerk. His private life was regular and he was diligent in his pastoral duties; though, like many competent administrators, he cared nothing for forms so long as he could get speedy results. That carelessness of forms, which are important or they would not have been devised, was later to be his undoing.

In the next year, 1048, the unwonted peace in the lands of the north brought renewal of an old trouble, one which we were beginning to think had passed away for ever. Since there was no fighting for them at home a fleet of vikings came to plunder along our coast from Essex to Southampton Water. The fleet made landfall at Sandwich, the usual port of arrival for ships from the Baltic. I don't know why this should be so; one would expect ships sailing from the north-east to reach Northumbria rather than Kent. Up in Jutland somewhere I suppose they have a set of sailing directions, telling them how to coast along the Frisian shore and then cross the Channel to England; that would be safer, though slower, than striking out across the North Sea.

When the King heard of these ravages he decided that he in person would lead his navy against the vikings. Of course Earl Godwin must come too, for he had commanded the fleet ever since it was formed in the days of King Canute; but the King did not wish him to gain more glory in battle. He was already too powerful; the Danish professionals who manned the long-ships must see that there was a King of the English to lead them.

The whole court moved down to Sandwich, where our ships were gathering to pursue the vikings. I was among the pages appointed to prepare the King's armour, but I was not one of those chosen to go aboard the flagship. I was then just twenty years old, and as strong and active as I would ever be; but I was glad to avoid the campaign. I have never felt any desire to go to war; partly because I am awkward at swordplay and might be laughed at, partly because I do not want to be hurt even to gain glory. On this subject plenty of other men feel as I do, but few of them are sensible enough to keep away from armies.

The King was as pleased and excited at the prospect of battle as if he had been a stripling instead of a middle-aged, white-haired and holy man. In his royal armour he made a most imposing figure; and all the time we were lacing him into his mailshirt he talked to us with the candid absence of self-consciousness that was characteristic of him.

'Isn't it strange?' he said, fingering his axe with a white, unweathered hand; but though his hands were white because a falconer must wear gloves, they were the strong capable hands of a good horseman. 'I am head of the house of Cerdic, a family who have been warriors for at least five hundred years. I am descended from Woden, a powerful and bloodthirsty demon. Yet purely by chance I have passed my forty-sixth birthday without ever striking a blow in anger. It is chance only. In Normandy I must avoid public notice for fear of Danish assassins, and since I became King of the English no foe has attacked us. At my age it feels queer to be a raw recruit. But I am confident that when danger appears I shall not disgrace my ancestors. If we were going out to make war on the army of some other Christian King I might not be eager to shed the blood of my fellow-men. But we are to hunt vikings, enemies of civilisation, beastly robbers who would rather steal than plough their own land. Drowning is too good for such savages. I hope we catch some of them alive, so that I can hang them before a crowd of the peasants they hope to pillage. Even if I did not look forward to it I should be sure that I am doing the right thing. This is not like a war of foreign conquest; a King who defends his people from vikings is doing no more than his duty.'

After these high hopes the King was greatly disappointed when the pirates did not stay to meet him. When they heard that our fleet was ready for sea they at once fled to shelter in the harbours of Flanders. We expected that Count Baldwin would drive them out, so that our ships might still catch them as they fled. Then we heard with disgust that the Flemings had bought very cheaply the bloodstained plunder of England; and that the vikings, rich and happy, had sailed home unmolested.

The King was especially furious. After a long and stormy meeting of the Council he strode into his bedchamber still muttering with anger. He carried a roll of papers, and expounded it to me since it had not moved his advisers.

'See, this is a map of northern Christendom, drawn for me by Bishop Robert of London. Here is the Baltic, where the Emperor is conquering the heathen Wends. Here live the Danes, who now call themselves Christians. All down here are the coasts of Frisia and Flanders, which have been Christian and civilised for the last three hundred years. And here, jutting out into the heathen north, is the island of Britain. Do you see how England is hemmed in by pirates on every side? On the west lies Ireland, where indeed the Irish are Christians of a kind; but their coasts are infested by Danish pirates, many of them still unbaptised. The north-west, is a scatter of islands, held by the same barbarians; and north beyond Scotland live the wicked vikings of Orkney and Iceland, the most savage of all.'

In his excitement he strode up and down the bedchamber.

'When you were born, young Edgar, England was part of this barbarous northern world. Canute conducted himself like a Christian King, I grant you. But he was also a Dane, and all his dominions looked to Denmark as their centre. We English are in some ways very like Danes, though of course not so wicked. If the wide realm of Canute had endured this whole island would have become an imitation of the north. God saved us from that fate, because the sons of Canute were not worthy of their father. God Himself sent me to rule the English, the crown falling on to my head without any effort on my part. Thus God laid on me the duty of bringing England into the civilised and truly Christian south. And He has shown me the means, ready to my hand. For just across the sea from us, here to the south, are a people who prove that even northern pirates can be tamed by good priests and good rulers. I have lived among them, and I know them. The Normans are of the same stock as the English; their forefathers were pirates, like my ancestor Cerdic. Now they are the most civilised men in the world. I have brought in Norman Bishops to reform the English church; if I am strong enough

I shall bring in Norman warriors to set an example to my unruly Earls. And it so happens that my nearest kinsman is a Norman, trained in all the arts of Norman civilisation. Ralph, my sister's son, is old enough to show his mettle. If I name him as my heir perhaps the Council will obey him when I am dead. But first I must make him known to all my Kingdom. I shall try to get him some fragment of Sweyn's Earldom; that is, if Sweyn's bloody kinsmen, Harold and Beorn, will allow me to dispose of it. Everything was going smoothly, as indeed it ought to when what I do is manifestly the Will of God. . . .

'And now that foolish greedy Count of Flanders has spoiled everything, by permitting savage pirates to sell their plunder in his markets. It is nearly always wrong to make war on the Emperor, the sword of Christendom; Count Baldwin actually sacked Aachen, as though to insult the memory of the great Charlemagne. Now he is the ally of pirates. I wanted to sail straight away to ravage his lands. But my foolish Council fears to mix in such a dangerous quarrel, and the great navy I inherited from Canute, the finest navy ever seen in the Narrow Seas, is to sit idle while pirates sell the stolen goods of Englishmen in a Christian market. It makes me despair. While I live I shall work to keep my country civilised, but after my death will come disaster.'

Throughout this long tirade I kept silent, thankful that the King spoke such dangerous words only to me. I agreed with nearly all he said, save that the Earls Harold and Beorn had done me no harm that I knew of and did not deserve to be called bloody. But if the Godwinssons and the other Anglo-Danes got to know the King's plans rebellion would follow.

The King had not sought my opinion, or my agreement. He had been giving relief to the emotions he must keep secret from his Council. Soon he was ready for bed, and as I lay on my pallet his mutterings died away.

By autumn the vikings had sailed home from Flanders, and England was at peace. Nothing else happened that year, except that I was promoted from page to chamberlain, though it was still my duty to prepare my lord for bed and afterwards to sleep on a pallet at his feet. The King felt shy when strange fingers touched him. I think he would have preferred to undress himself and then sleep completely alone. But such a striking breach of etiquette would have made his people think he had gone mad, so the next best thing was to have one familiar figure to perform these intimate services. I continued to carry out the duties of a page; in fact more than the customary duties, for every night I slept in the King's chamber with no colleagues to relieve me. But in my twenty-first year, with my moustache growing nicely, I must be called a chamberlain and draw the appropriate salary.

In another chamber the Lady slept among her women; but there were no separate female quarters barred off from the rest of the household, such as you still find in some old-fashioned halls. After four years of their queer imitation of married life husband and wife had grown extremely fond of one another, odd as that may seem to outsiders. She loved him as a dutiful daughter loves an indulgent father, and he took pleasure in the companionship of a graceful and good-humoured girl. She was always in and out of his chamber, even though he might be wearing only his bedgown; sometimes at night she helped me to tuck the coverlets round him. Both of them were so settled in the habit of continence that they were never tempted to infringe it. In public the Lady fulfilled to perfection the duties of a royal consort, and in private she was happy.

The King also was happy in private, for affairs were going well for his family. He had persuaded the Godwinssons to give up enough of Sweyn's land to make his nephew Ralph an Earl, though he was the poorest Earl in England. Earl Ralph was the son of Edward's sister Godiva and her first husband, the Count of Mantes. His father had died young while on pilgrimage to the Holy Land and his mother had married again; so that he had been brought up by his stepfather, Count Eustace of Boulogne. He had been trained as a Norman cavalier, and looked very well on his horse. It was hoped that he would defeat the raiding Welsh by bringing against them men trained to fight on horseback after the Norman fashion, and for that reason he had been put in charge of the defences of Worcester. We courtiers could see what was happening, though it was done so smoothly that the Council did not take alarm. The King was building up the greatness of Earl Ralph; but gently, so as not to antagonise Earl Godwin.

*

In the spring of 1049 Christendom united to suppress the disorders in Flanders, which Count Baldwin had turned into a refuge for pirates and vikings. The Emperor marched westwards through Lotharingia, and the English fleet sailed out to bar the Narrow Seas. Once more King Edward embarked on his flagship, fully armed; and I am sure that if he had encountered the enemy he would have fought with a heroism worthy of his ancestors. As far as I know not one of my ancestors was a hero. Therefore, since the King did not need me, I waited in Sandwich.

As it happened, the fleet returned completely victorious without a blow struck, which is the most fortunate outcome of any campaign. Count Baldwin submitted to the Emperor without fighting; he made restitution for the pillage of Aachen, and promised to send away all the pirates who sheltered in his land. It had been expected that he would try to flee to his barbarian allies in the north, but when we learned of his surrender the fleet put back to Sandwich. Many of the ships were laid up; but the King and the Earls remained in the port, with the regular squadron which was always kept in readiness, as it had been in the days of the warlike King Canute.

That was a sensible precaution; for of course the lawless fugitives expelled from Flanders all raided the English coast on their way to seek another refuge. Osgod Clapa, the Dane who had once been an English Earl, found himself at the head of a large band of homeless pirates; but after raiding in Essex most of these pirates deserted their leader, because he wished to use them in the civil wars of Denmark. They were thieves, not warriors; without Osgod they sailed aimlessly, plundering from village to village, until they were dispersed by the levy of the East Angles.

Sweyn Godwinsson had been one of the outlaws sheltering in Bruges. With a small squadron he sailed westward down Channel, hoping I suppose to link up with the vikings of Dublin. While the King and his court remained at Sandwich Earl Godwin led most of the regular navy in pursuit of his erring son.

Then we heard news that Sweyn, sheltering somewhere off the coast of the South Saxons, had sent messengers ashore to beg for pardon. That was what had been expected. No one imagined that Godwin would actually make war on one of his darling sons, but the fact that his father headed the pursuit would prove to Sweyn that even his family influence would not save him unless he sued for peace. The Council was summoned to meet in Sandwich, to settle the terms of Sweyn's pardon.

But this was the middle of the campaigning season, and some of the Earls were too busy to come to the Council. Trouble on the northern border kept Siward in Northumbria, while in the west the King of South Wales was stirring. Earl Ralph and Bishop Aldred gathered the local levies to oppose him; they also took into pay a large band of Welsh spearmen who claimed to be hereditary foes of the house of Griffith. So that on his flagship the King conferred only with Earl Godwin and the captains of his professional sailors.

While the Council was in session a messenger reached Sandwich with news of a grave defeat on the Welsh border. Exaggerated rumours ran through the town, but I heard the authentic version when I undressed the King that evening. He was in a truly royal rage, more angry than I had ever seen him. It is widely remembered that my lord was a very holy man, but his subjects forget that he was as hot-tempered as any member of his race; his virtue lay in this, that he allowed his rage to evaporate in harmless talk among his intimates.

In his chamber that night he let himself go.

'How can anyone rule this unfortunate country while Earl Godwin is the greatest man in it? That is why I was trying to build up my nephew Ralph as his rival. Ralph has been trained as a Norman knight. With his mounted followers I was sure he would win a few cheap victories over those barbarous Welsh, savages who fight in their shirts without armour. Instead he has allowed himself to be tricked by Welsh turncoats. As though even their horrid bloodfeuds would hold them faithful to an English Earl! On the battlefield our Welsh mercenaries joined King Griffith, and then Ralph fled at full gallop with all his men. It's disgrace that will always be remembered against him.'

'Did he behave worse than Bishop Aldred, my lord?' I asked, trying to look on the bright side.

'I suppose not, but in this world there's no justice. All the Council admire Bishop Aldred, because they think that when a clerk leads his men to war it shows courage. But they laugh at poor Ralph, just because he tried to fight on horseback in

60

what they call an un-English fashion. Someone said he ought to be known as Ralph the Timid, and if I know my own countrymen that nickname will cling to him for ever.'

In fact it did. It was all the more damaging because it proved to be true. Another man might have been spurred on by shame to fight like a hero in his next battle; Ralph just gave up trying, and the next time his life was in danger he fled even more disgracefully.

'Now that Ralph has been dishonoured Godwin will be stronger than ever,' the King went on. 'Very well, I shall face the fact. I shall leave everything in his hands. I shall ask him to make peace all round in any way that suits him. That's only common sense, though I hate doing it. Do you know what Godwin proposes? He suggests that his darling Sweyn shall be forgiven, welcomed to England, and given back his Earldom. Now, young Edgar, do you think that just?'

'Well . . . my lord,' I answered cautiously. I knew what the King wished me to say, but even in the privacy of this chamber I did not choose to speak openly against the great Earl Godwin. 'Well, it may not be strict justice, but as an act of mercy in an imperfect world it is not wholly imprudent. Sweyn has parted from his nun, and they will never meet again. He has been punished, and he has been frightened. If you give him another chance he may behave more wisely. It's not the best solution imaginable, but if his family plead for him I don't see how you can thwart them.'

'I can't please all the Godwinssons. That's the worst of it. Godwin wants me to forgive his son, and from the way he spoke I think he might go over to the Danish King unless he gets his way. But Harold, and that cousin Beorn who is always with the Godwinssons, refuse to give up Sweyn's lands which they have parted between them. They had the impudence to suggest that I find another Earldom for Sweyn, at the expense of Leofric or Siward. I refused, but in the end I may be driven to it. My first duty is to hold on to the crown of the English and so keep out the barbarous Danes. If necessary I must allow the Godwinssons to hold every Earldom in England, rather than drive them into opposition. I hate to see injustice done, the blameless Siward weakened to please the wicked Sweyn. But anything, even injustice, is better than civil war.'

In the end Sweyn was given a safeconduct to come and

make his peace with the King. He came and put his hands within the King's hands, swearing to be his loyal servant. But because Harold clung to them he was not at once granted his lands, and he went back still an outlaw to his ships off the coast of the South Saxons.

Then stories of his doings came into Sandwich thick and fast. Vikings from Dublin had been raiding in the west, and various Godwinssons were scattered with small squadrons of warships all down the Channel. The Earl himself led the main fleet, but Harold, Beorn, and even young Tostig in his first command, guarded various exposed harbours. The eight pirate ships which followed Sweyn lay off the port of Bosham, which had been for many years in the Godwin family. The sailors took advantage of this to go shopping in a town which favoured their leader.

On the evening of the day on which Sweyn left Sandwich we heard that he had encountered Beorn on the road; after a friendly meeting the two cousins were riding in company to Bosham. At once the King took alarm, and very reasonably. On the Downs beacons were lighted, and the levy of all southern England was summoned to muster under the King's standard. Housecarles stood guard at the closed gates of Sandwich, and we all prepared for civil war. The King retired early, and as he prepared for bed the Lady joined him in his chamber.

I was there, so much a part of the ordinary furniture of the chamber that they both spoke freely before me. 'You must not believe that we are all traitors,' the Lady began in great distress. 'You can count on Tostig absolutely, now and always. He has sworn loyalty, and he will never break his oath. I wish I could say the same of my father, but in honesty I can't. All the same, his family is now divided, and I think that for the present he will support his daughter's husband. Harold also is true. I don't say he would never change sides; but if he changes he will do it openly. He will defy you in form before he rebels. In any case, as the holder of Sweyn's Earldom he ought to be Sweyn's enemy.'

'You might say the same of Beorn,' the King pointed out. 'He also stands to lose if Sweyn returns to power. Yet he has ridden with Sweyn to Bosham.'

'Perhaps he is still trying to make peace,' I put in. 'He may be arguing with Sweyn, advising him to accept the King's pardon even without his lands.'

Neither of them would consider such an unlikely explanation. They said that Beorn, like most warriors, would see things in black or white. To him, his cousin Sweyn was an outlaw and an enemy of the King; if he rode with him it must be because he had decided to join the King's enemies.

In spite of their vows the King and his Lady passed that night together. But neither made any preparations for bed. The King sat on a stool by the fire while the Lady crouched at his feet, and together they reckoned the forces of every magnate in England and every halfhour sent me out to inquire if fresh news had arrived.

This showed me the Lady in a new light. I had thought of her as a nonentity, who did whatever she was told. In most matters Edith was in truth indifferent, and did as she was told to save herself the bother of rebellion. But sometimes she made up her mind, and then she was immovable. Now she had decided to stand by the King, even against her family.

Soon after midnight a messenger rode in to say that both Earls had boarded the pirate ships in Bosham harbour. Then the crews had been called from the waterside taverns and at sunset the squadron had sailed. As they reached open water the ships headed west, but night was falling and that might be a ruse. They could not be going far, for they had sailed in a hurry, with little water on board.

The pirates might intend to raid Sandwich and capture the King while his navy was scattered. At dawn we stood to arms; the King went round the ramparts in full armour, carrying a great axe. But daylight showed an empty sea, and we all went to sleep until dinner.

Two days later, while the levies of southern England were beginning to come in, we heard further news of Sweyn; news so terrible that at first we could not believe it. The pirates had called in at Dartmouth, and there put ashore the dead body of Beorn. He had been killed with an axe, while his hands were bound behind him.

Even without this corpse there was no concealing the disgusting truth; for Sweyn's conduct had been too much even for his pirates, who deserted him in Dartmouth and told all they knew. Sweyn had encountered Beorn by chance, as he rode back from the Council at Sandwich; and Beorn, moved by no motive but friendship, had tried to persuade his cousin to come into the

63

King's peace. Sweyn had agreed that this was a wise plan, but said that his mind was not yet made up; he would like to discuss it further with his cousin. But all the time he remembered that Beorn was one of the two Earls who now occupied his land, and who had advised against his reinstatement.

People said afterwards that Beorn was foolish to trust Sweyn. But consider the position: Sweyn was his cousin, as close to him as a brother; Sweyn had just offered to come into the King's peace, and though the proposed treaty had not been concluded negotiations were still continuing; Sweyn led eight shiploads of foreigners, not even his own sworn comrades but casual pirates picked up in Bruges; the Godwinssons were hunting him with forty ships of their own, helped by the regular navy of England. Beorn may have feared that he would sail away as the foe of King Edward and of his own father; he could make his way down Channel to the Danish harbours in Ireland and so north-about round Scotland to the breeding-place of pirates in the Sound. But Beorn could not have foreseen that his cousin, his ally, his comrade in arms, would murder him shamefully in time of truce.

At Bosham Sweyn asked Beorn to visit his ship. When Beorn refused pirates fell on him, bound him, and carried him off. As the squadron put into Dartmouth Sweyn slew him with an axe.

In Sandwich the army roared its disgust. Such treachery was unprecedented; not even heathen Danes would behave so. Of course Sweyn must be outlawed. There would be no lack of volunteers to take up the bloodfeud, for though Beorn was childless he had cousins and comrades who had loved him. But outlawry may come to any warrior; many outlaws are men of honour who have put themselves beyond the King's peace by honourably killing their enemies when the law says that they should have accepted money in place of blood. The army felt that something more must be done, to mark the contempt which every warrior felt for Sweyn the murderer. In a solemn assembly it was solemnly proclaimed that Sweyn Godwinsson was *nithing* – worthless. His oath was of no value, no warrior would seek his help, when he spoke it would be assumed that he was lying. It did not matter what he should do with the rest of his life, whether he outwitted the avengers or was knocked on the head by some public-spirited stranger. He was nithing, not worth bothering about.

By the old law of King Alfred a freeman who refuses to join the levy in time of war may be proclaimed nithing; but since no English freeman ever refuses to fight, though some of them fight on the wrong side, the penalty has not been inflicted within living memory. The compensation for wrongfully calling a man nithing is as heavy as if you had killed him, since honour is as precious as life. The word is seldom heard in a lawful assembly.

The Godwinssons were bitterly ashamed that one of their kin should have thus disgraced the honour of their house. They made what amends they could by burying Beorn very splendidly in the Old Minster at Winchester, and for a few weeks Earl Godwin himself was too abashed to appear in public. But for him the interests of his family came second only to his own; soon he was urging Bishop Aldred, that famous peacemaker, to get a pardon for Sweyn. That scoundrel himself cared nothing for his disgrace; he went back to Flanders, the refuge of all scoundrels, and passed the winter in comfort in the hall of Count Baldwin.

Earl Harold alone benefited from this cowardly murder. Now he could keep undisturbed his share of Sweyn's lands, and in addition he received part of the lands of Beorn; though the rest went to Leofric, just to prove that there could be great men in England who were not kin of the house of Godwin.

The amazing thing is that within a year Godwin managed to win a pardon for his eldest son; or rather Bishop Aldred did, who could compose any quarrel. The murderer was restored not only to the King's peace, but also to his Earldom.

As the King gained in assurance (for he had been very shy when first I knew him) he bothered less about whether his behaviour might seem eccentric. Especially in his bedchamber, among his intimates, he would say whatever came into his head. So I was not particularly surprised when one evening, while we were at Winchester for the Easter crownwearing of 1050, he asked me gravely whether I had ever seen the Devil. I answered that since I had come to court I had met many of his servants, but that I had never seen the Fiend in person.

'I saw him this morning,' the King said simply, 'and he was really so ugly that it was hard not to feel sorry for him. Perhaps

5

he wasn't Satan himself, for there was no pride in the creature; yet he was certainly one of the princes of Hell. God's foe for all eternity – what a fate! No wonder there was a hangdog air about him. But he got into that condition of his own free will, and now it's too late to pity him.'

'Good Heavens, my lord, where did you see him and what did he do to you?' I asked in amazement. The King had spoken as casually as if relating that he had heard an early cuckoo.

'Come, Edgar, use your head. Where would he be, in a court like this, where in general we try to keep the Commandments? Not sitting on the edge of a bed, waiting for the wrong partner to creep in. He was in the treasury, of course, with his hairy arms wrapped round a sack of silver. This year's wartax has just come in, and poor dear Hugolin asked me to come and help him gloat over it. I like Hugolin, and he's as honest as anyone of his trade can be. But after all he is a Norman, and the only weakness of those fine fellows is that in general they are a little too fond of money. Hugolin is very proud of his full treasury; he told me that no other treasurer in Christendom could show the like. Then he added that no other King in Christendom has the right to levy a wartax in time of peace, and when I thought it over I had to agree with him. All taxes are devilish things, but a wartax in time of peace reeks of the Pit. It's no wonder the Devil approves, and helps us to collect it.'

'But what did you do, my lord? How did you get rid of him?'

'I didn't. I left him sitting there, just beyond that wall. As things are, he has a right to sit in my treasury. Next year he will have to leave. When that money has been spent there will be no more of those sacks of silver under my roof, handy perches for the chief devils in Hell. At tomorrow's meeting of the Council I shall abolish the wartax. I have been stupidly slow to see that such a tax ought to be abolished. Besides the wickedness of the whole conception of it, collecting money in peacetime to pay idle soldiers who have no enemy to fight, the tax is a reminder of the saddest and most shameful epoch in the history of the English. Do you know that it was first collected by my father? King Ethelred used it, not to pay soldiers, but to bribe Danish pirates to go away. He did that year after year until the thing became a custom. Of course Canute, though in many ways he was a good man, was too greedy to end a custom that brought so much money into his treasury. But I shall end it. The pirates may never come again, now that most of them are Christians of a sort. If they come the whole levy of the Kingdom will be called out to fight them, without wages, as is the duty and privilege of free men. No more wartax. As King I must sometimes be stern and ruthless; I must hang robbers, even though they rob only because they are hungry; I fear that Godwin and his sons sometimes do much worse things in my name. But for one good deed I shall be remembered by posterity. I shall be remembered as the only King in history who abolished a tax he could have collected, just because he did not need the money.'

'Posterity will indeed be grateful, my lord,' I said soothingly. I did not add that it is not so easy to abolish a tax as the King supposed, for that might have upset him and spoiled his sleep. In fact, though my holy master never again levied the wartax, his Council insisted on putting on record the assessment, so that it might be collected again in an emergency; and as you all know it is now collected every year, whether in peace or war.

The King said no more about the abolition of the tax. He had announced his will, and he was certain that it would be carried into effect. He very seldom interfered in the daily details of administration, leaving all such matters to his Council; which meant in practice to Earl Godwin. But when for once he did decide to make a change he was inflexible. He knew that the great Earl would be sorry to see the tax ended, but he also knew that it would never again be levied during his reign.

The visible apparition of the Devil interested him much more than the tax; and rightly, for taxes are all about us but we seldom see their author, the Devil.

'Now why do you think,' he continued, 'that the Devil showed himself to me, while Hugolin the treasurer could not see him? It might be for one of two reasons. Either I am such a wicked King that the Devil is sure of me, and because he likes to pester any baptised Christian he chooses to give me a fright while I am still in this world; or my patron in Heaven, St Peter the Prince of the Apostles, has the will as well as the power to send me a warning, so that I may mend my ways before it is too late. The second is a much more comforting explanation, isn't it? I hope it is the right one.'

'It must be right, my lord,' I said eagerly. 'For one thing, the Devil is no fool. He appears to wicked men as they lie dying, but he would not warn you of your errors while you still have time to repair them. Besides, you are not a wicked King. St Peter is your patron. To save you from wrongdoing he has opened your eyes to the presence of the Devil, who of course finds himself at home in the treasury of every King.'

'An empty treasury won't be nearly so cosy for him. When that money has been spent he will go away. In the meantime I must tell the clerks that the treasury is an unchancy place, and that they must be sure they are in a state of grace while they work there. So we've decided, haven't we, that St Peter sent me that warning? Oh dear, that reminds me; I am getting deeper and deeper into his debt. Years ago, when I was frightened and miserable in Normandy, with no future after Duke Richard was dead and Danish assassins always on my track, I made a vow to St Peter, and I have never paid it. I vowed that if ever I was given my rights as King of the English I would go to Rome in all my state, and pray at Peter's tomb. Lots of my predecessors did it, from Egbert right down to Canute. But with the threat of invasion from Denmark always hanging over our heads I don't see how I can leave this country. St Peter won't go on sending me these most helpful warnings unless I soon pay him his due.'

'St Peter does not demand the impossible, my lord. And he has left a representative on earth, who may act in his name. The next embassy you send to Rome should ask the Pope to commute your vow.'

'That's a very good idea. The Pope can fix things up for me. There! Now everything's settled and I can go to sleep. The Devil may be squatting in my treasury, but that's on the other side of the party-wall. I shall put my image of St Peter over my bed as usual.'

'One thing is still unsettled, my lord.' I thought it better to warn the King of a trouble he was sure to meet in Council, rather than have him taken by surprise in the presence of all the magnates of England. 'The wartax pays for the regular navy. When the tax is gone how will your sailors be paid?'

'My sailors will have to earn a living in some more honest fashion. If they are willing to plough I shall give them land; if they insist on cutting throats for a wage they must seek it from some other lord. Luckily the tax for this year has already been gathered, so they will have plenty of time to plan their future. My future is already planned. For the next eight hours I shall be asleep.'

At the next Council the King carried his point. The tax was suspended, and it was agreed to disband the regular navy. The King was inclined to be ruthless to professional fighting-men, whom he regarded as no better than hired killers; but they enjoyed the sympathy of the magnates, who saw that they were treated generously. Most of the sailors were given a full year's notice to seek another lord (for of course none of them chose to earn their bread by sweating on the land); faithful veterans who had served in the wars of the great Canute were kept on for two years, by which time they were old enough to retire anyway. There were enough of these elderly warriors to man five ships and the King could just manage to pay them from his ordinary revenue. After these two years were up the last ships of the regular navy which had been founded by Canute, King of the North, were laid away to rot in deserted creeks.

During this same stay at Winchester there was another incident in the treasury. The strongroom where the silver was lodged lay next to the King's chamber, and now that we knew a Devil lodged in it also it was naturally never out of our thoughts. One day the King had a cold, and the weather was wet; so in the afternoon, instead of hunting, he lay down on his bed to rest until supper. For once I did not remain in the room with him. There was a pair of new hunting-boots to be oiled, and fish-oil has a nauseating stink; he told me to get on with the messy business in the open air. It was the middle of the day and the hall was full of guards, so I did as I was told. If there had been the slightest danger of assassination I would have disobeyed him, or at least sent for another chamberlain to take my place.

I was criminally careless (and never again was the King left alone in his chamber). That morning Hugolin had opened the treasury to fetch silver to pay the housecarles; then the King returned to his chamber unexpectedly, and rather than keep him waiting while the door was barred and fastened the treasurer went away, leaving the strongroom open. There was no way into it save through the King's chamber, and we all thought it safe enough.

Presently the King rang a little handbell, as a signal that he wished to get up. I came in to dress him, and Hugolin followed me to close the treasury. First he looked inside, as he always did; and at once began to clamour that three sacks of silver were missing.

'I saw the thief,' he lamented. 'In the hall I passed a stranger, and noticed that he was carrying a bag of the standard treasury pattern. I took it for granted that some rich housecarle was carrying home his pay untouched. What a fool I was! I saw the thief and let him go. But you, my lord, were not asleep all the time. Did you perhaps see him?'

'Yes, I also saw him,' said the King with a chuckle, 'and I also let him go. If the treasury has been robbed I am to blame. He was such a miserable sooty little man, I suppose a scullion from the kitchen. He peeped through my door and saw the treasury open behind my bed. He tiptoed into my chamber, looking ludicrously frightened and ludicrously greedy at the same time. I nearly raised the alarm, and then I thought of what would happen to the poor frightened thief. Blind him, cut off his right hand, then turn him out to beg; that's the penalty for robbing the treasury, isn't it? And if I caught him in the act I should look silly if I pardoned him. But it's all wrong that *I* should have a man hacked about so just for stealing from *me*; though I see that loyal servants who guard the possessions of their lord may have a different duty. So I decided to pardon him in advance, without telling anyone. I stuck my nose in my pillow and snored like a pig. The thief crept through my chamber, grabbed a bag of silver, and slunk out again. Then he came back for another load, and I thought that was going too far. It's one thing for a starving pauper to help himself rather than die of hunger, and quite another for a greedy rascal to make a fortune out of one chance-opened door. Unfortunately it took me some time to make up my mind, and to think of a way of frightening him off without getting him arrested. On his third trip I called out to him, but only in a whisper: "You and I are safe here, but I hear Hugolin coming. Be off before he catches you." He ran away as though the Devil were at his heels.'

The King smiled happily. 'As soon as that treasury is empty the Devil will leave it. Cheer up, Hugolin. Tell me frankly, is there still enough money for you?'

'Yes, my lord. With care there will be just enough.'

'And there is enough for me, because I can manage on very little. And there was enough for that thieving scullion, since he has not come back for more. Do you see, Hugolin? This is the richest treasury that ever was in Britain. It holds enough to content three greedy men. There's glory for you. You may boast yourself the most prudent treasurer in the world. Don't bother to chase that thief, though I hope the silly man remembers to call on a priest. He ought to know that he is in mortal sin. What a pity St Peter didn't allow him also to see the Devil. St Peter has been very good to me, and I must not forget that I owe him a pilgrimage.'

The next embassy to Rome obtained a commutation of the King's vow of pilgrimage. In place of the long and arduous journey the King was commanded to build a great minster in honour of St Peter. The change pleased everyone. Earl Godwin did not want the King to go abroad; and the King, though disappointed of an interesting tour, was happy to devote his energies to making the ancient and holy shrine of St Peter at Westminster the most splendid foundation of modern times. I have already told of its miraculous consecration at the hands of St Peter in person, so no place could have been more appropriate. It was handily situated, near London which the King visited every year. There was enough land and enough money, and when the time came there would be no difficulty in collecting enough devout monks.

For the rest of his life the King's main interest and hobby, after hunting, was the building of St Peter's at Westminster.

CHAPTER IV

The Fall of Earl Godwin

Before the Christmas crownwearing of 1050 I was promoted to be the King's cupbearer. King Edward was a jumpy, quick-tempered man who did not like strange faces near him, and I was one of his favourites. This was not because of any special virtue on my part; I was no more fitted than any other chamberlain to be the confident of the sovereign. But in the first place I never asked favours. A bachelor and an orphan, I wanted no more than the good food and fine clothes which were my due so long as I remained in the royal household. Since I did not beg for landed estates for myself, or for benefices in the church for my kin, no other courtier was jealous of me; and the King himself was never compelled to deny me a boon and then look for something surly in my bearing. In the second place I had made a good beginning. Under the eye of a new page the King felt unpleasantly self-conscious; it so happened that I had met him for the first time when he was too excited by his raid on the Old Lady to have time to be shy. During that first anxious night at Winchester I had struck just the right note of deferential intimacy. He knew that he could say what he liked in my presence, and that though I would never betray his confidence I could give him a sensible answer if he sought it.

King Edward would have preferred to go to the barrels and fill his own cup from the spigot, as he had done when he was a poor exile in Normandy. Since his position required that his cup should be filled by a servant in a fine livery he wanted to have a familiar figure at his elbow. My promotion meant that I was even more in my lord's company; I could have easily made a fortune if I had been trying to make a fortune at all. It also meant very much more work. I still slept every night in the royal chamber, though other chamberlains now cared for the King's clothes; and in the daytime I stood behind his chair when he sat in state at formal dinners and suppers.

At most of these Councils the King took no greater part than his cupbearer. He would sit in his carved throne, his pale fingers caressing the untouched cup before him. His usual cup was a great aurochs-horn which had belonged to King Canute; its rim was of silver-gilt, and a gold band round the middle supported silver-gilt legs like those of a goat. Long ago a Varang had brought it to Denmark from Constantinople. But if politeness required that he should drink many healths he would use a great cup of pure gold, chased with the image of St Peter holding the keys; the small bowl above the elaborate foot held no more than an eggshell, and the King might drain it repeatedly without taking more wine than he cared for.

Meanwhile great men would dispute hotly about the boundaries of their jurisdictions, or strike bargains about church preferment for their kin. The King would sit staring up into the rafters while the squabbles continued, only coming to life if someone mentioned hunting; and I also would stare into the rafters, holding a silver pitcher which probably would not be needed to refill the royal cup, no matter how long the feast might last. These long bickering Councils seemed to be a shocking waste of time; but, as the King once said to me, the bargains struck by the Earls would be even more shameless if the King were not present.

Sometimes really important matters came up to be decided at these Councils, and then it could be seen that the King ruled the English. I remember especially the Easter Council of 1051, for it marked the beginning of the great struggle with Earl Godwin. The metropolitan See of Canterbury was vacant, and at this Council the next Archbishop must be chosen.

The Archbishop of Canterbury is the second potentate in England, the King's greatest subject. If he is to carry out his task as the King's most trusted adviser he ought to know something of politics and administration, and of the other lands of Christendom. The Church in England, which has had so many ups and downs, also needs a holy and vigorous head. Because it is so difficult to choose a worthy Archbishop nobody wants Canterbury to be vacant again shortly after it has been filled; it is the custom to appoint a young and healthy clerk, who has the prospect of a long tenure. Knowing that in all probability another vacancy would not occur for some years, the magnates were anxious to choose someone who would fit easily into his place in the Council; but the King was all the more eager to choose someone who would enforce true discipline in the Church.

Old Archbishop Eadsige had played his part worthily; his influence had done much to bring about the peaceful accession of King Edward. But he was rather too much the Bishop of the men of Kent, living beside his minster instead of coming to the Council wherever it might be held. For a long time he had been ailing, and a few years ago his successor had been chosen; the Council appointed a coadjutor, who would step into his shoes when he was dead. But the Archbishop, after the manner of permanent invalids, took such good care of his health that it seemed he might live for ever; Bishop Siward died before him, and the Archbishop hung on until the autumn of 1050.

The vacancy of Canterbury had been considered at the Christmas crownwearing, but such a great position must not be filled in a hurry. A decision was postponed until the next meeting of the Council, at mid-Lent. In the meantime great men jockeyed for an advantage in the race, and as might have been expected Earl Godwin tried to steal a march on his rivals.

There was no formal crownwearing at this mid-Lent Council. But it was important as the chief business meeting of the year, just before the opening of the campaigning season; the Earls would decide whether armies should be raised against the Welsh or the Scots, and discuss the latest news about the plans of the northern vikings. In 1051 this Council met in London, because the King was already occupied with plans for his new buildings at Westminster; all the great Earls were there.

As was the custom at these meetings, the really important discussion took place during dinner. The King sat as usual at the high table on the dais, with Earl Godwin on his right and Earl Siward on his left; it was a long table, and there were many other great men at it. Earl Leofric sat beyond Siward, and beyond Godwin his sons Harold and Tostig (Sweyn had the grace to keep away). I stood behind the King's chair, where I could hear the discussion so clearly that sometimes I found it hard not to add my own views to those of the rulers of the English.

When everyone had eaten enough and it was time for serious business I could see the great men brace themselves to discuss the burning question of Canterbury. Then suddenly a chamberlain called for silence, and there entered a procession of monks; it was a solemn procession, with incense and a crossbearer, not a mere deputation. The magnates muttered among themselves that here was the King wasting time again, introducing religious exercises into the ordinary work of the world; but I could see that the King had not expected the interruption.

It turned out to be a procession of the monks of Christ Church, Canterbury, who are much too fond of visiting the courts of Kings instead of staying at home and obeying their vow of stability. They came to announce that they had held a canonical election, and had chosen as their next Archbishop one Aelfric, a monk of their community. Would the King be so good as to invest him with ring and staff, and thus put him in possession of the lands belonging to his See?

The King was taken aback. As everyone knows, the theory is that Bishops ought to be chosen by the monks of their minsters; once a monk told me that this is ordained in the Gospel, though when I asked him for the reference he could not find the passage. But everyone knows that Bishops are in fact appointed by the King; it would be impossible to govern the English if the most powerful figures in the Church were chosen by monks who know nothing of the world. Here was a dilemma. Either the King must defy canon law, or the first subject of his realm would have been chosen, from among themselves, by a small chance-gathered community living in a remote corner of Kent.

Earl Godwin was the first to speak. 'I came here expecting a long discussion, but these holy men have saved us the trouble. Canterbury has been filled. We may as well proceed to the next business. What measures shall we take this summer to protect the west country from the vikings of Dublin?' His voice, as usual, was quiet, and as usual he smiled; but his smile was remarkably smug.

Harold and Tostig glanced first at one another, and then at their father. They also seemed pleased, and Tostig smothered a giggle.

Siward glanced round the company, pulling down his bushy eyebrows. Suddenly he barked at the prior of Christ Church: 'This Aelfric, is he a man of good birth?'

'Oh yes, my lord,' the monk answered happily. 'We would not elect a churl to the throne of St Augustine. He is descended from the noblest house among the South Saxons.'

'That would be the house of Wulfnoth Child. So he is your cousin, is he, Godwin?' asked Siward with a frown.

'Permit me to congratulate you on this further honour to your noble kindred,' added Leofric with a beaming smile.

'He is your cousin, Godwin?' said the King, suddenly alert. 'Then I am afraid we must quash the election. Please don't think that I impute improper influence, but you must see, Godwin, that to the authorities in Rome this hole-and-corner election will look very odd. The monk elected is your kinsman. You happen to be the greatest Earl in England. Furthermore, you happen to be Earl in Kent among other provinces, and it happens that your family estates are mingled with those of Christ Church. An enemy might proclaim that you had bought the Archbishopric; and we must admit that such an enemy would be believed. It's a disappointment, I know. Console yourself with the reflection that Aelfric, if he is really a devout monk, will be glad to escape such a great responsibility in the secular world.'

Godwin still smiled, meeting the mocking smiles of the other Earls. In Council he never lost his temper, never wasted energy by struggling to win a lost fight. What he saw now convinced him that the time had come to give way. He shrugged his shoulders, speaking in a casual tone.

'It's hard luck if the most suitable candidate must lose the Archbishopric just because he happens to be my cousin. But, as you say, lord King, no one in Rome would believe in the honesty of the election. Very well. Let it be recorded that Aelfric has refused consecration. Who else have we who would make a good Archbishop?'

'Robert of London, of course. He's the best Bishop in England,' said the King defiantly.

'We can't have a foreigner,' Siward objected.

'Why not? Wasn't St Augustine a foreigner, and Theodore after him? Robert has been baptised, ordained, and consecrated. Although he was born in Normandy, as Bishop of London he is already my subject. Siward, you understand the Northumbrians. I understand the Church. Let us each stick to what he understands, and the English will be well governed.' The King glared stubbornly.

'I was baptised when Canute commanded it, you know, and since then I have gone regularly to Mass. Nowadays I am not a heathen pirate. All the same, I see what you mean. I won't stand out if the others favour Robert.'

Siward could not be browbeaten, but he did not take religion seriously enough to quarrel over a Bishopric.

The others were at it hammer and tongs; some praising Robert, some objecting that a Norman would not be able to rule English clerks. There might yet have been a quarrel if Leofric had not interjected: 'If we promote Robert that will leave London vacant. We must decide who steps into his shoes.'

He glanced slyly at Godwin, who at once cleared his throat to speak: 'The Abbot of Abingdon is a good man of business. He is English on both sides of his family, as it happens; and, I may add, no kin of mine. I have thought for some time that he is worthy of a Bishopric.'

You could see the bargain struck, in sidelong glances and suppressed shrugs; though no one put it into words.

Presently the Council rose; but in the afternoon all the Earls rode hunting with the King, and the discussion continued until supper-time. By then all had been arranged, and the evening meeting of the Council was devoted to lesser matters; notably an arrangement with Dover and some other towns of the south coast whereby they should always have ships ready for the King's service, to take the place of the disbanded regular navy. In return the burgesses of these towns were granted various privileges, though it seemed to me that they got the worst of the bargain.

While he prepared for bed the King explained the day's events to his Lady.

'The only man I blame is that foolish prior of Christ Church. Of course your father would have liked to make his cousin Archbishop. Who wouldn't? It's natural. But he hadn't yet gone so far as to mention his name. The premature election forced his hand, before he had time to talk us round. He may have been quite right. It's possible that Aelfric is really the best man for the post. But the monks chose him because he is your

77

father's cousin, and for no other reason; and that I can't allow. I have vetoed an irregular election. I hope I myself have not chosen an Archbishop for unworthy reasons of personal friendship. Robert is my friend, and I am glad to promote him. All the same, I *think* that wasn't why I chose him.'

'I'm glad you don't blame Father, and I'm glad he gave way gracefully when he saw the Council was against him. I spoke to my brothers for a minute before they went home, and I can assure you that there will be no hard feelings. Tostig declares that you were guided by justice, and justice is all he cares about. Harold was a little stuffy, but even he admits that it's for the King to choose his Archbishop.'

'I can hear Harold saying it. He always stands up for the rights of the King against his Council. That's not the way most Earls talk. It's more like an atheling who hopes that one day he himself will be King.'

'Harold a King? After all the Cerdingas, and the house of Canute, have been wiped out by some pestilence, I suppose?' answered the Lady with a laugh. 'Seriously, it's a very good thing that my brothers can't claim kinship with any royal house; otherwise it might be suspected Earls with all that vigour and ambition are aiming at the throne.'

'That's the great argument for a hereditary Kingship,' said the King ponderously; he seldom gave a frivolous answer to a frivolous remark. 'So long as the crown goes by descent the King can trust great men. Silly courtiers sometimes remind me of what Macbeth did to King Duncan. I always answer that the English are not Scots. I need not be jealous of your father, because the Cerdingas have ruled here for five hundred years and the English like to be ruled by the children of Kings. Even Sweyn the father of Canute was a King in his own land before the English accepted him. In England no one can start a new dynasty.'

I did not care for the tone of this speech, and I think it made the Lady uncomfortable also. The King must in fact be a little jealous of Earl Godwin, or he would not so strenuously deny it.

Archbishop Robert was as competent as most Normans. He soon left for Rome, to fetch his pallium, the emblem of his metropolitan authority. He travelled swiftly, and was back in England by the end of July. As soon as he had taken possession of his minster he travelled on to Wessex to call on the King, who was hunting on Cotswold.

The court was stopping in a small hunting lodge, and the great Earls were all in their governments; for July was in those days the height of the pirate season, when shire-levies must stand ready to defend the coasts at short notice. With the King was the Lady, and his clerks under the supervision of Regenbald the Norman, who had recently been granted the high-sounding foreign title of Chancellor; otherwise there was no one at court except servants and a small bodyguard. For supper the King and the Lady sat side by side at the board, as though they were ordinary folk.

Suddenly the main door was thrown open and the Archbishop of Canterbury was announced, to the great inconvenience of the cooks and the household staff. Nowadays, at the end of my life, I have grown accustomed to this Norman habit of hurtling from place to place, riding all day and then working hard by candlelight. But at that time we kept to the dignified English custom; great men travelled no more than twenty miles in the day, and gave long notice before they visited the King's court.

The King, delighted to see Archbishop Robert, commanded him to sit beside the Lady. I was thankful to be on duty as cupbearer; with a clear conscience I might continue to stand behind my lord, while other servants worked hard to prepare supper and lodgings for the Archbishop and his suite.

Archbishop Robert would not begin a description of the wonders of Rome and the papal curia, which was what the King wanted to hear. Instead, in the Norman manner, he plunged straight into business.

'My lord, in one matter the Pope has overruled you. Therefore you must set a good example by obeying his authority. I got my pallium without any trouble, but the Pope has directly forbidden me to consecrate the Bishop-elect of London. You will have to find someone else to follow me in that See.'

'Dear me, how very tiresome. Rome doesn't often interfere in little things like that. I wonder what went wrong? Still, I must obey the successor of St Peter, if the Pope is really in earnest. Now whom did I choose for London? Of course, I didn't choose him. That's why I can't remember. It was part of a deal with Earl Godwin. The man he recommended is

Abbot of Abingdon, and that's all I know about him. But if he were openly scandalous someone would have told me. I can't even recall his name.'

'I don't know his *Christian* name,' said the Archbishop with a sneer. 'Everyone, even the monks of Abingdon, calls him by the nickname of Spearhavoc. That shows what kind of man he is. Not scandalous, perhaps; just a lay warrior who has been pushed on in the Church by his influential kindred.'

'Was this known in Rome before you arrived? Are the failings of the Abbot of Abingdon common gossip throughout Christendom?' asked the Lady, in careful but accurate French.

'The Pope asked for my opinion of the new Bishop, and I gave it to him frankly. That was in the course of my duty, as head of the Church in England.'

'The trouble is,' said the king, 'that this fellow, this Spearhavoc, already holds the lands of the Bishopric. I gave him possession just after Easter, never thinking that Rome might object. He holds St Paul's minster also, and it will be an awkward business getting him out of it.'

'Very often God's business is awkward business,' answered the Archbishop. 'But you swore to do it, when they made you King of the English. You must appoint a worthy Bishop, and I shall consecrate him. Then every true clerk in Christendom will help us to dislodge this worldly Abbot.'

'Whom shall we appoint? It must be someone I know personally, for fear of another mistake. Have you any suggestions? No? Then what about my chaplain, William?'

'Another foreigner? My brothers won't like it,' said the Lady.

'Nor you father either, my dear,' the King answered stubbornly. 'But we want the best man. William is a Norman, certainly, but that is in his favour. Norman clerks make good Bishops.'

'Then that is settled,' the Archbishop said hastily, for fear that the King might still change his mind. 'One of my clerks shall draw up the appointment this evening, and I shall consecrate him next Sunday. It's time there was a proper Bishop in London.'

'This will disappoint my father-in-law,' said the King doubtfully. 'I'm sorry. Spearhavoc's promotion was the price I offered for his agreement to your nomination, my dear Robert, and it may seem to him that I have broken my word.'

'It's a great pity that you had anything to do with it, my lord,' snapped the Archbishop. 'A lay ruler has no right to interfere in religious appointments. At present Rome submits to this invasion of her rights, but change is in the air. We ought to get back to canonical election, as it was in the days of the primitive church.'

'Aelfric?' whispered the Lady under her breath, smiling.

That silenced even Archbishop Robert. He was a stout upholder of 'the plentitude of papal power', in those days a new phrase and a novel doctrine; but he could hardly insist on unfettered canonical election when he owed his own advancement to a royal veto.

At last the King could ask questions about Rome, and about the Norman court at Rouen which Robert had visited on his journey. For the rest of supper he listened to traveller's tales with all the enjoyment of the stay-at-home.

When supper was ended the King as usual retired to his chamber, and the Archbishop also was shown to his apartment. Half an hour later, as the King was getting into bed, I heard a knock on the door. Outside was a housecarle, holding the Archbishop of Canterbury by the elbow.

'I saw this man creeping along the passage. He claims to be one of the King's friends, but he doesn't know the password. Shall I send him in, or shall I hit him a clout with my axe?'

Since Robert could not speak English he was in fact in considerable danger. But to all the household I was known as the King's favourite attendant, and even housecarles would take orders from me, in private; though of course in public their prickly honour would have been slighted. I rescued the Archbishop from the sentry, and brought him into the chamber.

'Is the Lady here?' he asked.

'No, we are quite private,' answered the King. 'You need not bother about Edgar. He knows all my secrets, and he never tells them.'

'It would have been better if we were quite alone. But Kings are never alone, as I know. There is something I must tell you immediately, and it would be prudent to keep it secret from your Lady. Your talk of a bargain with Earl Godwin has decided me to open your eyes. You cannot continue to work with that man. He procured the murder of your brother Alfred.'

'Now that's not true,' the King said angrily. 'I've heard the story dozens of times, and it's mere malicious tittle-tattle. Alfred was killed by the followers of Harold Harefoot, Godwin's enemy; and he was killed at Ely, which then was garrisoned by Harefoot's men.'

'I didn't say Godwin killed him. I said he procured his death. In Rouen I heard the full story. It was told me by the only companion of Alfred who escaped. This man said that the atheling met Godwin in Sussex, and agreed to go in his company to visit the Lady at Winchester. But at Guildford Godwin's housecarle's treacherously attacked the atheling's Norman escort. Godwin himself bound Alfred, and delivered him to Harefoot.'

The King sat down, staring. 'But Godwin was at war with Harefoot,' he said slowly.

'Godwin was fighting on behalf of Canute's legitimate son, Hardicanute, against Canute's bastard, Harefoot. It didn't suit him that a third claimant should appear, to remind Englishmen of the claims of the Cerdingas. It didn't suit Harefoot either. Even though they were at open war, they worked together on the murder.'

'And my mother? Both Alfred and Hardicanute were her sons.'

Robert nodded grimly. 'She was faithful to the memory of Canute. She tried to carry out his will. By her advice Alfred trusted Godwin.'

'Perhaps she was deceived. Let us hope so. In any case I never see her nowadays, even when I visit Winchester. But look here, Robert, Hardicanute inquired into all this. Godwin was charged with the murder. He cleared himself by his oath and the oaths of his oath-helpers. All the magnates of England swore with him. Godwin would perhaps lie to save his head but why should all the other Earls support him in a false oath?'

'The oath was not exactly false. He was accused of murder and he did not murder Alfred. He handed him over, bound, to those who would kill him. The magnates knew the truth nearly everyone knows it. But no one wanted to stir up civil war between Hardicanute and the great Earl who had been Canute's favourite.'

'I suppose all England knows it, except the King. I believe you. But I also cannot accuse Godwin, unless I am willing to begin a civil war. I shall say nothing, unless he puts himself outside the law and gives me a genuine excuse to attack him. Oh, do you think Edith knows of her father's crime?'

I had heard this story years ago, like everybody else in Winchester. Perhaps it was a good thing that at last the King's eyes had been opened. But I could not stand by and see all his happiness destroyed. I joined in this exchange between the King of the English and his greatest subject.

'The Lady probably suspected her father – as you, my lord, suspected your mother. You were careful never to inquire into the part played in the tragedy by the Old Lady, for fear you would find out too much. Perhaps the Lady also was reluctant to learn the whole truth.'

'Leave me, both of you. Tonight I shall sleep alone. If I am murdered in consequence I hope you are both impaled on blunt stakes. Now go away, leave me.'

I slept outside the door of the King's chamber. He did not sleep.

During August the King was continually called from his hunting to judge disputes about the boundaries and immunities of the Archbishop's lands in Kent. These disputes arise every time a new Archbishop is appointed, especially if he is an energetic man of business. There is no room in one small province for a metropolitan Archbishop and a great Earl; the sensible solution would be to make the Archbishop ruler of all Kent, as the Bishop of Durham rules the patrimony of St Cuthbert; but no one more important than a chamberlain has ever thought of this simple remedy. It made the dispute more bitter that the Earl of Kent, the rival of Archbishop Robert, happened to be Godwin. But there would have been trouble even if a devout lay warrior had been responsible for the secular affairs of the district.

Earl Godwin was used to having his own way whenever he chose to stand up for his rights. He was surprised to find the King hostile to him, and he made little effort to conceal his anger. Harold and Tostig were even more outspoken. Among the clergy there was strife between the supporters of Spearhavoc and those of William, the King's chaplain. Altogether it was an uneasy, unhappy time. The royal household was gloomy and upset, until we all cheered up at the news that the Count of Boulogne was coming to visit us.

83

Whether it is pleasant to obey a Norman master is a question on which two opinions can be held; but there is no doubt that Normans are stimulating guests. They are alert and full of exciting modern ideas; they consider it part of good manners to be amusing, while many English magnates of those days held that pompous dullness was a sign of deep wisdom.

Count Eustace was the King's brother-in-law, and stepfather to Earl Ralph. I suppose he came on business, probably to put in a good word for the young man who had shown himself so incompetent as a defender of Wessex against Welsh raids; but his business was discussed privately, while he hunted with the King, and I never learned of its nature. In the end Earl Ralph was further than ever from a formal nomination to be the King's heir; but he was consoled with a royal licence to build castles to defend the district round Hereford. In those days castles in England were a novelty, and the peasants disapproved of them as a likely shelter for outlaws; but they kept out the Welsh as well as the sheriff which made them useful on that troubled border.

Then Count Eustace set out for home, with his great company of foreign knights. A few days later he was back, riding up to the King's hall in Gloucester in the gathering dusk. The King had just sat down to supper, and I stood behind his chair.

We were startled to see armed men enter the hall at that late hour, and a glance showed that they had ridden hard after a hard fight; some were wounded, and all were exhausted. But since the King and Count Eustace conversed in French there was little excitement among the common housecarles at the lower tables.

'My lord,' began Count Eustace, 'it seems we must fight our way out of your country. The coastlands are in revolt. You said your writ would get us free quarters in Dover. It didn't. Then there was a bit of a brawl, with a score of men killed on either side. I didn't want to sack your town without consulting you; so I broke off the action and hurried here.'

'Dover shall be sacked, never fear,' answered the King, his eyes flashing. 'I shall send off a messenger tonight, commanding Earl Godwin to burn it. The town lies in his government, and he must take responsibility for the evil deeds of its burgesses. What an ungrateful set of men! When the fleet was laid up I gave them extra privileges on condition they kept ships ready for my service. They enjoy more freedom than any other

84

borough, and they use it to make war on the guests of the King!'

'They are useful warriors,' said Eustace professionally, as one leader to another. 'You don't often find axemen who will stand their ground against cavalry. I could have scattered them in the end, if I had tried hard enough. But it seemed wasteful to send in valuable warhorses to be killed in street fighting.'

'My lord, you are a Christian King. You can't wage war on your own subjects just because some of your guests have been hurt in a riot. There are two sides to every quarrel. Send for the portreeve of Dover, and hear his excuses before you pronounce him guilty.' That was Archbishop Robert, speaking from his place at the King's right hand; he could follow this French conversation while the English courtiers sat with puzzled frowns.

'I do not wage war. The sacking of a town in which the King's guests have been injured is the penalty laid down by English law. King Hardicanute sacked Worcester because two of his housecarles had been killed there. Godwin commanded the troops who did it, so he will know how to do it again. You don't need a formal inquiry before sacking a town as the penalty for riot. In any case, no lives will be lost. None were lost when Godwin sacked Worcester. The burgesses will run away, and there will be no pursuit. Their houses will be burned, and that will be the end of it. I know I am right on the point of law. Edith, that is the law, isn't it?'

'Yes, that's the law, or that's what it used to be. If the King's officers are attacked in a town, that town should be burned. All the same, Edward, these gentlemen are not exactly your officers, and my father won't be pleased to sack a town which has been under his special protection for more than thirty years.' In her excitement the Lady rose to her feet, and spoke loudly in English so that all the hall could hear.

There was a buzz of conversation among the lesser courtiers. Perhaps the Lady had not intended to stir up discontent, but her plea for the men of Dover sounded as though she thought they were in the right.

'The law is the law, and never changes,' said the King fiercely. 'Men have been killed, and a score of them were within the special peace of the King, his guests journeying from his court. Robert, get one of your clerks to make out the order at once, before we finish supper. Edgar, see that the messenger rides tonight, and reaches Earl Godwin without delay.'

'I don't like it. You are behaving like a bloodthirsty tyrant,' muttered the Archbishop.

'I don't like it. All England will see that you back foreigners against true Englishmen,' murmured the Lady.

'I don't like it. You try the Earl too high, and he may not carry out his orders,' I grumbled under my breath, though of course no one heeded my opinion.

But we were none of us prepared for Godwin's answer, which was to gather an army on Cotswold.

It was done quite openly, without subterfuge. Sweyn and Harold marched to join him, with the men of East Anglia and Danish Mercia. They issued a manifesto, saying that they 'wished to meet the King and his Council and consult with them concerning the disgrace that had been brought on the King and all his people by the wicked attack of the Count of Boulogne'. In other words, they did not seek to depose King Edward, but merely to deprive him of his royal power.

To give him his due, Godwin never aimed higher than that. He never tried to make himself King of the English; he was content to be the King's master.

In Gloucester we were cut off from the rest of England. The King had no army with him. Luckily, when Earls ride in arms other Earls muster their men. Ralph of course was with us, and his small force of mounted Normans; Siward and Leofric came up by forced marches with the men of Northumbria and English Mercia. By the end of August the King also had an army, strong enough to march against the rebels on Cotswold.

On the 1st of September we marched. In this crisis even I bore arms, carrying an axe in the rear flank of the King's body-guard. My lord looked very warlike as he rode at our head, with a long lance and a great five-foot shield; he proposed to fight on horseback after the Norman fashion. But all the talk in the army was of the disaster civil war would bring to the English, who must be conquered again by the Danes as soon as our best warriors had killed one another.

That was what they were saying also in Godwin's army. When it came to the point no one was willing to fight. We saw them, drawn up in the shieldwall on a ridge by Beverstone; and very unpleasant they looked, so that I tried to edge farther to the rear. Then Earl Siward sent out a mounted man waving a green branch, and though the King fretted and wished to lead a charge by himself very soon all the Earls were meeting at a peace conference between the armies.

Siward, who feared no man, was chosen to tell the King that peace had been made with the rebels. He rode up to the body-guard with a cheerful grin, though I noticed that his toes were free of the stirrups and that his great axe dangled from his wrist by a short thong. He was a Dane of the old-fashioned kind, who prefer to fight on their feet.

'No heads loosened as yet, my lord,' he called gaily, 'though before the month is out there may be killing enough to content even your Norman cut-throats. In three weeks from now we meet Godwin in London, and each side brings all the men it can. That means that Godwin has lost, though so far he hasn't seen it. He has his whole power on the ridge over there, and in three weeks' time his men will be anxious to go home. Half my Northumbrians haven't yet found their marching boots; northerners are always slow to start. They will be in London, ready for any excitement, just when Godwin's men are wondering how the harvest will be got in without them. You'll see. Every day our strength will grow, and Godwin's will dwindle. By the way, I had to promise in your name that Godwin may come safely to London. I hope you consider yourself bound by that promise. At my time of life I should not care to be forsworn.'

For all his carefree voice he looked straight at the King from under bushy brows, and his hand touched the haft of his axe.

'If peace has been promised in my name I must keep the peace; though this is a just war,' my lord answered. 'Yet even if the land has peace these rebels deserve punishment.'

'Their leader shall be punished, if we can get the better of him. The ordinary axemen shall be spared, to fight under your banner and maintain the Kingdom of the English. If we kill them Hardrada will add England to his dominions, and that would not please even the Anglo-Danes.'

'Then go away and ratify the truce in my name. Tell all my loyal Earls to meet me tonight, so that we can plan our march on London. So after all I am not to fight a battle. Where's Edgar? I may as well get out of this cumbersome armour.'

The King drooped in his saddle. He looked suddenly miserable, like a child disappointed of an expected treat. I realised that he had been genuinely looking forward to leading his first charge. He was a good man, not eager to shed the blood of his own people; but he was also descended from a line of warriors, and he hated Godwin as a personal enemy.

'It's all over,' he said as I disarmed him, 'or rather, it never began. For eight years I have been King of the English, I am nearer fifty than forty years old, and I have never struck a blow in anger. Do you think I shall be remembered by posterity as the only King of the English who never risked his life on the field? If only God would permit me to share in some little unimportant skirmish, just to prove to the world that I am not a coward.'

'Posterity will remember you as the good King who kept peace and reformed the Church,' I answered soothingly, for I myself was delighted to be saved from a dangerous battle. 'And if you really get the new minster going outside London,' I added cunningly, 'that great building will keep your memory green for ages to come.'

'Ah, the West Minster,' said the King, brightening at once. 'Archbishop Robert and Bishop William are here with the army. Tonight we shall talk over our plans once again; and in three weeks I shall be in London, where I can mark out the foundations on the ground. I hope those Earls don't interrupt our discussion by talking endlessly about warfare.'

The army that rode with us to London was splendidly armed, but not very large. In September it is useless to call up the general levy of all free men entitled to bear arms, because peasants will not answer the summons in harvest time unless their own fields are menaced by hostile ravaging. Behind the King rode Bishops and abbots, for the Church was solidly on his side. The loyal Earls, Siward, Leofric and Ralph, brought their housecarles and the free thanes of their shires; in addition they brought other well-equipped warriors, thanes from every corner of the land who had commended themselves to these great men after the new fashion of service. But in our host there were hardly any foot, and wherever we halted we could find provisions to feed us.

We travelled slowly, to allow time for the men of the farthest Northumbria to join us. Our line of march lay north of the Thames, and at Oxford we halted for two days to organise the army. Meanwhile we had word that the Godwinssons were marching eastward a few miles south of the river. Earl Godwin had built a great hall at Southwark, facing London, and there he would stay while he drew up his men at the southern end of London Bridge.

The rebel army comprised the free thanes of all the God-winsson shires, East Angles and South Saxons and those Mercians who obeyed Sweyn. The dismissed sailors from the fleet and certain others of the old housecarles of Canute also joined the great man who had been Canute's minister. It seemed likely that by Michaelmas a great battle would be fought, and it was not at all certain that the King would win it.

But as we passed Reading armed men came to us from the far side of the river, waving branches to show that they came in peace. Earl Leofric rode out to parley with them, and then came bustling up to the King in high spirits. Among all the magnates of that time Leofric was the only true Englishman, born and bred in England; he was more eager for peace than Siward the Dane or Ralph the Norman, or than the King who had been reared oversea.

'It's the beginning of the rot,' he shouted gaily, telling his news to all who would hear. 'By the time Godwin reaches Southwark he will have no army. These men have been rebels, but now they wish to join us. They are the free thanes of Kent and the South Saxons, and they have been considering their rights and obligations, as free thanes should. When their Earl called up the levies of his shires they came to the muster, as was their duty. But they are not commended to Godwin, and now they see that duty does not compel them to follow their Earl against their lawful King.'

'Of course. That's true of free thanes anywhere,' said the King placidly. 'If we point it out to the thanes of East Anglia they may agree that Siward is as good a Dane as Godwin, and also come over. I'm not so sure about the men who commended themselves to Godwin. I suppose they ought to follow their lord in any quarrel. If we try to win them over we may be procuring perjury, and that would be sinful. But I don't understand the ins and out of commendation. When I was a young man they were doing it all over Normandy, but in those days I was not interested in military affairs. Ralph, do you know how we ought to treat men who have taken oath to Godwin or one of his

89

sons? Must we make war on them, or can we honourably ask them to desert their lords?' He spoke in English, out of courtesy to the English Earls round him; but Earl Ralph knew something of his mother's language.

'You may not steal another man's vassals. But if Godwin yields we can compel him to release them. It's really quite simple. He gives them back their oath, and then they commend themselves afresh to the King.'

'And after that they must follow me against any foe. Very well, that's what we'll do. No need to punish them for rebellion. Just ask them to swear another oath. I like this commendation business. Properly managed, it can give the lesser landowners a stake in the government.'

'If they did their duty they would have that already, in the shire court,' grumbled Earl Leofric. 'Nowadays no one bothers to attend, and it's all left to the Earl and his housecarles.'

'Ah, the shire court is English, and commendation is foreign,' chuckled the King. 'That's all Leofric thinks about. Never mind. I don't propose to alter the Law of the English. I could if I wanted to, for that matter. We shall just encourage commendation as a personal obligation, quite outside the law.'

By the time we reached London Godwin's army had dissolved. A few housecarles and the more honourable of his vassals stayed with him; but even they stayed only to protect his person, not to wage war on the King. The Council which assembled in St Paul's minster did not need to plan a campaign; it had only to decide on the punishment of the rebels.

Of course I was not present at the Council; but the King told me all about it that afternoon, as I helped him to remove his robes of state. Or rather, as usual, he talked to himself and allowed me to overhear him.

'Sweyn has been outlawed, of course,' he said, rubbing his hands with glee. 'A man who has once been forgiven for raping an abbess can't expect to be forgiven for rebellion as well. About the rest of them the Council were very stubborn; Godwin may be unpopular, but an Earl will always stand up for another Earl in trouble with the King. They want him to stand a formal trial; which means that every perjurer in England will rally round to help him with his oath.'

He was silent as I pulled his silk shirt over his head, and then helped him into a linen one.

'A formal trial,' he went on. 'Yes, but they can't try him until he appears to answer his accusers. That's it. If we frighten him, or make him lose his temper, he may disappear of his own accord rather than face trial. I shall send him a very rude message, and I won't let him bring a bodyguard when he comes to seek my peace. Now whom shall I send to carry the message? Archbishop Robert speaks well, and he isn't afraid of Godwin. But perhaps the Archbishop of Canterbury is too great a man to be sent on an errand.'

In a lower tone he ran through several names. 'Siward would hit him with an axe, and that would never do. Leofric would just smooth things over, and I don't want peace with Godwin. Ralph might be afraid to deliver my message properly. No, such a go-between ought to be a clerk. Which clerk? Bishop William? A foreigner, ignorant of English law; Godwin would browbeat him. The same applies to all my Norman clerks, though they are cleverer than any Englishman. Ah, I've got it. Bishop Stigand.'

He saw my surprise and now spoke directly to me, no longer uttering his private thoughts aloud.

'Stigand is Godwin's creature. He wants to bring Godwin back into the King's peace. Whatever message he carries, he will help Godwin to find the right answer to it. The point is, Edgar, that if I order him to carry my message he can't refuse; or at any rate he won't refuse, since at the moment I am stronger than Godwin. Can you imagine Stigand quarrelling with the fount of promotion? So he goes to Godwin, to tell him of the King's anger. What will Godwin think of that? An Anglo-Dane, Canute's faithful henchman, a hater of Normans – if there's anyone in England who should support Godwin it's Stigand. When Godwin sees that even Stigand obeys me he will understand that all England has turned against him. That's it. Now all I have to do is to think of a really unpleasant message.'

The negotiations on the next day were immediately made public. The mighty Earl was falling into disgrace, and the Council wished that London and all England should know it. The messages that had passed between the parties were read publicly at Paul's Cross in London.

First Godwin proposed that he should stand trial before the King's Council, first receiving hostages to guarantee that he might leave the trial a free man. Since this would have been a guarantee that he would not be punished even if found guilty it was of course refused. Then Godwin offered to bring oath-helpers to swear to his innocence. This also the King refused, though I am not sure he was within his rights; the law as I understand it allows a culprit to clear himself of any accusation if the oaths on his side outweigh the oaths of his accusers. Probably Godwin could have gathered oaths heavier than the accusations of all the other Earls and Bishops; so perhaps the King was prudent to forbid a trial which might have ended with axeplay in the Council chamber.

At last Godwin, losing patience, asked what he must do before the King would receive him into his peace; and Stigand gave the barbed answer: 'You will enjoy the King's peace and favour as soon as you bring to him the atheling Alfred and his companions, alive and well.'

That was how matters stood when the negotiations were published to the Londoners. It was late in the afternoon, and no one expected more to be done that day. But the King was in an exalted frame of mind. While he sat at supper he turned suddenly to Bishop Stigand. I was standing behind his chair, and I heard everything.

'I've got another errand for you, my lord,' the King announced out of the blue. As always when addressing Stigand his manner was constrained; he could not bring himself to be rude to a consecrated Bishop, but he felt the utmost contempt for Stigand as a man. 'I want you to cross the bridge now, tonight, and give Earl Godwin in Southwark my final answer.'

He rose, and stood to look down the hall as Archbishop Robert beside him rapped for silence.

'As King of the English,' he said formally, 'I am especially charged with preserving the peace among my subjects. Earl Godwin has repeatedly injured that peace. Now he refuses to answer for his crimes before the court most competent to try him. Therefore he and all his kin have put themselves outside my law. Their lands are forfeit. As outlaws they have five days in which to leave my dominions. After that any man who wills may slay them without blame.'

As he sat down he grinned at the Bishop of Winchester. 'Go and tell that in Southwark as soon as you can. The days of grace have already begun to run.'

Siward and Leofric looked sour; custom decrees that the

Council should be consulted before a great man is outlawed. The Archbishop and the other clerks were delighted, and the warriors at the lower tables beat on the board with their drinking horns and cheered for war.

Almost at once I must fill the King's cup. Before he pronounced sentence he had not touched his wine; now he took a deep draught, and called for more. He looked white and shaken. He must have wondered, up to the very last moment, whether his Councillors and housecarles would ratify the downfall of the great Earl.

When Siward spoke we all relaxed, for his first words showed that he accepted the King's decision. 'We must send mounted men to watch the gates of Southwark. It's just possible that Godwin will turn pirate where he stands, and ride out to ravage the south. Until he has begun his journey to the coast we can't be certain that he has chosen exile.'

The King nodded agreement. The magnates of England sat around the supper tables, waiting the return of the Bishop of Winchester.

Within an hour Stigand was back, angry and ill at ease and a little frightened. 'I delivered your sentence, my lord,' he said sulkily. 'Godwin took it very hard. In his rage he overturned a table, and in the heat of the moment he said things which I shall not repeat. But he obeys the King's decree, though he protests that he has been treated with injustice. Before I left he had begun to collect his gear.'

'He must do that, whatever he does after. He can't stay quietly in Southwark,' objected Earl Leofric. 'We shan't know whether he really submits until our scouts have seen him ride out.'

'We shall wait here for news, until dawn if need be,' said the King.

The housecarles cheered this announcement also, either because they admired the stern hardihood of their King or because they relished the prospect of an all-night session with the ale-casks.

The King sat happily on his throne, a new look in his eye. He was triumphant, but he was also responsible; for the first time in his life truly King of the English, with no minister to do his work for him. He drank very little; but he was alert, chatting happily about affairs of state.

Before midnight we heard news of the Godwinssons. First came a message from the portreeve of London, saying that Godwin himself, his wife Gytha, and four of his sons, Sweyn, Tostig, young Gyrth and little Wulfnoth, had all ridden out on the road to Bosham. They took with them a few horseloads of treasure, and Judith the young Flemish princess who had recently been married to Tostig; but no housecarles, save for a small escort to guard the treasure. They rode quite openly, and had sent for the portreeve that he might bear witness that they were travelling peaceably to Flanders.

'All the same, it was bad manners to set out in the middle of the night,' said Leofric. 'They could have waited for dawn and still have reached Bosham with time to spare. Either the old fox judges you by himself, my lord, and fears murder; or, more likely, he wants people to think he flees in fear of his life, so that they will blame you.'

'Never mind,' Siward put in. 'It would be odd if Godwin behaved frankly. Have you noticed that no one saw Harold in that party? He's a dangerous man. I wonder what he's doing? He may be trying to raise the Londoners in rebellion.'

'The Londoners wouldn't follow him, or I don't think they would,' answered Leofric. 'Tostig now – he could gather an army anywhere, because the people like him. It's lucky for us that he chose this month to get married. He must take young Judith to safety before he sails on viking cruise.'

'We shall wait for news of Harold all the same. I shan't go to bed until I know that all the Godwinssons are safely on the way to Flanders.' The King spoke firmly. 'There's another one old enough to bear arms, isn't there? What's his name, Leofwin?'

We had grown very bored and sleepy by the time our scouts brought tidings of Harold. It was well that Earl Siward had remembered to post them; for the portreeve of London thought only of avoiding trouble for his town, and feared to make enemies by revealing more than he had been told to tell. Siward's horsemen reported that Harold and Leofwin had ridden westwards, alone.

'Now what can that mean?' asked Earl Leofric. 'They must be planning something, or they would have ridden with their father. Young Harold is amazingly self-confident, but surely even he can't be trying to raise the West Saxons, of all people, in rebellion against the house of Cerdic?'

'Even he wouldn't try that,' the King agreed. 'But Harold is a romantic young hero. He won't go tamely into exile. Perhaps he will wander over the western moors like a real wolfshead, instead of guzzling in Bruges through the winter with no work and no excitement.'

'You are too kind to Harold, my lord,' said Earl Siward in his harsh practical Danish voice. 'He looks like a hero, and he's as brave as any young viking. But though he will run risks without flinching he always has some commonsensical object in view. . . . What can it be this time? Ah, I just said it myself – viking. He isn't riding into Wessex, he's riding *through* Wessex to join the vikings of Ireland.'

'And he has five days' grace,' added Leofric regretfully. 'A pity. He knows the coast of Devon. Probably he has agents in the towns. If he brings a viking fleet against the west country he can do us a great deal of harm.'

'Then why should he have five days' grace?' asked the King sharply. 'As I understand the law those days are a favour accorded to a peaceful exile, so that he can collect his baggage and go oversea in comfort. Strictly speaking, an outlaw is a wolfshead from the moment sentence is pronounced. Furthermore, a traitor riding to join the vikings may be killed by anyone who meets him. Isn't that so, Earl Siward? What do you think, Bishop Stigand? Our laws against vikings are more Danish than English, and I will accept the opinion of the two leading Danes in my Council.'

Siward answered briefly: 'You may cut off his head, if you catch him.'

Stigand looked uncomfortable. He hated to condemn a Godwinsson, and perhaps the King was cruel to make him express an opinion. But the law was plain, and he could only nod agreement.

'Then order the scouts to ride after them,' commanded the King. 'They are to take them if they will yield, and cut them down if they resist.'

'No good, my lord,' said Siward at once. 'Those scouts have been mounted since dusk. They will never catch two travellers who ride fresh horses. Send a single messenger, with a warrant to impress horses on the road. Let him warn some magnate already in the west, and tell him to catch these pirates.'

'That's it,' said the King. 'Send the messenger to Bishop

Aldred. He is guarding the Severn, and his housecarles will be ready.'

Stigand sighed with relief; Leofric looked doubtful, but said nothing. It was notorious that Aldred the Peacemaker never caught any criminal who had the good sense to run away; every outlaw has kin who may avenge him, and the Bishop did not like to make enemies.

Later we heard that the two Godwinssons had sailed from Bristol unmolested.

Next morning the King slept late, though when he called to me to dress him he was fully awake and bubbling with excitement.

'For the first time I am really King of the English,' he exclaimed. 'For eight years I have been afraid of that terrible Earl Godwin, and when at last I pluck up my courage to attack him he flees without a drop of blood spilled. Now I can do whatever I like. I can crush those raiding Welsh, I can bring the Scots to order. I can hire Norman experts to teach my men how to fight on horseback. Best of all, I can nominate my successor.'

'Yes, my lord, it is indeed a splendid prospect. Shall we be staying long in London, or will you now return to the Lady in Gloucester?' Perhaps that was unkind, but I wanted my lord to apply his mind to a problem that seemed to have slipped his memory.

'Oh dear, the Lady. . . . Yes indeed, that will be an unpleasant meeting. Yet why should I meet her? She has shown herself content to live a virgin, if she may live in luxury. The place for her is a comfortable easy-going nunnery. I shall make no move to put her away, though Rome will give her an annulment if she chooses to apply for one. She remains the Lady of England, but she lives in a convent while I go hunting. . . . That's fair, and it will satisfy everyone. Do you agree, Edgar? Then go out and find a clerk, and tell the clerk to tell the senior chaplain to tell the Archbishop of Canterbury that I would like to see him. Do it properly, mind. The Archbishop is not to be summoned by a mere chamberlain.'

The King grinned broadly. Now that he was the real ruler of England he enjoyed the etiquette which had irked him when he was a figurehead for Godwin.

CHAPTER V

The Return of Earl Godwin

By the time we got back to the King's favourite country, the hunting lodges of Cotswold, the Lady and her women had retired to a suitable convent. Archbishop Robert arranged it without bothering the King. It was unkind of him to send her to the strict community of Wherwell, but I suppose when an Archbishop hears that a grown woman wishes to try the religious life he takes it for granted that she is eager for its full rigour. As soon as she asked for a change she was sent to Wilton, her old school. In after years she never complained of her treatment, so she must have been reasonably content.

It was the happiest winter of the King's life, and of mine. The King passed every morning in some church, every afternoon hunting, and every evening discussing intellectual riddles with learned men. I very seldom went out of doors, and had plenty of time to look after the jewels of the regalia; but at night the King would speak to me freely, and I knew all the secrets of that blameless and godfearing court.

Luckily the land was at peace, and there were few problems of government; for when problems arose the King was not clever at dealing with them. On the brink of his fiftieth year he had never learned how to manage men; on broad questions of principle he saw where the right lay and pursued it unswervingly, but when it was a question of some nice little office that must be given either to A or B he hovered undecided and then plumped for the wrong man. He had never before dealt with efficient rascals, or with soldiers who were at the same time loyal and avaricious. He could squash an obvious scoundrel, and trust an honest man; most ordinary Englishmen are something in between, and they baffled him.

In these matters he took the advice of Archbishop Robert, which was usually bad. The Archbishop was well-educated, practical, and experienced in administration. But he was a foreigner, impatient of English prejudice, refusing to bother his head with the ramifications of English feuds. I once heard Bishop Aldred trying to explain to him that Earl Alfgar, son of Earl Leofric, must naturally be preferred to Earl Odda, who had risen solely by royal favour; and that it would be risky to set either of them to rule Anglo-Danes, who despise all Mercians. Robert answered shortly that Odda was a good man, chaste and charitable; the Danes of Mercia must obey him, or take the consequences.

The King remained immensely popular, whatever he did; to the English it seemed novel and invigorating to be governed by a thoroughly good man, even if he made mistakes. Those who thought themselves ill-treated blamed the Archbishop for misleading the King; it became a popular catchword that Canterbury ought to be ruled by an English Archbishop.

Meanwhile the King continued to work at the project nearest his heart, without consulting his Council. He made his arrangements secretly, and told us only when everything was ready. I remember the first I heard of it, one evening in Advent when I was preparing the King for bed. He opened the subject in a roundabout way.

'Edgar, you are a real West Saxon, aren't you, from the old stock that made England one Kingdom? Suppose I should drop dead this minute, who would you cheer for as my successor?'

The King was asking a serious question. I did not waste his time by denying that one day he would die.

'I haven't an idea, my lord,' I answered. 'I suppose any Cerdinga who had the backing of the great Earls.'

'There isn't one, you know. I am the last of my house. Well, that's not quite accurate. I may have a kinsman somewhere in Hungary. My eldest half-brother, Edmund, had a son who was smuggled oversea as a baby for fear of the Danes; and the story goes that he fetched up in Hungary. It's odd to think that I may have a nephew nearly as old as I am. But if that baby lived he will now be completely Hungarian. That's a very foreign kind of foreigner. I don't think the English would care to be ruled by him.'

'Perhaps a Hungarian won't do, my lord. All the same, anyone would be better than a Dane. To keep the Danes out of England even I would carry an axe.'

'Luckily the house of Canute is as extinct as the house of Cerdic. There's no one in Denmark with a reasonable claim; unless indeed the King of the Danes maintains that his crown makes him also the King of the English. Someone might say that, just because Canute once united the two peoples.'

'Then I don't know what will happen when you are dead, my lord. Perhaps there will never be another King of all the English. The Earls may rule on their own, without a King.'

'Oh no, Edgar, remember the vision of Bishop Britwold. God has already chosen my successor. But it is the duty of every Christian to further the Will of God. Therefore, if I think I know who ought to succeed me, it is my duty to help him to the throne.'

'Who is he, if he isn't a Hungarian or a Dane, and there is no Cerdinga in England? Have you other foreign kinsmen?'

'Of course. I was born of a mother, though to hear the Earls discussing pedigrees you would think Kings came into the world without help from any woman. Poor Ralph is out of the running, though he is my sister's son. He has shown himself cowardly in battle, and that bars him. But the Old Lady, my mother, had a brother who was Duke of the Normans. He is dead now, and so are his sons. He left a single grandson, who is now my nearest kinsman after poor Ralph. That is Duke William of the Normans, a fine ruler whom I propose to make my heir.'

'He is no Cerdinga,' I objected.

'Neither is anyone else, outside Hungary; and that's too far away to count. In the male line there are no more Cerdingas. If you count females you will find dozens of them, but in England no one reckons female descent. All the same, it's worth mentioning that William's children will be Cerdingas in the female line. He plans to marry Matilda of Flanders, who can trace her descent from King Alfred. They are only waiting to clear up some little difficulty with the Pope.'

'That will help him in Wessex, my lord, if the common people should know about it. It's not the sort of thing they would know unless they are told. But it won't carry much weight with the great Earls.'

'Archbishop Robert has shown me how to deal with them. It's a new dodge of statecraft, already common in France and the Empire. I shall invite Duke William to visit me for Christmas, and while he is at court I shall ask the magnates to swear that they will support him as my successor.'

'Is that worth doing? They will swear to please you, and then say afterwards that their oaths were worthless, as taken under duress.'

'Duress? From fear of *me*? They may say they were frightened, but no one will believe them.'

I argued with the King, considering this to be my duty; if he sought my advice I must give it frankly. But he was in love with his new up-to-date scheme, and could not understand that fairly honourable men might swear falsely to avoid a direct collision with their lord. He would not recognise that even good men may have some evil in them, though he was quick to see the few good qualities of the wicked.

Duke William came to the Christmas crownwearing, a short dark warrior of twenty-three, quick in his movements and interested in everything. He made a good impression on the lesser thanes, for he rode gallantly in the hunt and was sober and courteous at table. The King told me that the Earls and Archbishop Robert had all sworn to make him the next King of the English. But this was done in private, and no record was kept; so that later men denied it. I am certain the King told the truth as he saw it; perhaps some of the magnates did not understand what they swore, or swore with reservations.

After a short stay Duke William and his followers went home to their own country, bearing rich presents.

The Old Lady died in March 1052, and was buried beside King Canute in the Old Minster at Winchester. The King arranged for Masses and put his servants into mourning, but he did not pretend to be stricken with grief. On the contrary, at this time he was blithe, and perhaps almost too pleased with himself. He put a new design on his coins, showing himself as a warrior glaring out from a helmet, in place of the old picture of a crowned King. With Godwin in Bruges, and his mother in the grave, he was completely his own master.

His only complaint was that the business of ruling the

English took him from his hunting. It was known that Harold and Leofwin were gathering a fleet among the vikings of Ireland; so the western coast must be guarded. A more serious threat appeared in the spring. News came that Godwin himself was recruiting among the pirates of Flanders; he might be planning a descent on the coasts of the South Saxons, the ancestral home of his house. The King gave orders that an English fleet should be collected and held in readiness at Sandwich, the usual base. But here my lord, still inexperienced as a ruler, made a grave but natural mistake. He put in command of this fleet the two Earls who had shown themselves most loyal to him, Ralph and Odda. But these were the Earls of Hereford and Somerset; their absence left the Welsh border undefended, and at once King Griffith of the North raided fiercely as far as Leominster.

While the levies of Mercia were busy with King Griffith the Dublin pirates sailed up the Bristol Channel and landed to ravage in Somerset. Harold himself led them, and at Porlock defeated the Somersaetas with great slaughter. Meanwhile our fleet, and the King's housecarles, lay at Sandwich with no enemy in sight. Old men began to say that the days of Ethelred were come again, when if pirates landed in the west the King and the army of England were always in the east.

The royal household remained in London. At first the King had wished to sail out into the Channel with his ships, but he had been persuaded that this would be too great a gamble. In the open sea there is always a way round, and Godwin with his pirates might have appeared before London while the power of England was cruising off Kent. In London we were kept busy fitting out a reserve army, made up of those lesser thanes and free peasants who come to the muster, ill armed, only when there is a serious threat of invasion.

My lord was in a warlike mood. 'If Godwin lands I shall meet him in the field,' he declared as he sorted the spare swords in his treasury. 'We must arm every man who is willing. I don't trust the sailors, who are mostly Danes. On land we Englishmen will make an end of the Danish Godwinssons and their Flemish pirates.'

Presently it began to appear that the fleet was in the right place after all. News came that Harold had rounded Land's End and was coasting up Channel, while his father prepared

101

to cross from Flanders to join him. At Sandwich our ships lay between the two squadrons, and might with luck catch them separately.

We had no luck. At midsummer Godwin sailed from the Yser, and the Earls Ralph and Odda put out from Sandwich to meet him. Then a great storm blew up. In the murky weather our ships could not find the pirates, and when the wind abated both fleets had been so gravely damaged that they must seek harbour immediately. Ralph and Odda struggled round the Foreland into London River, while the pirates limped back to Flanders.

All this excitement was bad for the King. He had been sitting in London, organising his troops, while in the Channel two great fleets manoeuvred and every day might bring news of a decisive battle. His throne, perhaps his life, were at stake; but he had been persuaded to leave the management of the campaign to others. Now it seemed that his chosen lieutenants had failed disgracefully, and he could not make up his mind whether the fault lay in their incompetence or their disloyalty.

He was at dinner when we told him that his battered ships were dropping anchor in the Pool. At once he burst into loud complaint: 'It's absurd, fantastic! Midsummer, on the sheltered coast of the South Saxons, and these lubbers muddle themselves into such an unseaworthy condition that they must come to London for repairs! I suppose Ralph got his feet tangled in his spurs! But Odda is a West Saxon, an experienced sailor. At midsummer he ought to be able to dodge Beachy Head! Whoever heard of ships putting in for repairs after a cruise in the Channel in June! I must find other commanders to lead my navy.'

'That's sound sense as far as it goes,' said Earl Leofric coolly, 'but where will you find them? Don't appoint me, my lord. With King Griffith on the rampage I must hurry back to Mercia.'

Earl Siward grunted agreement. 'I must keep an eye on the north. I haven't time to go on viking cruise, even if the King commands me. Get rid of Ralph by all means, but why not leave Odda in charge? That storm was really dangerous, you know. Godwin has scuttled back to Bruges, and his sailors are Frisian pirates.'

'They must go, both of them,' my lord said obstinately.

'This afternoon I shall dismiss them, immediately after dinner.'

Archbishop Robert's cupbearer had been bending over his lord to translate these passages of muttered, grumbling English. Now the Archbishop spoke quietly into the King's ear, in swift French which the Earls could not understand: 'Ralph and Odda are your loyal servants. Don't you see that these other lords will not fight for you against Godwin?'

The King slumped back in his chair, silent.

All through July and August our army mustered in London. Harold and his Dublin vikings continued eastward along the south coast, ravaging as they came; while the English fleet remained at anchor in the Pool. Ralph and Odda had been dismissed to their Earldoms in the west, but no other commander had been appointed. None would undertake the task. Our veteran sailors deserted, for they were Danes who would not fight against Godwin; the fishermen and upland thanes who were set in their place dared not face the open sea in long unstable warships. The King talked it over with the few deepsea sailors he could trust, and decided to keep the ships in the sheltered waters of the Thames; there they could be employed to defend the Port of London, if Godwin ventured to come so far.

For Godwin was again on the move. He had collected more Frisian pirates, and his ships were ravaging the Isle of Wight. Whenever he wished he might link up with Harold, for there were no English warships south of the Thames.

In London we waited nervously. The King sat long in Council, and every day visited his army on the open plain west of the city. But as harvest drew near the men grew restless, until the daily desertions outnumbered the day's recruits.

Undoubtedly the King was behaving like his father, sitting still with a great army while pirates ravaged his lands. Without a fleet what else could he do? If he marched south Godwin would sail round the Foreland to enter an undefended London. Of course the common people grumbled, and since they must have a scapegoat they fixed on the Norman clerks whom the King had promoted. Feeling grew so strong that Archbishop Robert thought it prudent to keep away from formal meetings of the Council; instead he would slip round in the evenings to confer with the King in his bedchamber.

I recall the last of these meetings, since for once the King did not bother to send me away. The campaign must soon reach its climax. Godwin and Harold and all the pirate fleet had sailed past the Foreland and were ravaging Sheppey. Within a week the decisive battle must be fought before London. The Archbishop came disguised in the cowl of a simple monk, while the King prepared for bed.

'What's the news?' asked Robert as soon as he entered.

'It might be worse,' the King answered with a worried frown. 'The men of Sheppey stood to defend their crops, though of course the pirates got the better of them. At least they didn't welcome the invaders, like those treacherous South Saxons.'

'Frankly, do you think your army will join Godwin?'

'Join him, no. Perhaps they won't fight against him. My mistake was to gather them in London, which is nowadays more Danish than English. Godwin governed it for many years, and the burgesses are disloyal. I should have mustered my men in Wessex, where the glories of the house of Cerdic are still remembered. Look how gallantly the western thanes fought against Harold at Porlock! In the west they will still die for their rightful King. Now it's too late to move. If I march west while the foe are in the Thames it will look like a retreat, and all the waverers will desert the losing cause.'

'What a people you have been called to govern! Tailed Englishmen, always ready to change sides! They deserve to be ruled by Godwin and his sons, and I can't wish them a worse fate.'

'Not all the Godwinssons are scoundrels,' said the King, looking on the bright side. 'Young Tostig is an honest man who does justice, and they say he lives faithfully with his Flemish wife.'

'But think of Sweyn and Harold and Leofwin and Gyrth! How can a land prosper which has such magnates to rule it?'

'Sweyn is no longer a viking. He has gone to Jerusalem on pilgrimage, to seek forgiveness for his sins. I always thought there was good in that boy. About Harold and the others I agree with you.'

'But what will you do, my lord, when these savages invade England?'

'What *can* I do? I can't run away. I am the King appointed by God to rule the English, and I may not abandon my duty.

When the time comes I shall take up my axe and fight at the head of those willing to fight for me. At the best I shall be killed in battle; if I am captured I shall meet a worse fate, like my poor brother Alfred. He did his duty, hoping to free his people from oppression by Danish pirates. What he did was righteous – and it brought him death by torture.'

It was not my place to interrupt, but I could not leave the King in this agony of despair. 'My lord,' I cried, 'Godwin and his pirates cannot overthrow you. The English will have you as their King until you die. The Earls refuse to fight against other Englishmen only because Hardrada and his Danes will come over and conquer us if the defenders of England kill one another.'

The King heard me patiently, and then explained in French to the Archbishop. 'Edgar says that the English will never desert me. But they would rather accept Godwin than fight a great battle which would leave England a prey to Hardrada and his Danes.'

'Perhaps Godwin's followers will also refuse to fight?' Robert suggested.

'No, they are pirates, willing fight anyone.'

'Then Godwin does not care what happens to his country, so long as he himself remains rich?'

'That is so, lord Archbishop,' said the King sadly. 'Godwin is a wicked man, and in this world the wicked flourish like a green bay tree. He will come back victorious, to enjoy his estates as before. I can do nothing against him. But if I remain King of the English there will be some flicker of good government in the land. Since my army will not fight I shall work with Godwin, and do what I can to restrain him.'

'You will protect me, my lord, and the other Norman clerks who serve you?'

'I shall protect you if I can. First of all I must keep my throne.'

On the next day, the 14th of September, the pirates rowed under London bridge, hugging the south bank of the river to avoid our arrows. Godwin landed at Southwark, and fixed his head-quarters in his own hall by the river bank, whence he had fled a year ago. The levies of Kent and the South Saxons joined him as soon as he was ashore. Then the Frisian ships rowed across the river to attack the English fleet anchored off London. The peasants who manned the King's ships were no match for veteran pirates, and to prevent a useless slaughter of loyal Englishmen the King signalled for a parley.

The Council met next morning. In the evening it was proclaimed that Earl Godwin had answered all the charges brought against him, clearing himself by his own oath and the oaths of his helpers; therefore he was to be inlawed and granted the full friendship of the King, and the lands and offices of all the Godwinssons were to be returned to them. Furthermore, since the King had been led to persecute this innocent man by the advice of evil counsellors, those evil counsellors, and especially the Norman Bishops, must immediately go into exile. Peace was now secure throughout the land, and every warrior should go at once to his own home.

Robert of Canterbury, Ulf of Dorchester, William of London, all Norman Bishops, fled in a small boat that very night. They feared that the King would be unable to protect them for the legal five days of grace granted them to gather their goods.

In the evening the King told me to make a bundle of his weapons and mail and take it to Hugolin the treasurer. 'That axe is a work of art,' said he, 'and so is the helmet. They are too good to throw away, but I shall never again need them. In future if there is fighting to be done Godwin will do it for me. I have done my duty, at Sandwich and here in London; but either we failed to find the pirates or when we had found them the army wouldn't fight. Has there ever been such an unlucky King? But this is my fate, and I must make the best of it.'

When he was in bed he went on talking to himself.

'I must fetch the Lady from her convent. Poor girl, I was hard on her, but what else could I do? You can't have a Lady ruling at court while all her kin are outlaws. No, I can face Edith. The real trouble will be sitting with Godwin in Council. He must rule the country, since he is so strong that I can't prevent him; but must I talk to him by the hour? I must, at least when I wear my crown to discuss affairs of state. Well, I shall cut the Christmas feasting as short as possible, and perhaps in these troubled days Godwin will be too busy to come to Gloucester.'

He was silent for so long that I thought he had gone to sleep. Suddenly he spoke again: 'I shall do whatever Godwin advises. But I must make it clear to all my people that I am following his instructions. Then they won't blame me for his evil deeds, and perhaps one day honest men will rise against him. Even when he seizes Bishoprics to reward his followers I shall not complain. I shall wait until ordinary laymen notice the contrast between Danish adventurers and godfearing educated Normans.'

Next day I understood this new grievance. Before the court left London Godwin intruded his follower Stigand into the Archbishopric of Canterbury. That was a scandalous appointment, which shocked even tough Anglo-Danes. There could be no pretence that the See was vacant; the Archbishop had been driven out only by threats of murder. Stigand was notoriously a hanger-on of the Danish faction, unfitted in character and education for such high office. He knew that it would be vain to seek a pallium from Rome, so he took possession of his minster wearing the pallium which Robert had left behind when he fled to save his life. Thus he was correctly dressed. But no one was deceived. Bishops-elect, even if they were of Godwin's party, in future sought consecration from Cynesige of York or from some Archbishop oversea.

When the court moved down to Cotswold for the winter hunting it was no longer the centre of English government. Godwin ruled, and he preferred to stay near London. The Lady was the only member of her family living permanently with us, and she was quickly on good terms with the King again. During the troubles she had been loyal to her husband. If she had to choose she would support him even against her kin. But now all parties were friendly, on the surface. She had enjoyed her visit to Wilton, and she need never fear a rival. It is astonishing what men will put up with when they have grown used to it; Godwin and the King were now partners, and they managed to rub along.

About this time we heard that there was one Godwinsson less in the world. News came that Sweyn had perished in a storm, as he journeyed through Greekland on his return from Jerusalem. But in the Holy Sepulchre he had been shriven of all his sins, edifying his companions by the fervour of his contrition. A trader from the east told the story in the King's hall, and when he enlarged on this contrition there were sniggers. The King silenced the mockery, standing in his place to make a formal pronouncement.

107

'We are Christians in this hall, and we believe that every man is endowed with free will. We have sinned, and it would be well for all of us to show contrition. Never mock at a penitent sinner. But in this case mockery is not only unseemly, it is mistaken. Sweyn was a man of great fortitude; whatever he set out to do he accomplished. When he raped an abbess, when he murdered his kinsmen under truce, he did what he willed without counting the cost. When he journeyed to mourn at the tomb of God do you think he went lightly? He reached Jerusalem, and there his sins were remitted. Perhaps it was God's mercy that led him astray in that tempest, before he could blacken his soul with further crimes. As things fell out he made a good end, and I shall pray for his soul.'

This speech pleased the Lady, who loved her brothers; and it made things easier when next Godwin came to court. That was not why the King said it. In matters of religion he spoke his mind fearlessly, however he might compromise in secular affairs.

There was one secular affair on which the King would not compromise. He had chosen Duke William to be his heir, and he was determined that all the magnates should swear to carry out his will. For the Easter crownwearing of 1053 he assembled all the great men of the south, though Earl Siward and Archbishop Cynesige remained in York. Stigand was with the court, for even after he had seized Canterbury he kept his lawful Bishopric of Winchester; and naturally he felt more at home in the minster which was his by right than in the greater minster he had stolen. The King told me with great delight that he had persuaded Stigand to swear that he would support the claim of Duke William. Stigand had baulked at a public ceremony, but in the King's chapel he had taken oath with his hand on the gospel.

My lord was so pleased with this success that I had not the heart to remind him that Stigand would swear anything, in private; but that the oath of a man who had sworn canonical obedience to Archbishop Robert and now wore his lord's stolen pallium was not worth striving after.

During Holy Week the King extracted the same oath from Godwin; but again it was sworn in private and therefore unlikely to be kept. Godwin was not quite so unscrupulous as Stigand, and if he had promised publicly shame might have kept him true to his word. But an oath sworn in private could later be denied; and if witnesses came forward to prove it Godwin might plausibly plead that an oath in the King's chapel, with the King present, had been sworn under duress.

'All the same,' answered my lord gaily, when I had hinted my doubts, 'after I am dead these men will have to do as they have sworn. For where else can they find a King? A Dane could not come in, save by bloody conquest. There is no other Cerdinga nearer than Hungary.'

'No, my lord,' I said to comfort him, 'there is no other candidate. Duke William must be the next King of the English – if the English have another King,' I added under my breath.

After my lord was dead I did not think there would be another King of all the English. Already the country was falling apart, as the great Earls became stronger and the crown weaker. Siward of Northumbria made peace or war without reference to his lord in the south; the men of Lothian, from hatred of the Danes in York, had given their allegiance to the Scots; Chester was as much an outpost of Man or Dublin as a seaport of the northern Angles; English Mercia, jealous of the Danish half of the old province, made overtures to Griffith the King of North Wales. It seemed likely that after the house of Cerdic had passed away Wessex and the Saxon south-east would continue the tradition of the ancient Kingdom of Winchester, while the outlying districts joined up with powers beyond the English border.

But it was important that King Edward should enjoy peace of mind; for he was a good man, and I loved him. I listened without interruption while he sketched the glorious future of his native land, in which Norman commonsense and efficiency should be blended with the characteristic English mastery of beauty in the arts.

The famous and terrible judgement of God struck on the Thursday after Easter, the 15th of April 1053. Earl Godwin and his two elder sons, Harold and Tostig, had lingered at court after the rest of the Council had gone home. I can remember it all, for at that famous dinner I was the King's cupbearer.

It came about by chance, unless indeed I brought it about. Most unusually, the King called for more wine. It irked him to sit talking to the Godwinssons, and in his nervous irritation he had drained his cup merely to find something with which to occupy his hands. Of course he was not drunk; but normally he drank very little, and thus it happened that the small pitcher I carried must be replenished. When I had walked down the hall to the tapped cask at the far end the butler gave me more wine; but he filled the pitcher overfull, and I had to watch it carefully. I could not look at the floor; so it was that as I stepped on the dais, coming back to the high table, I stumbled and nearly spilled the wine. I managed to change legs like a horse going over a bank, and my pitcher remained upright. I hate making a mistake when I am waiting at table; even a servant has his pride. In my relief at seeing the wine unspilled I exclaimed aloud, though at the high table that was a breach of etiquette.

'Up we go, one brother helping the other,' I said as my left leg righted the blunder.

To my amazement, the King answered me. 'One brother helps the other. Alas, I have no brother to help me. Many years ago poor Alfred was murdered.' He turned to stare full in the face of Earl Godwin, seated at his left.

It was a pointed remark, especially as it had nothing to do with what had been said before. It was designed to vex Godwin, and he was vexed.

'My lord,' he said angrily, 'I did not murder your brother even though slander still whispers that I did. Twice I have solemnly cleared myself from the charge, by my oath and the oaths of my helpers. How many more times must I deny it before I am believed?'

The King shook his head with a sad, sweet smile of resignation which must have been intensely irritating. It showed more clearly than any words that he would continue to believe in Godwin's guilt, and yet nothing was said which Godwin could answer.

'Very well,' said the Earl, fuming. 'This has gone on long enough. Pay attention, all of you.' He snatched up a little roll of white bread. 'Now I shall swallow this roll. If I had any guilty part in the death of the atheling Alfred may it choke me so help me God.' He glared defiantly at the other great men seated at the high table.

'Wait a minute,' said the King, as calm as if such appeals were heard at every meal. 'We may as well carry out the rite properly

In the old days there used to be a formal ordeal by bread, as some of you may remember. Before Godwin eats that roll it ought to be blessed, and then we beseech God to come down and do justice. Archbishop, will you perform the blessing?' He turned to Stigand, who sat in the place of honour at his right.

Stigand looked uncomfortable. He was Godwin's man, and he did not care to join in this baiting of his lord. 'The custom is no longer used,' he said apologetically. 'I am told that Rome frowns on these ordeals, and indeed it seems presumptuous that Christians should call on God for a miracle whenever it is convenient. I can't remember the old blessing, and I am not scholar enough to compose a modern version here and now.'

'Ah, the Archbishop scruples to countenance a rite which Rome might view amiss,' answered the King with heavy irony. The whole world knew that Rome did not recognise Stigand's promotion. 'Very well. These ordeals are after all a custom of the laity, which the Church has never encouraged. But we must not disappoint Earl Godwin, who has challenged that piece of bread to be his oath-helper. Since this is a matter for laymen, a layman shall pronounce the blessing. I am the most eminent layman in this hall. Godwin, will you please hand me that roll?'

Taking the little round loaf in his right hand the King stroked it with a ring that he wore on the middle finger of his left. We all knew this ring, which had been made by one of the great craftsmen of old; the stone had been carved with a figure of St John the Apostle, and under it was kept a most holy relic. Then he held the roll in his left hand and made the sign of the cross over it, at the same time looking up to Heaven. 'May God display His power by means of this piece of bread,' he prayed. 'For as bread is the support without which men cannot continue in the world, so truth and fairdealing are the supports without which men cannot live justly. Therefore through the power of God bread, though a mere creature, may on occasion uphold truth and fair dealing.'

Clothed in his robes of state, with his long white hair flowing below the crown and his long white beard covering his breast, the King looked like some great Prophet painted on a church wall. The whole company watched in an awed silence.

Holding the bread in both hands he turned to Godwin. 'Take and eat,' he said solemnly. From another mouth that might have sounded blasphemous; but the King was in earnest and the echo deliberate.

Godwin looked red and selfconscious. He also looked very angry. He had been trapped into making this exhibition, which could not clear his damaged reputation. In law he had been cleared by his oath and the oaths of his helpers; the fact that he could swallow a mouthful of bread without choking would not convince anyone who still believed him guilty. And of course there was just the bare chance that something might go wrong, for the blessing of King Edward was known to be a thing of power.

As the Earl crammed the roll into his mouth the King once more sketched the sign of the cross in the air. I was the only man in the hall still looking at the King; then I saw his expression change, as he leaned forward in amazement. Following his eyes, I also stared at Earl Godwin.

The Earl's face was purple; on the table his hands clenched themselves into gnarled fists. He leaned forward, then levered himself upright on arms knotted with muscle. For a moment he stood erect, his head thrown back, his fingers clawing at his throat. Then he fell sideways, all in one piece, without any bending at the joints. He seemed to fall from his toes, like a tree felled close to the ground.

After the crash of that fall there was a moment of awed silence. Then the King spoke cheerfully to Stigand: 'Well, Archbishop, he asked for the judgement of God, and he got it. The ordeal was his suggestion. I did not force it on him.'

Harold and Tostig hastened to their father; from the women's table by the wall the Lady came running. In a moment the prostrate figure was hidden by the group of his children and attendants. I glanced quickly round the hall. The King sat smiling placidly, as though this were an expected event – and a pleasant one. The Archbishop, and the other clerks, were muttering prayers. The lesser courtiers sat upright on their benches, trying to keep all expression out of their faces; as yet they could not tell whether the correct reaction to this catastrophe would be rejoicing or mourning. The captain of the housecarles was very properly hurrying up to the dais; when anything unexpected happened his first duty was to guard the person of the King.

I slipped from my place to intercept him. 'Keep an eye on

Earl Harold,' I whispered. 'He's Godwin's heir, and he may think it his duty to exact a life for a life.' The captain nodded, and went over to join the group round Earl Godwin; unobtrusively he took up a position between Earl Harold and the King.

Presently Earl Harold straightened up and spoke: 'My father still breathes, but death cannot be far away. With your permission, my lord, I will take him to his chamber. Perhaps the Archbishop will order a tomb prepared in the Old Minster.'

'Drag out the stinking dog,' I heard the King mutter under his breath, then he spoke courteously and aloud: 'If he still breathes it is right that the Archbishop should shrive him. Carry him away, and do what you can. Dear me, what a sudden and terrible event! There will be great changes now. Earl Harold, when you have taken leave of your father I should like to consult with you in private. Will you come to me in my chamber as soon as is convenient.'

In his chamber, where only I could see him, the King did not attempt to hide his joy at Godwin's death. 'The scoundrel has been punished as he deserved,' he said gleefully. 'Mind you, Edgar, I am not rejoicing at his damnation. That would be a terrible thing for any Christian man to do. By the providence of God he may yet creep into Heaven. He was struck down as he boasted of his crimes; but he still lives, and there is time for repentance. There is sure to be a gleam of consciousness before the end, and with all those clerks round him he will die shriven. If for an instant he regrets the murder of my brother Purgatory is the worst that can come to him. There will be Masses for his soul, and we may pray for him without blasphemy.

'And at last I am free of a nagging temptation,' he went on after a pause. 'I have never been able to make up my mind about the bloodfeud. My ancestors for the last five hundred years call on me to avenge my murdered brother, and at the same time I know that God has forbidden murder. It was nothing but a quirk of honour that saved me from mortal sin. I used to remind myself that a King cannot engage in a fair fight with his subject; if I had revenged myself on Godwin I should have been crushing an inferior. But the excuse wore thin as he grew more powerful, until if he had continued to prosper I might have arranged to have him stabbed in the back. Now that has been settled for me. Godwin is dead, and

113

all the world will know why he died. Yet my hands are clean of blood. . . . Now all I have to do is to settle the government of his Earldom. I hope Harold proves reasonable. He's a bloody pirate, and I shall never forgive his ravaging of Somerset. But I don't want to make war on him if I can decently avoid it.'

Soon Earl Harold was announced, and I was sent out of the room while the conference was held in private. But that made no difference, for the King told me all about it as I prepared him for bed that night.

'Harold also has his quirk of honour,' he said with a sigh of content. 'He wishes above all things to avoid even the appearance of profiting by his father's death. He must succeed to Godwin's Earldom of Wessex; I can't refuse him that unless I declare him outlaw. But when he takes over the West Saxons he will give up the East Angles. Both together would be too much for any subject. So we have agreed to offer the East Angles to Alfgar, Leofric's son. When Leofric dies Alfgar will succeed him in Mercia; then East Anglia will be vacant, as promotion for some other promising young nobleman. In the meantime it's nice to think of all those Danish pirates on the east coast being ruled by a true Englishman. Siward has a son, who must succeed him; but in any case the north goes its own way. A King in Winchester cannot control York. But now we have arranged things so that they will last my time, without danger of civil war.'

As he got into bed he summed up. 'Harold will be the greatest man in England, perhaps more powerful than the King. But he has foes among his own house. Tostig hates him, and the Lady sides with Tostig. The Godwinssons are too wicked to remain united. What an exciting day – but on the whole a pleasant one.'

The King slept like a child.

CHAPTER VI

The Rise of Earl Harold

The removal of Godwin did not leave so great a gap as might have been expected. Perhaps if the King had tried hard he might now have made himself the real ruler of the English; but he did not try. He had seen, only a year ago, that the thanes of England would not follow him in civil war, and the disappointment had sapped his will.

In the old days he had refused to admit that Godwin's power was greater than his own. He had seen himself as the supreme lord, delegating details of administration to a useful servant. He may have wondered from time to time whether he was strong enough to dismiss this useful servant; but after Godwin had failed to keep order in Dover it had turned out to be quite easy.

Then, only a year ago, the King's power had melted away as soon as he leaned on it. Never again would he call on his followers to muster in arms; never again would he risk humiliation.

Therefore Earl Harold stepped without friction into his father's shoes. He was first in Council, warleader, in peace the dispenser of all civil patronage (for the King himself looked after ecclesiastical appointments). But though Harold wielded all his father's power he did not, in the summer of 1053, overshadow the King as Godwin had overshadowed him.

His age made a difference. He was in his early thirties, and I think younger than his sister, the Lady. It may seem to you odd that I cannot be certain on such a point, which must have been well known to many; but I never met the Godwinssons until they were grown up, and a chamberlain cannot ask that kind of personal question. Anyway, Harold was the King's brother-in-law, and young enough to be his son; which gave him a very different status from that of a father-in-law who was ten years his senior. Harold was also younger than the other two Earls who might in certain circumstances become his rivals; both Siward and Leofric could remember him as a boy. Though he proved ruthless in war he was always pleasant and urbane in Council, and he behaved with great deference to the King. Above all, he could not be blamed for the murder of the atheling Alfred, since in 1036 he had been too young to bear arms.

Thus during that summer we lived happily. A stranger might suppose that the mighty King of the English ruled unquestioned, merely delegating day-to-day business to a trusted subordinate. It was not immediately apparent that if it came to a clash the minister must prevail.

The King prayed, and hunted, and in the evening discussed learning and the wonders of the ancient world with his favourite Norman courtiers. If things were done in his name of which he might have disapproved they were not brought to his attention.

One eminent member of the court was discontented – the Lady. Of all her brothers she liked Harold least; Tostig was her favourite. Yet in the new distribution of power Harold had all and his brothers nothing. The circumstances of their exile had divided the Godwinssons. Harold had joined the Dublin vikings, the most bloodthirsty enemies of the English; he had taken Leofwin with him, but Leofwin was too young to have a mind of his own. Tostig had stayed with his father, waiting decorously in the Christian land of Flanders until the threat of civil war brought him home. As the Lady saw it, Tostig had behaved like a responsible statesman, and Harold like a ruthless viking.

'She won't face facts,' the King complained to me when we were alone one evening. 'Like so many women, she makes a picture of the world as it ought to be, and then complains because reality disappoints her. She spoke to me again this afternoon, asking me to give Tostig a great Earldom. She won't see that there isn't one to give. Siward rules the north, and when he dies it must go to his son. Even Harold is not strong enough to disinherit that family. I rather like old Siward. He's a barbarous hero from the old epics, perhaps a little out of place in

116

modern civilised England; but you know where you are with him. He may be a killer, but he's honest. In the same way Leofric is rooted in Mercia. He isn't a man to make himself beloved like Siward, but the almsdeeds of Godiva will never be forgotten. Alfgar will inherit his mother's popularity and his father's prestige. With Harold in Wessex and the south, that means that all England is occupied.'

'Besides,' he continued, 'Harold is not quite such a ruffian as I had supposed. The Lady won't see that even his past wickedness works in his favour. Since the battle of Porlock he is hated in the south-west, which means that his own Earldom wouldn't follow him in revolt. He can never attempt to displace me, any more than I can get rid of him. Tostig, who hasn't an enemy in the world, would be a much more dangerous minister. But there, you can't argue with a woman. The Lady will never be convinced.'

It seemed that all England was settled and at peace, under the rule of great Earls who would transmit their governments to their sons. Harold alone had no heir, because he was not yet married; though it was an open secret that he kept a favourite concubine in a fine house at Canterbury, and had bastards growing up all over the country. However, there were plenty of younger Godwinssons who could succeed him if necessary.

There was also no heir of the house of Cerdic. Among the Godwinssons only Tostig agreed with the King's choice of a successor. At every Council the question cropped up.

Then someone remembered the refugees in Hungary. It must have been Harold who thought of them in the first place, but he was too cautious to appear as the originator of the idea. Bishop Aldred was the first to speak of them, one evening during the Christmas crownwearing of 1053.

Bishop Aldred possessed every quality necessary to a statesman, except foresight. He could genuinely understand the point of view of an opponent, which made him good at arranging treaties; his memory was clear, he never delayed in answering letters, and in money matters he could not be cheated. But so long as no one was fighting he was satisfied; not true peace, but the mere absence of war, was his highest aim. He never asked himself whether by getting an agreement today he was laying the foundation of a savage war in the future; he had no policy except delay, and he negotiated as though all the great men who now ruled England would live for ever.

That evening he spoke persuasively. The King was childless. In Hungary lived the son of the great English hero, Edmund Ironside. It was shameful that a genuine Cerdinga should be the pensioner of a foreign court. The young man must be weary of exile, and now that all England was at peace he should be invited to return. He might scruple to make the first approach, because that would look like begging for an English pension. But if the King would send a formal invitation he would surely hurry to revisit the land of his birth.

When the Bishop finished speaking I saw Harold smile encouragement; the other Earls made not very enthusiastic noises of assent. No one would oppose in public such a harmless suggestion, though Ralph looked surly. The King stared up at the rafters, and I guessed that he was praying for guidance. He wanted this Hungarian to stay in Hungary, but he could not withstand the unanimous desire of his Council.

'I know nothing about this Edward,' he began, 'except that he is the son of my half-brother Edmund. But if the King of the Hungarians keeps him in luxury he must be of good behaviour. I suppose my treasury ought to support him. Let me see, would you call the son of a half-brother a nephew or a half-nephew? Anyway, he is the only male Cerdinga living, except myself. Very well, we shall send him an invitation. But we must go carefully, for fear of offending powerful neighbours. We can't write direct to the King of the Hungarians, you know. He owes allegiance to the Empire, and the Emperor would feel insulted. There is no hurry. This atheling has lived abroad since Sweyn the father of Canute overthrew my father, and a few more months will not matter. How would this do? Let us send an embassy to the Emperor, asking him to ask the King of the Hungarians to send Edward here. When everyone concerned has agreed, we can send a formal embassy. Who shall go as ambassador? Why not Bishop Aldred, since he was the first to show interest in this remote question?'

The Bishop preened himself; it would be pleasant to visit the Emperor as envoy from a great and friendly King. Earl Harold looked less pleased, for the King would remove from the Council one of his most useful supporters. But it was a suggestion that no one could oppose. The clerks were ordered to begin the complicated draft of the ambassador's instructions

118

and to look up the precedents for his letter of credence to the Emperor.

That night the Lady came into the chamber to chat with the King as he prepared for bed, and my lord returned once more to the subject of the Hungarian exile. 'In Council I kept my temper, and I hope someone in Heaven made a note of it. It's Harold's idea that this atheling should return, and of course he would like to make him my successor. A foreigner from Hungary, knowing nothing of English affairs! He would be Harold's tool, just as I was the tool of Godwin his father. But that sort of thing can't go on generation after generation. Look at what happened to the Franks! The Merovings had even more prestige than the Cerdingas; in the old heathen days they had been sacred rulers, and they still observed the old ritual prohibitions against getting their hair cut or riding a horse. They were so scared that they must have a Mayor of the Palace to make their mistakes for them, since a sacred King cannot make a mistake. Then the Mayors of the Palace took over, and there were no more Merovings. Of course that wasn't the end of it. What the Carolings had taken by usurpation they lost to usurpers.'

He spoke more rapidly. 'That's what will happen among the English, you mark my words, if the Godwinssons make themselves into hereditary chief ministers. But the world grows worse every year, and I expect it will happen more quickly than in France. Harold will rule for a few years in the name of this atheling. Then he will make himself King of the English. But his posterity will not keep the crown.'

'He doesn't think so far ahead as you suppose,' answered the Lady. 'This idea of bringing over the Hungarian was his, I grant you. But don't you think he suggested it only to annoy, because he knew you wouldn't like it? It pleases him sometimes to show that he's master, but he's clever, and cautious, and always makes sure of popular support before he suggests anything. He can't hope to be King of the English himself; and he can hardly be plotting for his grandchildren, since he has never bothered to marry.'

'That's another thing,' said the King, who could easily be persuaded to drop one grievance by the mention of another. 'Your brother Harold is setting a shocking bad example, and I wish you could persuade him to stop. In Canute's time marriage went clean out of fashion. He himself lived honestly enough with my mother, but half his Councillors kept to the old heathen ways. For the last twenty years and more every Bishop in England has been telling his flock to marry for life, or else live chaste. It's a great pity that laymen should see the most famous English layman openly keeping a Danish concubine. I don't ask Harold to observe all the Commandments all the time; there would be no harm done if he had one or two mistresses in the country and visited them quietly. But if he is going to live with one woman, why on earth can't he marry her like a Christian?'

'It's late in the day to ask that of him,' the Lady objected. 'When the connection began Edith Swan-neck was very beautiful, and they are still fond of one another. But Harold would look ridiculous if he offered to marry a thirty-year-old concubine who had already borne his children. Besides, this Edith has no kin of any consequence. So long as my brother remains unmarried he has something in reserve. In a tight place he could marry into some great house, and gain an ally.'

'Everything about Harold is unsatisfactory,' my lord grumbled. 'It's hard luck that I should be landed with the worst of the Godwinssons as chief minister. If only Tostig had been born second instead of third! Or, for that matter, if you had been born a boy!'

'Tostig and I will work together against Harold,' the Lady answered in a soothing voice. 'Somewhere you must find enough land to make Tostig a great Earl. Then we shall gradually overshadow Harold, without driving him to extremes or putting him outside the law. I don't want to outlaw my brother, but I agree that he's not worthy to rule England in your name.'

The house of Godwin was now openly divided. The younger brothers, fascinated by Harold's greatness, still clung to him; but Tostig and the Lady were firmly on the side of the King.

Although the plan had been settled in principle at Christmas 1053 it was not until the following summer that Bishop Aldred was free to journey into the Empire. Presently he came back to say that the Emperor had sent word into Hungary, and that the atheling would come when he was ready. He implied that this would not be for some time; Bishop Aldred wove his complicated plans as though all his contemporaries were immortal.

In the meantime a war had broken out in England, though we in the south were little affected. Malcolm, son and heir of the murdered King Duncan of the Scots, persuaded Earl Siward to join him in an attack on King Macbeth. The poets sing of it as a very great war. The vikings of Orkney came in force to help the Scots, and in the battle thousands were slain on either side; though in the end the Northumbrians gained the victory. King Macbeth got away alive, but only to lurk for another year or two in the far north. Malcolm was anointed King on the old magic stone of the Scots. The Northumbrians took a great booty that made many of them rich for life. But what mattered to us in Wessex was that in the battle Osbern Siwardsson was killed.

It was characteristic of Siward, that antique hero, that when he learned of the boy's death he asked only how he had been killed. When they told him that the corpse was everything it should be, lying on its back with all its wounds in front, he went on to win the battle unmoved. Siward had another son to carry on his line; yet this Waltheof was a child, too young to govern an Earldom, and Siward was old.

'At last there is an opening for Tostig,' said the Lady when she heard the news.

In the same autumn there happened a remarkable event, of which the like had not been known since the Romans left Britain; all the Welsh were united under one ruler. King Griffith of the North made war on King Griffith of the South, and killed him. The southern King left no son to succeed him, though he had kin to keep alive the family claim. The faithless Welsh submitted to the victor, who ruled without opposition from Chester to the Usk.

It had been a restless year, and there was more trouble at the Lent Council in the following spring. In the first place Earl Siward was too ill to attend, and it was said that he would never recover. The great Earldom of Northumbria must go to a stranger. If Tostig were promoted, would that mean a doubling of the power of the Godwinssons, or would Harold find a rival who would presently surpass him? All the magnates were touchy and bad-tempered, and at the lower end of the hall their housecarles bickered until the chamberlains were hard put to it to keep the peace.

The great man whose nerve was the first to break was not one of those we had been watching. While we feared a desperate quarrel among the Godwinssons, the housecarles of Earl Alfgar came storming through the passages, crying that they must load their master's baggage without delay. Then the Council adjourned until next morning, and it was publicly proclaimed that the Earl of the East Angles had been outlawed for treason.

I wish I could explain this episode, but I can't. It is unlikely that Alfgar expected to get Northumbria, when obviously he must have English Mercia as soon as his father was dead. On the other hand, it would be a very strange coincidence if he happened to plot an independent treason when everyone was thinking about the succession to Earl Siward. I am not even sure that he was justly called a traitor. The King himself could not make up his mind on the point. On different occasions I heard him say that Alfgar had been condemned by false oaths, and that he had admitted his guilt. Perhaps his enemies slandered him while he was planning some other treason that was never discovered.

At all events, if Alfgar was falsely convicted he had taken precautions against such a misfortune. Recently he had given his young daughter Edith in marriage to the much older Welsh King, and he used his five days of grace to flee not to the nearest seaport, but westward into Wales. His housecarles remained faithful to him, and the thanes of English Mercia would fight for the son of Leofric against all comers. He was soon at the head of a powerful army.

In the middle of this crisis came news that Siward was dead and Northumbria without a ruler.

Tostig was the only successor available, as even Harold must admit. Leofric was suspect, and his son Alfgar disqualified. Harold was by this time on bad terms with his brother, but he had to approve his appointment as Earl of the Northumbrians.

When the King went to London to wear his crown at Pentecost 1055 the war had not yet begun, though it was known that King Griffith and Alfgar would invade before winter. All the Earls were free to come to the Council, even Tostig who had just taken possession of his new Earldom. He and Leofric brought their wives with them; for the Lady had come to

London with the King, and merchants from oversea, knowing the movements of the court, had imported special cargoes of fine silk and Greek jewellery. It was a very gay crownwearing, for those who enjoy the company of pretty women; and I enjoyed it also, for I like to see handsome clothes of the latest fashion.

It seemed that in those days everyone was building churches. Earl Leofric, or rather Godiva his wife, had just finished their great foundation at Coventry; I have never seen it, but I am told it is very splendid. The Lady had rebuilt the chapel at Wilton, in gratitude for the community's generous hospitality while her family were in exile. Oddly enough the most fashionable convent in England, with a membership drawn from noble houses, had hitherto made do with a little wooden chapel. Unkind neighbours whispered that this was because the nuns devoted all their spare money to the refectory, but I think it was just an example of the English habit of putting up with an old unsatisfactory building rather than bring in crowds of workmen to wander all over the place. Anyway, the Lady replaced the wooden chapel with a fine one of stone, taller than anything of the kind I had seen before. Bishop Hermann consecrated it in a ceremony of great splendour when the court passed by on the way to London. Everybody liked poor Bishop Hermann, though the affairs of his diocese were always in confusion. I remember the consecration, and the feast afterwards when we ate sugar cakes cooked by the nuns themselves; and if the Lady had to pay some bills that she thought Bishop Hermann had paid already, the money was there and it was not enough to mar the feeling of festivity.

In London we heard that even Earl Harold was contemplating the foundation of a great church; though in general he was stingy with the clergy, always disputing their immunity from taxation. Just to be different his new foundation at Waltham would not be a minster; instead he would put in canons who followed one of the new foreign rules.

Of course Tostig had not yet had time to found anything in his new Earldom, but he talked largely of his plans when the magnates supped with the King on the eve of Pentecost. It was a cheerful and good-tempered gathering, even though Earl Leofric sighed from time to time at the absence of his son. While they were discussing the great shrines of Northumbria Judith joined in from the women's table with a story of her own.

'St Cuthbert protects all the north, and so long as he stays with us we shall be safe from raiding Scots. But I wish they would find a better place for his relics. They have been moved often enough in the past. Do you know, lord King, that they are kept inside the monastic enclosure, so that no female may approach them?'

'But they make an exception for the wives of rulers, don't they? That's the custom in most religious houses,' said Bishop William in French from the high table. Bishop William had been recalled by his flock soon after his flight with Archbishop Robert; he was such a good Bishop, even though a Norman, that the Londoners could not get on without him. Now he was trying hard to learn English, in gratitude. He could understand the language, especially when spoken by Judith the Fleming, but he could not yet trust himself to speak it.

'The monks made an exception for me,' answered Judith, smiling. She continued to speak English, for she wanted the whole company to understand her story. 'Unfortunately St Cuthbert didn't. The burgesses of Durham warned me that he might be angry, even after his prior had given me permission to enter the enclosure. So I took the precaution of sending my maid before I paid a visit myself. She came back from the shrine most distressed, saying that as she knelt unseen hand had pinched and beaten her all over. After that I wouldn't risk it. Though I made a good offering I have never seen St Cuthbert. Don't you think, lord King, that the shrine ought to be moved to the nave of the minster?'

The King chuckled. 'Those monks carried St Cuthbert from Lindisfarne. We can't deprive them of the relics they guarded at the risk of their lives. Anyway, young Judith has only herself to blame. The prior gave her permission to enter the enclosure, because she is the wife of a ruler. Instead she sent her maid. Naturally St Cuthbert was angry. I hope Tostig made amends with a really good offering.'

'It was a costly one, my lord. The prior was satisfied, and he speaks for St Cuthbert. So all should be well.'

The King often spoke of saints as though they were still fallible mortals. There was no irreverence in it; he thought of

124

the saints every day, and he seemed to understand their characters as though he had known them on earth.

Next morning, when the court went in state to the High Mass of Pentecost, we were still thinking of religious affairs. Harold and Tostig went to St Paul's, to please their friends the Londoners; Ralph had been detained in the west by the threat of Welsh invasion; but Earl Leofric and Godiva came with the King and the Lady to Westminster.

Nowadays I was always close to the King on formal occasions. The treasurer looked after the regalia while it was in store, but what the King was to wear was handed to me. Since I was responsible for the crown, orb and sceptre I stayed near them while they were displayed in public. On that morning I stood against the wall, while the King sat on a throne in the middle of the chancel; but I was level with him, and I did not take my eyes off him for long.

The King prayed with devotion, as always. But at the Consecration his manner changed. I saw him glance at the Host, as we all do, and expected him then to bow his head. He bowed his whole body until he was almost prostrate on the ground, and his shoulders shook with emotion. He did not straighten up until the *Ite* had been sung, and then his face was changed; he looked as though he had been frightened, and awed, and at the same time comforted. I glanced quickly round the other magnates. Most of them were as usual, but Earl Leofric and Godiva remained prostrate even after the King had risen.

When we got home after Mass I helped the King to disrobe, and took the precious regalia back to the treasurer. During the day I waited at dinner and supper, and stood in an anteroom during the private discussions of the Council; but I never had a chance to speak to the King until he was preparing for bed. Even then the Lady came into his chamber, to discuss the singing they had heard that morning; as a rule the King liked to talk about the chant, but tonight he answered shortly and let the Lady see that his mind was not on music. When she left he went straight to his little figure of St Peter; but before he could begin his prayers I said what I had been bursting to say for the last twelve hours.

'My lord, this morning did you see a vision? If a messenger

came to you from Heaven, surely you have a duty to announce his message to your people?'

'Now what put that into your head? I suppose it showed in my face. All the same, at the most solemn moment of the Mass you ought to be looking at the altar, not at the King.'

'My lord, that's not fair. You know that I follow the Mass. I don't talk to my neighbours or say my private prayers like an old woman. Today I looked at the altar when it was time for the Consecration; but I also glanced from time to time at the crown of England for which I am responsible.'

'Yes, well then, of course, you saw that something had happened to me. It wasn't anything very strange or unusual, now that I have had time to think it over. It gave me a shock when I saw it, naturally. But there was nothing that you could call a message, nothing that it is my duty to pass on to my people. So I shall say no more about it.'

'Please, my lord, tell me what you saw. You saw something. And I think Earl Leofric and Godiva saw it also.'

'You notice too much, Edgar. But if you noticed it others may have done the same, and queer rumours will be flying about. Perhaps I should tell you. You won't sleep until you know all about this, as you know all the other secrets of the court. But then you never pass on those secrets to others. It's a venial fault in a loyal servant. Very well. . . . '

The King paused to find the right words.

'This morning in Westminster I saw God. That's nothing extraordinary, is it? Remember, you saw Him too, and so did everyone else who paid attention while the priest consecrated the Host. We all saw God's body, everyone in the crowded minster. The only difference was that to you He looked like a wafer, and to me, just for once, He looked like a beautiful child. That's what I saw the priest hold in his hands. Leofric saw the same, and Godiva also. I don't think anyone else did.'

'My lord. . . . ' I could say no more.

'Now don't make a fuss about this, Edgar. I did not see God in all His glory, as St John did on Patmos, and perhaps other great saints. I saw Him in the form of a child, as anyone could have seen Him who happened to be living in Nazareth at the right time. There's no favour in that, you know. In fact you might call it evidence that God doubts my faith. You believe in the Mass, and don't need a miracle to prove it. Poor old Edward needs one . . . or that's what they think in Heaven. It's nothing to be proud of.'

'It was a miracle, my lord, a favour shown to a holy King, a favour shared by the righteous Earl and his charitable wife.'

'Yes, that makes it seem a compliment, doesn't it? I'm proud to think that my guardian angel puts me in the same class as the charitable Godiva. But let's say no more about it. It was not important.'

The King would never speak of it again.

On the first Sunday after Pentecost we were still in London, and of course the King went to hear High Mass at Westminster. On this ordinary Sunday he did not wear his crown, and therefore I was not on duty; but I went in his party, because I had to hear Mass somewhere and I liked the chant at Westminster. No Earls rode with the King, only a small bodyguard of housecarles; and behind them a little group of courtiers and servants.

In the open space before the minster we found the usual crowd of beggars. The housecarles hustled them aside to make way for the King. But every beggar got at least a silver penny, which those who turned up regularly regarded as their due; and a few, who had made long journeys to tell the King of their misfortunes, were given quite substantial sums of money. Beggars collected whenever it was known that the King would appear in public; for even wicked and avaricious Kings must distribute largesse.

These beggars were so much part of the expected background that no one paid them much attention; until we became aware that one man was resisting the housecarles, refusing to get out of the way. They were gentle with him, since he could not be dangerous; his legs were so twisted that his feet seemed fixed to his buttocks. Writhing on his knees, he waved his hands in the air and cried out in an unknown tongue.

The King reined his horse, waiting quietly for the path to be cleared. No one wanted the cripple to be hurt, and it was difficult to move him gently. All the time he was shouting, evidently one phrase repeated again and again; a housecarle listened, understood, and laughed.

'Who's this man, and what's he asking?' called the King sharply. 'He must want something more than money. If you can understand him find out what it is.'

'He is Irish, my lord,' answered the housecarle, looking a little abashed. 'I know something of his language because as a lad I sailed with the Dublin kings. Of course that was years ago, and I gave up piracy when I joined King Hardicanute's bodyguard. I laughed because this Irish beggar is proclaiming that he won't get out of the way until the King of the English has consented to carry him into the minster riding on his shoulders.'

'So that's what he's saying, is it?' answered the King mildly. 'You can speak to him in his queer language? Well, we can't get on while he lies in the way, and I wouldn't like to see a beggar beated by my bodyguard while we are all on our way to Mass. Ask the man exactly what he wants, and why he wants it. But even if he has come all the way from Ireland I won't give him more money than is fitting.'

The housecarle spoke to the beggar, who squatted on his twisted legs under the nose of the King's horse. The beggar replied with great animation, waving his hands to emphasise his story. With a shrug the housecarle turned to the King, smiling at the absurdity of what he must say.

'This man is named Michael, and he has been deformed from birth. He has visited all the shrines and holy places of Ireland, with no success. Two months ago St Peter appeared to him in a dream, and told him that he would be cured if he prayed before the new altar of St Peter in Westminster in England. But a condition was attached to this assurance. The cure will work only if Michael visits the altar in the way specified. He must be carried up the whole length of the church on the shoulders of the King of the English.'

Everyone laughed, but the King pursued the subject. 'Ask him how he got here.'

'He says he begged a passage from Cork to Bristol. Trader from the west let him ride on a packpony from Bristol to London. He has never walked a step in his life. But from London to Westminster he dragged himself on his knees.'

'Was it an English ship, and an English packtrain?'

'Yes, my lord.'

'Then I shall do what he asks of me. For the love of God my subjects carried him all the way from Cork to London. After such an example of charity it would be shameful if their King refused to carry him a mere hundred yards. Hold my horse, one

128

of you. Michael, sit quiet. I won't crouch down because sometimes that makes me dizzy. Let two housecarles pick him up and put him on my shoulders.'

The King slid from his horse, and leaned forward like a boy playing leapfrog. I ran out to drape my cloak over his shoulders, for the beggar was very filthy and the King wore a fine red tunic. Then Michael, a skinny starved little man, was hoisted aloft, his grubby hands clasping the King's neck. My lord stumped sturdily through the west door of the minster.

In the nave we took up our usual formation. The customary procession approached the high altar, candle-bearers, thurifers, the bodyguard, courtiers and an almoner carrying the special Sunday offering; in the midst the white hair and white beard of the King of the English were almost hidden by the grey frieze rags and grimy legs of a filthy beggar.

The King dumped his burden before the high altar, and then went to the throne prepared for him. The Mass proceeded as usual. When it was time to leave we all waited for the King to make the first move; but Michael leapt to his feet and capered down the nave, shouting that he was healed. The monks and the whole congregation began to praise God, and there was a great deal of noise and confusion. Through it we heard the King's voice shouting:

'Bodyguard, escort me from the church. It's dinner time, and there is no reason for delay.'

We pressed our way back to the King's hall in London through an excited crowd which swelled every minute as the news spread. But when onlookers praised the King as a worker of miracles he grew angry.

At dinner he would not speak of the cure. That evening, in his chamber, he returned to the subject. I think for the last time in his life.

'Edgar, see that this man Michael gets back to Ireland as quickly as possible. He's a beggar by trade, and he will think that because he was cured at Westminster the monks are obliged to keep him for the rest of his life. I don't see why the Irish should not care for the Irish poor; we have enough of our own in England. Besides, if he stays in London Bishop William will make a show of him. Now don't you ever let me hear you say that you have seen me cure a cripple! Michael was cured by St Peter, after he had carried out St Peter's instructions. I did

9

less than the English skipper who carried him to Bristol. No one says the sailor worked a miracle. No one even bothers to find out his name.'

'All the same,' he went on, now talking to himself, 'St Peter did not forget me. He has given me a valuable lesson in humility. Just think of it, I was tempted to refuse to carry the wretch! The Devil whispered to me that a starveling Irishman was trying to make the King of England look ridiculous. How shameful if I had yielded to the tempter! Any Christian ought to be willing to help another Christian over a journey of a mere hundred yards. If one Christian is a King and the other a beggar that should make no difference. Any of my courtiers would have done as much, had they been asked. That beggar is a very lucky man, to have his cure granted on such easy conditions.'

It seemed to me at that time that the saints took an unusual interest in King Edward. Before he came to the throne there had been Bishop Britwold's vision, and later King Edward had seen the death of the Danish King. Now St Peter had intervened in a very striking fashion. But these were favours granted by King Edward's advocates in Heaven, not signs that God Himself was specially pleased with him. He was a good man who did as the catechism commanded; he never missed Mass; he tried to examine every problem from the point of view of a Christian. If he persevered in this way of life he would end up in Heaven; but so far there was nothing to suggest that his virtues were heroic.

By midsummer the court was back among the forests of the west country, where religion did not occupy our thoughts as it did at Westminster.

Everyone had expected trouble in the north now that the great Siward was no longer there to overawe the Scots; instead Tostig brought a firmer peace than the oldest Northumbrian could remember. The King of the Scots owed his throne to an English army, and that helped; but in addition Tostig went out of his way to make friends with Malcolm. At York the two rulers performed some old pagan ceremony that made them blood-brothers, so that it would be a crime against kinship if they made war on each other. King Edward disapproved when he heard of it, for Christianity is not as firm in Northumbria as it ought to be in the land of St Oswald King and Martyr; too many new-settled Danes live there, who still remember Odin and Thor. But even if the ceremony gave scandal the friendship endured; King Malcolm never made war on Tostig, though he raided over the border on one occasion when the Earl was absent from his government.

Though the north was quiet a dangerous storm was gathering in the west. News came that Alfgar and his Mercian adherents had recruited eighteen shiploads of pirates from Dublin. That shocked the King even more than Alfgar's alliance with the Welsh.

'In my youth such treachery would have been unthinkable,' I heard him say to Earl Harold, who had called in at court to discuss the defence of Wessex. 'Anglo-Danes would sometimes seek help from their heathen cousins, but to all Englishmen the pirates of Dublin were enemies. Alfgar owes me no loyalty, since I have sent him into exile. But he owes a loyalty to Christendom, unless he is prepared to deny his baptism and become a heathen himself. For an Englishman to lead vikings against Englishmen is such wickedness as our ancestors never knew.'

Harold blushed, fingering his cup as an excuse to turn his eyes away from the King. 'Sometimes an Englishman loves England so much that he will seek the help of any allies to return to his native land,' he mumbled awkwardly. Then he spoke more briskly, with a resolute mien. 'We shall beat Alfgar in the field, and then we'll pardon him. Put him back, and he'll rule his own people well enough. Perhaps I made a mistake when I advised you to declare him outlaw. . . . That's it, we shan't wait any longer. If he doesn't invade I shall bring up the levy of Wessex and seek him out in Wales. One smashing defeat, and he will have learned his lesson.'

'Don't do that yet,' the King answered at once. 'The Welsh have not attacked us, and I will not begin an aggressive war against fellow-Christians. Besides, Earl Ralph has been entrusted with the defence of the border, and if you come to his help unasked it may seem that we doubt his competence.'

'We doubt it, don't we?' said Harold curtly.

'He is the son of my sister, and a loyal vassal. In theory his measures for the defence of Herefordshire are perfectly sound. Castles keep raiders out of Normandy, and if they break through in spite of the castles mounted warriors defeat them.

131

I saw it, when I was in exile. Ralph has been unlucky. Next time he should succeed.'

'His measures may be excellent,' answered Harold, 'but he will never persuade his thanes to carry them out. Some men can make themselves obeyed, others can't. Country thanes don't ride well enough to fight on horseback, and even Ralph's paid housecarles will think it is a crazy notion.'

'Give him his chance, all the same. Oh dear, those Dublin vikings! They make everything so complicated. We can cope with the neighbours of England, but when they bring in allies from abroad we need more than ordinary shire-levies.'

That second reminder of his shocking treason at the time of Godwin's exile silenced Earl Harold; as indeed it was meant to do. So far the great Earl had displayed his prowess only in sacking the farms of Englishmen. That was the weak point in his political position, and the King never tired of reminding him of it.

In October, as a consequence, when King Griffith and Alfgar marched to the harrying of Herefordshire they were met by the shire-levy alone, without help from Wessex. The court was on Cotswold, and we had early news of the fighting. On the 24th a messenger told us that Earl Ralph and all his men were mustered outside the city of Hereford, awaiting attack by the Welsh. We sat up all night, hoping for news of victory.

It was nearly dawn when the second messenger arrived, and I took him straight to the King who still sat at the supper table. We could see bad news in his face, before he opened his mouth. But as his tale proceeded we were shocked at the extent of the disaster.

'We were ready, arrayed in our ranks, when the enemy came into sight. But the Earl had commanded us all to stay on our horses. When the trumpets sounded the horses began to gallop and our men could not control them. Most of the army had ridden off the field before a blow had been struck.'

'Wait a moment,' the King interrupted. 'Who are you? Whom do you serve? Where were you in this army?'

'I am Wulf, a free thane. But because I have commended myself to the Bishop of Hereford I fought with the levy of the minster. My horse ran away with the rest of them, though presently I was able to stop it.'

'What became of the Earl and his Normans? They are trained

to fight mounted. Their horses would not run away.'

'They left the field in good order, when they saw our army scattered. They did not return to the city. I think they hid themselves in Richard's Castle. No one in Hereford saw them after the rout.'

'A good knight would have charged with his household alone,' said the King aside in French. 'That's the end of Ralph as a warleader. Well, go on, Wulf,' he added in English.

'By the time the Welsh reached the city we had got rid of our horses. We stood to defend the hedges and gardens. But the wind blew from the west, and as the houses burned round us we were driven back. We hoped that the minster would not burn, since the walls are stone. When the rest fled the Bishop's men rallied to defend it, and the monks came out armed to join us. Presently the Welsh carried the west door, and I think the monks were all killed. When I swam the Wye the Welsh held all the town. They were binding the burgesses to sell them as slaves. On the far side of the river I found old Bishop Athelstan. Because I was the last man to get away unhurt from the sack he gave me a horse and sent me to tell the King.'

'I am glad to know the Bishop is safe. Are you sure the minster was destroyed?'

'Yes, my lord. When I looked back the whole roof was burning. With the Welsh were vikings, who know how to destroy stone buildings. Welshmen don't like cities.'

'You have done your duty. Go and rest. Treasurer, give this man a bag of silver. Chancellor, two letters must leave at once. Write to Bishop Athelstan, offering him the hospitality of the King's hall. Write to Earl Harold, commanding him to march immediately against the Welsh with the whole levy of Wessex. That's the best we can do. Now, if my chaplain is ready, I shall go to hear Mass.'

Suddenly the King was an old man. He shuffled to his chapel, bent and stumbling. I knew what had broken his spirit; for a second time his nephew had shown himself a coward, and the only man who could restore the situation was the hated Earl Harold.

Harold restored the situation with brisk efficiency. He gathered an army from all England; even Northumbria sent a contingent, now that it was governed by a Godwinsson. At the beginning of winter this great host invaded south Wales, and King Griffith dared not meet it in the field. By the time the court moved to Gloucester for the Christmas crownwearing a peace had been arranged.

'And I must ratify what the Earl has promised in my name,' the King complained to me on the evening he heard the news. 'Alfgar must be forgiven and restored to his Earldom. Harold easily forgives a traitor who led savage vikings to ravage his own countrymen, for Harold himself did it not long ago. My nephew Ralph, who has always been loyal to me, loses his Earldom; of course it goes to Harold. I can't complain of that, I suppose, since Ralph has shown himself utterly incompetent. But Alfgar the traitor is not punished at all. He paid off his vikings quite brazenly with the plunder of Hereford, and they have gone back to Dublin rich and happy. That means, of course, that they will gladly follow the next Earl who chooses to revolt against me.

'This is the end of the united Kingdom of the English,' he went on, half to himself, as he settled into bed. 'Never before could an Englishman call in the vikings and expect forgiveness. Anglo-Danes are not Englishmen, and have always been judged by a different standard. Henceforth it will be impossible to control the Earls. A rebuke, and the culprit will turn viking. I don't see how a King can come after me, for all that Bishop Britwold was told that God would choose my successor. I don't understand politics. I shall just carry on from day to day, and do my best for good order in the Church while under Harold the Kingdom falls to pieces.'

Yet even in Church matters, which had for so long been his peculiar province, the King could not always have his own way. In February 1056 died Bishop Athelstan, a sick old man who had never got over the destruction of his minster. For some years he had been so frail that a Welsh Bishop had helped him as coadjutor; but of course a Welshman could not be Bishop of Hereford. The King had promised the next vacant Bishopric to a Lotharingian named Walter who was chaplain to the Lady. Now Harold declared that the Bishop of Hereford must be an Englishman and a warrior; for he might be called on to hold the new defences of the city, recently completed at Harold's orders. There was hot argument at the Lent Council. As cupbearer I heard most of it, for the great men were too angry to be discreet. In the end the King gave way.

He did not give way gracefully. He complained about Harold to everyone he met. When the Lady came into his chamber that evening, to show him a roll of foreign silk, he told her his grievance as though she had been born an enemy to the house of Godwin.

'There's no Bishopric for your Walter. He's the best clerk in the household, and he has taken the trouble to learn English to fit him for a responsible post. But the great Earl of the West Saxons wants Hereford for a toady of his own. That's what it boils down to. Of course Harold began with a lot of nonsense about English Bishoprics for Englishmen, as though he had never supported Stigand the Dane. Tostig was foolish enough to agree with him; and even Odda, who genuinely cares for the welfare of the Church, said he thought Hereford was no place for a Lotharingian. I'm glad to say Alfgar sat quiet. Whenever that city is mentioned he blushes to the roots of his beard. Leofric won't talk about it either, for shame at the treason of his son. But since they did not oppose Harold I suppose they must agree with him. Then it emerged that Harold not only wants the See for an Englishman, he has already picked the Englishman who must have it – Leofgar, his chaplain. What a world we live in!'

'My brother is in general a good judge of men,' said the Lady coolly. 'This Leofgar may perhaps make an excellent Bishop.'

'You don't know him?'

'I can't recall him. But Harold's chaplains are usually respectable men.'

'Not Leofgar. He may once have been a respectable house-carle, but as a clerk he is downright scandalous. Harold pointed him out to me, and one look was enough. The fellow shaves his chin as a clerk should, but on his lip is a whacking great moustache sticking out beyond his ears.'

'Is that very terrible? Now I come to think of it, I have never seen a Bishop wearing a moustache. But there are holy men who dress curiously on purpose, to show their contempt for the ways of the world. Do you remember that Irish pilgrim, with a kilt so short it was positively indecent?'

'There's a canon of the Church forbidding clerks to wear moustaches, or at least I think there is. Anyway, it's the mark of a warrior, won chiefly by swaggering vikings. If Harold needs a warrior to defend his new wall at Hereford let him appoint one, and pay him from the revenues of his Earldom. What he has done is to appoint a commander, and arrange to have him paid from the patrimony of St Ethelbert.'

'An honourable housecarle might make a very good Bishop, if he has good advisers to keep him straight on tricky questions of ritual and theology. Harold may be too interested in the secular business of defence; but you say Tostig didn't object, and he is a sound churchman.'

'Ah, that's it. I understand. Tostig can do no wrong. I should have remembered. It's very hard that the Lady of England should be loyal to her brother, rather than to the King who married her.'

'Are we married? There's a problem that puzzled my father.'

The Lady swept out of the chamber, leaving that unanswerable query hanging in the air.

Thus the promotion of Leofgar was a project on which all the Godwinssons were united, and the King could not resist. By Easter the warrior-Bishop had been enthroned in his half-repaired minster, where he passed his time in training the burgesses in the old English method of fighting, on foot with a great two-handed axe.

Perhaps Bishop Leofgar clung to his moustache to keep himself warlike, not because he was by nature a warrior. In any case he was not so experienced in battle as the famous King Griffith. Within three months of his consecration, in June 1056, the Bishop and the levy of Hereford met the Welsh army at Glasbury-on-Wye, and the Welsh were victorious. The Bishop was slain, axe in hand; and with him many of his clergy, which proves that Leofgar was at least a leader who could make his clerks follow him. For the second year in succession Earl Harold and the whole levy of England must be called out to drive off the plundering Welsh.

It was a most unpleasant campaign, though I am thankful to say I saw nothing of it. The King would never again take the field. The shock of Earl Ralph's misconduct had made him an old man, and in any case he was now in his fifty-fifth year, which is too old to begin learning the military art. The court continued its round of hunting in the forests of Cotswold, and all we heard from the army was the endless plea for more horses to replace those that had died from the cold of the mountains.

136

Earl Harold penetrated the inmost fastnesses of Wales, and of course the Welsh dared not meet such a great army in the open field. By autumn both sides had had enough of the war, and Bishop Aldred, that experienced peacemaker, was able to arrange terms. They were not terms of which the English could be proud; King Griffith was undefeated, and if we wanted peace we must buy it from him. He came to Gloucester, and once more swore to be a faithful servant of King Edward; in return he was recognised as lord of all the lands of Chester beyond the river Dee (which he had conquered years before), and of Archenfield, the district between the Wye and the Monnow, which he had overrun as he marched to the sacking of Hereford. This peace left him with a more powerful Kingdom than any Welshman had ruled since the days of King Arthur.

One other man gained from these negotiations, the accomplished Bishop of Worcester. Once again the See of Hereford was vacant, and once again the Council was divided about the filling of it. To avert another quarrel between Earl Harold and the King it was agreed that Bishop Aldred should hold it in plurality with Worcester. Soon after he received yet a third Bishopric. Hermann of Lotharingia had worried himself sick; he could not make the most simple decision without groans and tears of self-reproaches. He retired of his own accord to a monastery oversea. But he kept the title of his Bishopric, so that Aldred was styled administrator only.

CHAPTER VII

The Rule of Earl Harold

It was becoming more and more difficult to govern England. Everyone knew that the King disliked Earl Harold, but Earl Harold was held responsible for every action of the government. About this time died Earl Odda, the only great man whom the King trusted thoroughly; he had always been devout and he made a most edifying end, actually taking the cowl of a monk as he lay on his deathbed. Earl Ralph was in disgrace, and his health was failing. He died in December 1057, as much from shame and disappointment as from any other cause; his son was a child, and his brother would not leave his County of Mantes in France. Harold Ralphsson now holds a great fief to the west of Hereford, but in those days it was never suggested that he should succeed his father.

Earl Leofric died in the same autumn, and England was the poorer for it. He was the last of the elder statesmen, the magnates who had been trained by King Canute when England was the centre of the northern world. He was a good Christian and a lavish founder of churches, and the influence of the noble Godiva had increased his beneficence. He had been a Councillor when the Council offered the crown to King Edward. A landmark was gone.

Of course Earl Alfgar succeeded his father in Mercia, where the family were almost hereditary rulers. He was not allowed to keep East Anglia as well, though he wanted to. All through the autumn there were long and stormy meetings of the Council; but with Leofric gone Harold could not be withstood. At Christmas the new division of power was made public, and 1058 opened with the house of Godwin supreme over the greater part of England.

Harold himself added Ralph's late Earldom of Hereford to the chief Godwinsson Earldom of Wessex. That could be defended on grounds of public policy, since Harold was the only English commander who could cope with the King of all the Welsh. Tostig remained in Northumbria, which also seemed reasonable; Tostig was a Godwinsson but he was rather Harold's rival than his follower, and he had been first promoted at the instance of the Lady, supported by the King. His personal friendship with the King of the Scots was a valuable asset, and he was beginning to bring order to the lawless north.

But the aggrandisement of the younger, untried Godwinssons was a naked display of Harold's power. Gyrth, a gallant warrior but in other respects quite undistinguished, was granted Alfgar's late Earldom in East Anglia. Leofwin, who had gone on viking cruise with Harold while Gyrth peacefully shared his father's exile in Bruges, was given a new Earldom which did not represent any one of the ancient provinces of England; he ruled over what had long ago been the independent Kingdoms of Sussex and Kent, together with several of the Danish shires north of London. The Londoners maintained that no Earl could rule them, for it was their privilege to serve only the King of all the English; in name their claim was recognised, but Leofwin's novel Earldom surrounded them on every side.

There was yet another Godwinsson, little Wulfnoth, the youngest of the family and still a child. When he was older Harold would find an Earldom for him, and unless he robbed his other brothers he must filch a province from Alfgar. It was natural that the thanes of English Mercia, and their Earl, should be restive under such a government.

I have forgotten to mention an unexpected appearance, and speedy disappearance, of the atheling Edward. That is because it did not affect the court, and we saw it only as a minor setback to the plans of the greedy Earl Harold. It happened in the summer of 1057, before the rearrangement of the Earldoms.

The King was then nearer sixty than fifty, and since the reign of the legendary Cerdic no King of the true English line had hitherto attained old age. The problem of the succession filled every mind except that of King Edward, who never worried over it. His chosen successor was Duke William, and he would further his cause in any way he could; but he trusted far more in the vision of Bishop Britwold, and often reminded his friends that the next King of the English had already been chosen by God.

Harold also had his chosen candidate, this foreign atheling. It was two years since Bishop Aldred had visited the Emperor, and still there was no news of the Hungarian. I wondered whether some friend of King Edward had passed on a hint to the Emperor; but I misjudged my lord, who was too straightforward for such diplomacy. In the summer of 1057 we were told that Edward the atheling, with his Hungarian wife and their two small children, had landed on the south coast.

It seemed odd that an exile should delay for two years before visiting the prosperous Kingdom where he had a very good prospect of the throne; but the excuses forwarded to court sounded reasonable. Armies had been ravaging on the borders of the Empire; then the elder child had fallen sick while the Hungarian princess gave birth to the younger; then Edward himself had been ill. He was still not fully recovered, his messenger informed us; as soon as he was strong enough for the long ride he would come to court.

As it happened, he never got farther than London. There Harold met him, and I suppose they had a lot to say to one another. For the plan, as anyone could see, was that this stranger should be chosen as the next King of the English precisely because he was a stranger, with no following in the country; he would reign as a helpless puppet while Harold ruled. All the same, this delay in London showed a lack of consideration for the King who was his host, and the West Saxons murmured against the foreigner who could not be bothered to look at the province which one day would be the heart of his Kingdom.

Then we heard that the atheling was dead, of the disease he had brought with him from Hungary. He was buried beside King Ethelred, his grandfather, in St Paul's minster, and the King granted an ample revenue for the support of his widow and children. At the time we heard all sorts of rumours about the wicked plots of Earl Harold, who was very much disliked by the West Saxons; of course it was said that Harold had poisoned the atheling, for fear that when he met his uncle the two Cerdingas would combine to overthrow the house of Godwin. But West Saxons will say anything, especially about an unpopular Earl; Harold had arranged to bring in the Hungarian, and his early death was a setback to a careful plan.

140

It did not distress the King, who had never seen his nephew. The court was not even put into mourning, though Requiem Masses were sung. King Edward had quite firmly made up his mind about what would happen to England after he was dead.

'Either I shall be succeeded by my cousin, Duke William, or there will never be another King of all the English,' he said to the Lady one evening, at a time when the death of the atheling was still fresh in our minds. 'Duke William is all that a King should be: strong and just and honest, and earnest to reform the Church. He is chaste also, which is regrettably rare in a great man nowadays, and his mercy is really remarkable. Do you know that in Normandy they have abolished the death-penalty? Rebels and brigands may happen to get killed in battle, but if they are captured their lives are spared. In all his reign the Duke has never hanged a man.'

'What is done to them, then?' asked the Lady, trying to show interest in a subject that did not really appeal to her. 'Does the Duke shaved their heads and put them in a monastery, or does he let them go free?'

'Neither, I am glad to say. Sometimes a wicked man may mend his ways if you put him in a monastery, but more often he corrupts the brethren he finds there. Of course William does not release the criminals he has caught. To do so would be unfair to his honest subjects. No, after a man has been found guilty he is blinded and castrated, and then turned loose to beg, a standing warning to all evildoers.'

'Is that merciful? Many thieves would prefer the rope if you gave them the choice. Anyway, I don't suppose the criminal lives very long after his punishment.'

'That's not the point. He lives long enough to repent of his sins, while in England many thieves go to the gibbet cursing God. Even if he does not repent, he is incapable of further harm. It is a most enlightened reform, and I wish I could introduce it here.'

'Do you mean you want to introduce it, but you can't because Harold opposes it in Council? Shall I persuade Tostig and get him to persuade Alfgar? I doubt whether Tostig would really approve, though he might back you to vex Harold. Tostig is all for justice, and for hanging every evildoer.'

'No, my dear, I shall not try to persuade the Council. It's

141

too much of an effort. If William comes after me he will bring in the custom. If he doesn't, each Earldom will soon be following its own customs.'

'Didn't Bishop Britwold see your successor chosen in Heaven? If that's so the Kingdom is destined to endure.'

'If that is what the Bishop saw there will be a King to succeed me. But we can't be sure it was a vision. He was asleep, and it may have been nothing more than a lying dream.' Animated, the King strode up and down his bedchamber. 'In the ordinary human world, without the intervention of a miracle, I don't see how England can continue as one realm. Never in the past have the Earls been so powerful, or so at enmity with one another. It's even more curious that the wardens of the threatened frontiers are making friends with the aliens over the border. Young Tostig is bloodbrother to Malcolm the Scot; Alfgar is father-in-law to King Griffith. Do you see where that leads? One day Mercia will join Wales, and Northumbria will join Scotland. Then there will hardly be room in Wessex for a King as well as an Earl, and very likely the Kingdom will be abolished.'

'Would that be a disaster?'

'I have no reason to suppose so. There was a time when the Emperor ruled all Christendom, and nowadays no one wants that unity to be restored. If there are to be many Christian rulers, who can say how many is the right number? I should be sorry to see this Kingdom dismembered. But that is a mere sentiment, on a level with my fondness for an old book or an old building. My mind can supply no reason why Winchester and York should obey the same ruler, when we are all agreed that it is right for, say, Wales or Orkney to have rulers of their own.'

'Then you are not really worried about what will happen to the English after you are dead?'

'I would like them to be ruled by Duke William, because that would be good for them. But it is not the guiding passion of my life. I am not a very effective King, and I am not very interested in Kingdoms. What matters most to me, as it matters most to every man and woman, is that I should scrape into Heaven after I am dead. At my coronation I took oath to guard the Church, and I cannot lay down that responsibility. I am also under a vow to found a great community at Westminster. If

142

anyone wants to rule the country, your brother Harold or your brother Tostig or some other, I shall not interfere. The foundation of Westminster, and my obligations as a Christian, will occupy the years I have left.'

The King was as good as his word. Henceforth he played little part in the administration of the country; though he used his great influence to appoint worthy Bishops, and his great wealth to found religious houses. All else was left to Earl Harold.

In the summer of 1058 Earl Harold went to Rome on pilgrimage. He was rich enough to travel in comfort, and he thought he could spare time for the journey; though in this he may have been mistaken. Clever politicians who always search for hidden motives tried hard to find some dubious secondary object for the pilgrimage, but sensible men will see that it needs no explanation. Wouldn't we all visit Rome if we had the time and the money? It was said that Earl Harold wanted to have a look at Duke William, and to stir up other Frenchmen to make trouble for Normandy. Of course he rode to Rome through France; perhaps he tried to conclude a few alliances that did him no good in the end. But he went to Rome because Rome is worth a visit.

He sought also a pallium for Stigand. Archbishop Robert had died in his Norman monastery; and if Stigand was not canonical Archbishop of Canterbury at least the Archbishopric was vacant. At Rome they granted whatever the great Earl asked. But Stigand never enjoyed the luck that such a painstaking intriguer might seem to deserve. Within a year the long-awaited pallium proved worthless, for it had been granted by the wrong Pope. During 1058 Benedict X held the Holy City; but in April of the next year he was overthrown, and Nicholas II reigned in his stead. Everyone now agrees that Benedict was a usurper; though he was not exactly an anti-Pope, for at that time there was no other claimant. Earl Harold, a layman, cannot be blamed for accepting the authority he found ruling in the Lateran; but the position of Stigand was now weaker than before. Hitherto he had been an Archbishop as yet unconfirmed by the Holy See; now he was marked as the adherent of a schismatic, probably himself in schism. Even in his own province no Bishop-elect would seek consecration at his hands.

While Earl Harold was absent on pilgrimage the Kingdom of the English was very nearly overthrown. The danger was soon past, and the fighting did little material damage; so the ordinary thanes of the countryside hardly recognised the peril they had escaped. At court we could appreciate it; we knew we had been saved from disaster only by the interposition of God, or by very good luck – which comes to the same thing.

It all began with a quarrel between the Earls Tostig and Alfgar. I don't know the cause of the quarrel, for it happened in Coventry while we were on Cotswold. Earl Tostig was honest and just and brave, but when he was on the scent of wrong-doing it was impossible to deflect him; the story I heard was that he had hanged some Mercian who was under the protection of Alfgar. When Tostig visited Coventry Alfgar reproached him for this, and Tostig retorted that Alfgar was a viking. Alfgar did not care to be reminded of his part in the sacking of Hereford, and one thing led to another until the Earls parted, vowing open war. Tostig had the greater influence in the Council; Gyrth, Leofwin and Stigand backed a Godwinsson, the King backed a lover of justice. For the second time Alfgar was outlawed, and once again he fled to his son-in-law, King Griffith of the Welsh.

An attack by the combined forces of Mercia and Wales could be very dangerous, as had been shown at the defeat of Earl Ralph. What made it much worse was that Magnus, son of Harold Hardrada King of the Norwegians, happened to be cruising in the Irish Sea with a great fleet of vikings. The rebels got in touch with him – and there was no one to lead the army of England. The King was too old for war, Gyrth and Leofwin too young. Earl Harold was somewhere on the Continent.

Stigand and Bishop Aldred came in panic to warn the King Our housecarles were equally alarmed, and talked of fleeing to the traditional stronghold of Athelney, where long ago King Alfred hid from the Danes. Tostig was mustering the levy of Northumbria, but it was known that the West Saxons would not follow him. In this emergency only the King kept his head. I heard him encourage the Bishops as they sat at the supper table.

'We are faced by three dangerous foes, I grant you,' he said cheerfully. 'But if you will stop and think you will see

144

that these foes cannot long remain allied. Magnus would like to restore the realm of King Canute; Griffith wants land unencumbered with English settlers; Alfgar wishes to expand the bounds of Mercia. Magnus will favour the Anglo-Danes, who are hated by all Mercians and Welshmen. Griffith and Alfgar must quarrel over the boundary of Mercia. After they have won a battle they will at once fight among themselves. But they may be unable to win the first battle. Combined, their armies would be formidable, but they are unlikely to march in company. Magnus will strike for Chester and the Anglo-Danes of Westmorland. Alfgar will march on York, to cut off the head of Earl Tostig. Griffith still hankers after Hereford. If Tostig can defend himself during the summer we shall spin out the campaign until Harold returns.'

As a matter of fact there was hardly any fighting. Tostig gathered a strong force in York, for his friendship with the King of the Scots made it safe to reduce his northern garrisons; Alfgar dared not march against him. King Griffith yet again wasted the countryside round Hereford; but the new walls of the city, and the neighbouring castles built by Earl Ralph, kept him west of the Severn. The incursion of the dreaded vikings was an utter failure. Magnus, hoping to gather recruits from among the Anglo-Danes, commanded his pirates not to plunder; of course they did not obey him, and their ravages set the men of Westmorland against him. But the mere issuing of the order displeased the vikings, who complained that they did not voyage overseas to conquer thrones for princes, but to win booty. Threatened by mutiny if he continued to march inland, Magnus returned to his ship and presently sailed off to plunder in Orkney. By the time Earl Harold landed at Bosham all the foreigners had gone, and the native rebels were eager for peace if it could be had without loss of dignity.

Bishop Aldred could always arrange that kind of peace. Soon Alfgar had been restored as Earl of the Mercians, and Griffith, King of all the Welsh, had once more promised obedience to the King of all the English. In the south it was not generally known that the vikings who had plundered Westmorland came from a great fleet commanded by a son of the King of the Norwegians. That was as well, for in those days an invasion of vikings was greatly dreaded by all Englishmen.

10

145

Earl Harold was a very competent ruler, chiefly because he had no other interests and dealt with any pressing matter as soon as it came to his attention. Even if King Edward had been supreme he would have needed someone to do his work for him; a man who prayed all the morning and hunted all the afternoon had no time for petty details of administration.

Earl Harold was temperate in eating and drinking; whenever he rode on a journey he carried a hawk, but he did not often ride out solely for sport; since his great private wealth supplied his needs he never robbed the treasury. If there had to be a minister no better minister could be found. But the King had not chosen him, and he never liked him.

Harold's gravest fault, as a nobleman and a Christian, was his custom of living openly and scandalously with concubines. Even in this he was no worse than many great men. He was reasonably faithful to Edith Swan-neck, who had a comfortable establishment in Canterbury; there were other girls dotted about in his provinces, but he did not give great estates to their kin. As I say, many great men live after this fashion, and no one takes it very tragically. But Harold was unlucky in that most of his eminent rivals lived much better. The King was a virgin; Tostig was completely faithful to Judith, whom he loved; the Norman clerks at court constantly reminded us that Duke William kept his marriage vows.

Sometimes the King would suggest to Earl Harold that it was time he married and settled down. But there was no house in England grand enough to furnish a bride for the great Earl, now that Alfgar and his kin were his implacable enemies; and if Harold should marry and still keep on Edith Swan-neck things would be worse than before.

For two years England was so peaceful that in truth the land had no history. For the Christmas crownwearing of 1059 the King of the Scots came to Gloucester and swore loyalty and friendship. It was a very magnificent embassy; with Malcolm came all the great men of the north: the Archbishop of York, the Bishop of Durham, and the Earl of Northumbrians. King Malcolm owed his throne to an English army. All the same, gratitude is a rare virtue in foreign policy, and I think his peaceful conduct was due rather to his friendship with Earl Tostig than to the memory of the gallant deeds of old Siward.

Earl Tostig was frequently at court. He was the Lady's closest friend, and even the King sometimes seemed to forget that he was a Godwinsson. In Northumbria he was doing very good work; he enforced such stern peace that travellers could journey singly, whereas in Siward's day men had not ventured on the open moors save in companies of at least thirty. Because of his love of order he cut off a great many heads, and his subjects murmured. He himself disliked living in the cold, unfriendly, crowded city of York. To keep order in the north would take all the time of an ordinary governor; but Earl Tostig was exceptionally efficient, and if he thought he could safely pay long visits to Wessex we took it for granted that he had judged the situation correctly.

The Archbishop of York was another frequent visitor to the southern province, a thing that I believe had never happened before. But then never before had southern England been stuck with an uncanonical Archbishop of Canterbury. Stigand would not resign peacefully, and Harold would not permit the Council to declare him outlaw. Stigand the Anglo-Dane had stood by Earl Godwin in the old days, and Harold would not desert any veteran adherent of his father. But even Harold had to admit that Stigand was no true Archbishop; when his new-built minster at Waltham was finished he brought Cynesige down from York to consecrate it. Cynesige was always being asked to come south to consecrate a Bishop or a church, or perform any of the other functions that must normally be done by a Metropolitan. It seems odd that Stigand should have swallowed these insults, especially as they came from an Anglo-Dane of his own faction; but he was a politician before he was anything else, and he valued the precedence in Council which he derived from Canterbury. Ill-wishers added that he valued Canterbury's own endowments, but I do not believe that weighed with him so much as the vulgar supposed. Even if he should resign Canterbury he would still be the undoubted and canonical Bishop of Winchester, which gave him an ample revenue. He did not need money, since his private life was chaste and he gave no scandal. If only he had submitted to the rightful Pope he would have passed anywhere as a good Bishop.

The court lived quietly; as he grew older the King hunted less and prayed more. But we remained in touch with the great events we could no longer control. Of course we saw

Stigand and the Godwinsson Earls at every Council; in addition Tostig, Alfgar, and the Archbishop of York came to us frequently on private visits.

Then, in December 1060, while the great men were assembling in Gloucester for the Christmas crownwearing, came news that Archbishop Cynesige was dead.

'Very distressing, but this is no time to discuss the virtues of the late Archbishop,' said Harold, after Stigand, a fine preacher, had held the whole supper table for five minutes with an extempore panegyric 'Before this Council ends we must choose a successor. I hope, lord King, that we can fix on an English clerk who is worthy to fill the great position.'

'Yes, there's no time to be lost. At Easter the holy oils must be blessed, and for that we must have another Archbishop with a genuine pallium from Rome,' said the King. Stigand blushed.

'An English Archbishop, a competent man of business familiar with episcopal ritual. He will have to be young enough to travel fast, if he is to be back from Rome by Easter,' Tostig put in. 'In a sense he will be specially the Archbishop of the Northumbrians, so perhaps I may suggest a name. Would Bishop Aldred accept promotion? I am sure there is no English clerk more worthy.'

The Bishop of Worcester gave a little start of pleasure; then pulled himself together to sit looking woodenly down his nose. He would be shamed if he accepted Tostig's offer, and then found it forbidden by the King.

'I won't propose a Norman, because popular feeling is against them,' said King Edward, 'but couldn't we find some energetic reforming Lotharingian? The north is so riven by bloodfeud that a stranger will suit it better than an Englishman. At present Bishop Aldred bears heavy responsibilities. It will be hard to replace him in Worcester, Hereford and Wiltshire. Do you insist on an Englishman, Earl Harold? Well, in that case I agree that there is no one more worthy than Aldred.'

King Edward could never manage men. In the same speech he reaffirmed his unpopular preference for foreigners, allowed himself to be overruled by Earl Harold, and paid Bishop Aldred a very left-handed compliment.

'There's no need to replace Aldred in any of his dioceses,' said Harold, as though his decision must be final. 'The Dane smashed up most of the churches in the north, and no one has rebuilt them. The Archbishop of York has a very small flock and a very small revenue. Aldred can govern York in his spare time, and the combined incomes of all his dioceses will enable him to live in the state proper to an Archbishop.'

'You are too gracious, my lord. But I think I could do all the work you propose,' said Bishop Aldred.

The King sighed. Even in religious questions, which interested him more than military or financial affairs, Harold had the last word.

'Then that's settled,' said Tostig cheerfully. 'How soon can you be ready to start, Aldred? I shall come with you. I've never made the pilgrimage to Rome, and Judith likes travel.'

'Can you leave the Northumbrians? Remember the mess I found when I got back from my pilgrimage,' said Harold with a frown. That made Earl Alfgar look uncomfortable; but then these meetings of the Council were never very friendly gatherings, and there were frequent sly reminders of past wars.

'The Northumbrians will have to manage without me. What's the use of being an Earl if you can't sometimes enjoy yourself? Of all the wonderful world oversea I have seen only Flanders.'

'You will find Rome very different from the viking camps of Bruges,' said the King sarcastically. 'I wish I could come with you. The English can spare me, now that Earl Harold takes so much work off my hands. But I fear I am too old to undertake the journey.'

By April 1061 Tostig and Bishop Aldred were in Rome; but it was proved that the Northumbrians could not manage without the protection of their Earl. The Scots poured over the border, ravaging far and wide. I heard afterwards that King Malcolm justified his attack by explaining that he was the sworn brother and friend of Earl Tostig, but not of his subjects. I am the unwarlike son of a burgess, and I shall never understand the code of honour that binds warrior Kings.

In Rome the pilgrims met with some curious adventures. Pope Nicholas II, who had recently replaced the usurper, was still busy reforming the abuses which creep back into the Church whenever the Keys of St Peter have fallen into unworthy hands. In particular the new Pope was hot against pluralism. When he learned that the Archbishop-elect of York,

149

come humbly to seek his pallium, intended to hold at the same time the Sees of Worcester, Hereford and Wiltshire, there was a frightful scene. At court we heard the whole story from a follower of Earl Tostig who had been present.

Poor Aldred had accumulated these preferments not because he was avaricious, but because he was a better man of business than any other English clerk. But the Pope gave him no opportunity to defend himself, and in the middle of the papal tirade some busybody voiced a doubt about the regularity of Aldred's consecration. The Pope seized the opportunity for a severe rebuke. Aldred was commanded to return to England a simple priest, not even Bishop of Worcester.

An accident afforded the Holy Father an opportunity for second thoughts. Outside Rome the returning pilgrims were attacked by the men of a local Count and robbed of all they carried. They went back to the Curia to borrow money for their travelling expenses. Then Pope Nicholas realised that Aldred had obeyed him without demur; if he was at fault he was willing to begin life anew as a simple parish priest. Such loyalty atoned for any irregularities in the past. The Pope still maintained that three Dioceses and a Metropolitan See were too much for any one clerk; but he himself repeated Aldred's consecration, to set all doubts at rest, and sent him back to England with the pallium of York. For the time being he was permitted to keep Worcester in plurality, until the revenues of York had recovered from the ravaging of the Danes. But Hermann was commanded to leave his monastery and take up his duties in Wiltshire; and for Hereford the Pope appointed without the formality of election, Walter of Lotharingia, the court chaplain whom the King had chosen when Athelstan died.

This last appointment was a splendid vindication of the judgement of King Edward. If the Pope, to whom Englishmen and Lotharingians are equally foreign, chose a Lotharingian for an English Bishopric it proved that the Lotharingian was the best man for the post. The Roman Curia avoids arousing opposition if it can; since Walter was the friend and chaplain of the Lady the Godwinsson faction did not object.

Thus in England we had once more a properly consecrated Archbishop, his obedience to Rome symbolised by his pallium

Without one we would have been in an awkward position. Even with Aldred to perform the functions of which Stigand was incapable the work of the Church was in many ways impeded. Stigand enjoyed the revenues of Canterbury, and in secular affairs took precedence as the first subject in the Kingdom. But no one accepted his authority as Metropolitan, though he was undoubtedly a priest and a Bishop.

In 1062 two legates arrived from Rome to clear up the tangle. This was a novelty. No papal legates had visited England since St Augustine was sent from Rome to convert our ancestors. The King approved the innovation, and Earl Harold did not openly object. It is significant that the legates did not attempt to remove Stigand; so long as the great Earl upheld him even Rome was powerless. Their most important task was to make sure that Aldred resigned from Worcester, and to choose his successor. The Bishop they chose was the holy Wulfstan, and his actions after he had been enthroned show how difficult it was for a clerk to steer his way through the tangle; for he must have consulted the legates before he behaved as he did.

Worcester lies within the province of Canterbury, but Wulfstan sought consecration from Aldred of York. He then went to Canterbury and professed canonical obedience to Stigand. If such a devout and fearless prelate, with legates to advise him, could not find a more tidy solution there was no easy way out.

At court we were not concerned. King Edward no longer ruled England; he had resigned the management of affairs to Earl Harold. We heard all the news, but we did not make it.

That was a kind of life which suited me very well. I like to know what is happening, but I also like to sleep safe. Our routine was as regular as if the court had been a monastery, except that every ten days we moved to another hunting forest. On our travels I rode a quiet horse, beside the carts which carried the King's robes of state. That gave me enough fresh air and exercise to keep me in health; except when we travelled I seldom went out of doors. In the morning I accompanied the King to Mass, and while he hunted in the afternoon I supervised the lesser chamberlains who cleaned and mended his robes and jewels. At dinner and supper I stood behind his chair. At night I prepared him for bed and then slept in a corner of his chamber. I was as close to him as a nurse to the infant in her charge, and almost as much in his confidence as if he had been my fosterling. I was on duty seven days a week and never had a holiday. But the court was my home and the wellbeing of the King my chief interest. If he had commanded me to go off and enjoy myself I would have pleaded to remain in his company.

The King's interests were narrowing. Since the visit of the legates he had abandoned his efforts to oversee the Church; by recognising the merits of Abbot Wulfstan, who was personally unknown to the King, the legates had chosen a better Bishop than he would have found by himself. Now that Rome took an interest there was no need for King Edward to intervene in what theologians are agreed is not the province of the laity. Though Stigand still kept his scandalous and equivocal position at Canterbury the Bishops and clergy of England were not obviously worse than those of other countries, and it was not for the King to make them better. His chaplains he chose with care, and he spent more and more time talking with them in private or praying under their direction; he was training the soul of Edward Cerdinga, instead of elevating the standard of religious life in his Kingdom.

In temporal affairs he hardly bothered to keep himself abreast of the news. Anything important was decided by Earl Harold, though in small matters of promotions and salaries and grants of land the King would sometimes exert himself to please the Lady or Earl Tostig. Alone among the magnates, Earl Tostig was personally a welcome visitor at court. I think he enjoyed these visits, but there was little the King could do for the great Earl of the Northumbrians. The Lady asked for a stream of little favours, and received them; she was too tactful to seek anything important, lest the King be driven to admit that it was no longer within his power to grant it. Perhaps if Tostig and the Lady had combined to work against Harold they might have weakened his position. But though they disliked him as a man (as did King Edward) they could not quarrel with his policy. Under his guidance the English lived prosperous and peaceful.

CHAPTER VIII

The Wars of Earl Harold

In the summer of 1062 there died Earl Alfgar of the Mercians, the only magnate of the first rank who owed nothing to Harold or to any other of the Godwinssons. His death was unexpected, for he was not yet old. Now Harold was without a rival, towering high above any other Englishman. There was no difficulty about the succession to Mercia; Alfgar had been the son and grandson of Mercian Earls, and of course the great province went to his son. But this Edwin was only just of an age to bear arms, and in Council no one heeded him. He was not on good terms with Tostig, the only other Earl who was independent of Harold.

In England the death of Earl Alfgar caused little stir; it was otherwise in Wales. King Griffith had never trusted in the friendship of the English, and of course he was quite right. Wales ought to be ruled by the King of the English, and the mountains that we cannot subdue ought to be divided among many petty chieftains; a King of all the Welsh was an anomaly and a perpetual threat to Wessex. For the last year or two King Griffith had kept the peace because he could rely on the friendship and protection of his father-in-law, the great Earl of the Mercians. Now he decided to attack before the English attacked him. In the depth of winter, just before Christmas, his men raided right up to the Severn and beyond.

We were in Gloucester for the Christmas crownwearing when we heard of this Welsh raid. All the Earls had come to court for the meeting of the Council; but naturally they had with them only the few housecarles of their bodyguards. At first we feared that the faithless Griffith might swoop on Gloucester and capture the King; then our scouts reported that the Welsh had turned for home, driving a great booty before them. The irruption had been a raid, not an attempt to drive back the frontier of England. Snow and mud would soon close the passes, and there would be no more danger until next spring.

The whole Council was furious with King Griffith, but young Earl Edwin was especially outraged. Alfgar his father had been Griffith's ally and protector, and for that very reason he had neglected the defences of Mercia. Griffith had no grievance against the Mercians, except the standing grievance of all Welshmen, that in times past the English drove them westward into the barren hills. It was decided that when spring came the whole levy of England should march into Wales, and remain there for as long as King Griffith lived.

'But I can't sit here, drinking the Christmas wine, while those plundering Welsh roast our stolen cattle,' said Earl Harold, looking round the Councillors as they sat at supper. 'Why should we leave them in peace for the winter? By spring our cattle will be slaughtered, and our fellow-countrymen sold as slaves to the vikings. To get back that booty we must strike at once.'

'This is Christmas,' objected young Edwin. 'The thanes are drinking, like everyone else. If you call them out in the middle of the holiday half of them won't come to the muster.'

'Exactly, it's Christmas,' Harold replied. 'The Welsh will have scattered to feast in their separate valleys. King Griffith will be drinking in his hall, with only his household to defend him. The housecarles I have brought with me will be more than a match for them. All my men are mounted, and on good horses. If the Council agrees I shall ride into Wales tomorrow, and come back with the head of King Griffith.'

'Can you make your men charge mounted? That would shake the Welsh more than anything else you could do,' asked the King wistfully.

'It would shake my housecarles also. I'm sorry, my lord. I know that's the way they fight in France, and there it's effective. But the French practise at it from the moment they are old enough to ride. One day, when I have time, I shall train my men in the art. For the present they had better make war after the fashion of their ancestors.'

'I wish you would listen to me. I'm sure it's the best way of fighting. But you are the commander of my levies, and you must do as you think best. Don't get caught in those Welsh valleys. Griffith can't kill you, but the snow can.'

My lord did not like Earl Harold as a man; but like everyone else in Gloucester he knew him to be the best warleader in the realm.

'Are you really going to ride from end to end of Wales in the worst of winter, with no following but the bodyguard you bring to a Council?' asked Tostig in admiration. 'That will be a famous deed, whether you come back triumphant or leave your head in the mountains. Shall I come with you?'

'Better not, brother. They need you in Northumbria, and if anything goes wrong we don't want all the warleaders of the English to perish together. Besides, if we can catch King Griffith in his hall my housecarles will be enough. But in the summer I shall be glad of your help, if the war isn't finished by then.'

'You shall have it, the pick of the Northumbrians. We shall ride on our best horses. Who knows, we might manage a mounted charge.'

I could see a wave of sympathy for Harold travelling through the hall. He was ambitious and unscrupulous and greedy for power; but he was also a hero.

Earl Harold was back in Gloucester soon after Epiphany. He had ridden through all Wales, from south to north, and by the speed of his advance escaped ambush in the passes. Spies told him that King Griffith was keeping Christmas at Rhuddlan, on the north coast; it was the ancestral seat of his family, from which he had conquered all Wales. The English housecarles swept down the valley, riding out from the mountains which have always been a protection to the Welsh; it was a direction from which attack was never expected. They very nearly caught King Griffith sitting over his wine; he had barely time to flee to the river-mouth and jump on the nearest ship. While he coasted west with a handful of followers Harold's men killed as many of his household as they could catch, sacked and burned his hall, and at leisure destroyed most of his ships, laid up in the river for the winter. Then they rode swiftly back to England; they were out of Wales before an avenging army could be gathered.

It was a mighty deed, and of course a deadly insult to King Griffith. War must follow. It proved to be a war without quarter, which the King thought unchristian and unnecessary. I heard Harold justify his policy at the Lent Council, while his men were gathering to march.

'The Welsh have been with us always,' he said heavily; he was then about forty years old, and beginning to affect the manner of a veteran. 'We shall have them with us always. They are a nuisance, but not dangerous. King Griffith is the exceptional danger, because he has united all his countrymen. But that unity will not survive him. Therefore, during this coming summer, we must abolish King Griffith. I shall proclaim to all the Welsh that my arm will remain in their land, ravaging and slaying, for as long as King Griffith lives. Then, if he won't face us in battle, and we can't catch him, some Welshman will kill him for us. We must finish this war as quickly as we can. The Danes and the Scots will invade us in the autumn if they learn that the whole levy of England is tied up in Wales.'

'You will be driving subjects to murder their lord, and that can never be right,' answered the King. 'In addition, you propose to ravage like a viking, killing helpless unarmed peasants. That sort of warfare may seem prudent and far-sighted, but it carries a curse with it. Unless God sends a miracle your housecarles must conquer the Welsh. But I feel it in my bones that, before their beards are grey, they will lie dead and defeated on some other field.'

There was a stir in the hall, for the King spoke as though he could foresee the future. Harold answered stoutly: 'My housecarles are warriors. Every warrior should be prepared for death in battle, on one day or another. Anyway, whatever the future holds for us, that is how we shall conquer Wales.'

'I don't like it. But you command my army. You must fight this war as you think best.' The King said no more.

Everyone else thought highly of Harold's plans, which were indeed well considered. He brought his own ships right round England from Bosham to Bristol. He filled them with picked men, housecarles and rich thanes, well armoured and well equipped. Such a small force could be fed even in the barren valleys, but it was stronger than any army the Welsh could bring against it; the men were his own commended vassals, and would obey him faithfully.

With this little squadron he sailed over to south Wales, the land which not long ago had been conquered by King Griffith and where many still disliked him. At the mouth of every valley the English landed, burned the houses and the crops, and killed every grown man; though King Edward had forbidden them to kill the women and children. In this crisis the conquered southern Welsh refused to fight for King Griffith; most of them fled starving to the mountain tops. Meanwhile Earl Tostig and a picked body of Northumbrians rode westward along the north coast from Chester. King Griffith lay with his army in the north, but he was not strong enough to challenge a pitched battle. He blocked the passes, hoping to delay Tostig; but the Northumbrians on their fine horses always found a way round the ambush, until presently the brothers joined forces in central Wales.

Then began such a devastation as the country had never seen. If the Welsh tried to hold a hill-fort Harold stormed it, and killed the defenders to the last man; if they fled they saw their crops destroyed, so that next winter they must starve. Embassies begged for peace, but Harold answered that while King Griffith lived the war must continue.

On Cotswold we heard nothing but admiring reports of the discipline and fortitude of the English; on scanty rations, in the appalling mountain weather, they marched for many miles and did all their leader commanded. But the messenger who told us this admitted in answer to the King's questions that the campaign had its compensations. Some old-fashioned housecarles liked to keep a tally of heads taken; now there was no more room for notches on the hafts of their axes. For others there was the amusement of rape, and the killing of prisoners by novel and striking methods. Wales is a poor land, but a lucky man might stumble on a hoard of plunder, stolen long ago from the English. Our warriors knew that they were enduring hardship like heroes; but the war was not dangerous, and it had its enjoyable moments.

'They are wrong. This is a very dangerous war,' the King said to me that evening. 'Cruelty and pride bring a punishment, even in this life. One day Harold and his followers will be ground down, even as now they grind down the Welsh.'

'They have beaten the Welsh until they cannot rise again,' I answered. I don't like Welshmen.

157

'There may come other foes, foes the English have never yet faced,' said the King bodingly. He was aware of coming evil; and long ago he had seen the death of King Magnus even while it happened hundreds of miles away. I shivered.

All the same, Earl Harold was a cunning warleader, and his ruthless plan succeeded. All summer the army ravaged Wales, until early in August a shamed and frightened Welshman brought Harold the head of King Griffith.

The court came to Gloucester to welcome the victorious army. Soon after we arrived a ship was rowed up the river from Bristol, bearing Harold's gift to his lord. It was the head of King Griffith, tastefully mounted on the beak of a war-galley which had been the flagship of the Welsh fleet. Before the ship was burned they had sawed off the carved beak, and a sharp spike at the end of it fitted neatly into the neck of its late owner. The whole made an elegant trophy.

The King was horrified when he saw it, and at once gave orders that the head be buried properly in consecrated ground. 'I am not a viking, to drink from the skull of my dead enemy,' he said savagely. 'If Harold is the kind of barbarian who likes to carve dead bodies into keepsakes he may eat dead Welsh-men as well, for all I care. That is the head of a Christian ruler who once feasted with me in this very hall. His only crime was that he made war on the English, and that may be the duty of every good Welshman. If Earl Godwin may lie under a splendid tomb in the Old Minster the head of this patriot deserves at least a Requiem Mass, with the whole chapter of Gloucester singing in choir.'

I was not the only courtier to think that the King was unjust to Earl Harold, who had crushed the Welsh and took a natural pride in his grim trophy of victory. But Harold's next exploit shocked even the ignorant commons.

During that autumn all Wales was in a terrible mess, so Harold returned to set the devastated country to rights. He gave the valleys of the south to the heirs of the chieftains overthrown by King Griffith. The land had been so depopu-lated that he encouraged Welsh widows to marry his followers, since otherwise there would have been no husbands for them. The ancestral lands of King Griffith in the north were divided between his kinsmen, who each swore loyalty to the King of the English. Of course the plain west of Chester, and the land of Archenfield between Wye and Monnow, were returned to their rightful owners. In the middle of this reorganisation the widow of King Griffith wandered, penniless and starving, into Harold's camp among the mountains.

Edith was daughter to Earl Alfgar and sister to Earl Edwin. She was young, and luckily childless. She expected to be treated with deference and sent back to her brother's hall in Mercia.

Instead Harold married her on the spot, against her will. There have been countless rumours about this dreadful affair. The story goes that Harold procured her assent to the marriage by leaving her tied up in the open until she gave it; another version says that she had to be tied to the bed on her wedding night. I hope this last is only an exaggeration of the first story, and indeed that seems probable; but in either case the widow of a King, the daughter and sister of English Earls, was tied up until she yielded to the wicked Harold.

It is hard to see what he hoped to gain from this brutal deed. Perhaps Earl Alfgar's daughter was especially pretty and desirable, a point on which I am not competent to pronounce. But if his motive was lust, why *marry* her? He could not expect that such a match would bring him the friendship of the Earls of Mercia; of course Edwin hated him fiercely for the rest of his life. My own belief is that Harold acted as he did to feed his abounding pride. The Godwinssons are descended from an ancient family of the South Saxons, but the South Saxons are not a very famous folk; Harold's mother was the daughter of a mere heathen viking. In the estimation of any Englishman the house of Mercia was second only to the house of Cerdic, while Godwin had been a new man. Harold would show the world that he was powerful enough to marry with the highest; his sons, when they came, would be very nobly born.

At this time Harold was so great that nothing could weaken him. But his marriage did not augment his strength, and it shocked the King as it shocked all honest men.

The Lady summed up the feeling of the court, discussing Harold's conduct one day with her lord as they walked back together from early Mass. I was walking behind the King with his kneeling-cushion, and I think they both forgot that I could overhear.

'Sweyn seemed bad all through; until at the end of his life he showed more than a spark of goodness. Tostig has as much

159

virtue as can be expected from any sinful mortal, especially in his dealings with women. He loves Judith, and lives faithfully with her. Harold, born between those two brothers, has in him a bit of both of them. He is ruthless, like Sweyn, and fair-dealing, like Tostig. Like Tostig he is loyal. But I fear he grows more like Sweyn every day. This poor Edith might be another Abbess of Leominster; except that Harold has married her for life, instead of sending her home after taking his pleasure. But that other Edith, the Swan-neck, still lives in great comfort by Canterbury minster.'

'It's a very bad example to lesser folk,' said the King with a sigh. 'Just when we are trying to explain to the Anglo-Danes what marriage means among Christians. I'm glad you consider Harold loyal. I sometimes wonder about that. I don't mean that he is plotting to displace me. After all, a man of his ancestry cannot himself be King, and he would gain nothing by setting up a Dane in my place. But if he is truly loyal he ought to pay more attention to my wishes, instead of running the country as he thinks fit.'

'He is obstinate. But he's a good minister. England prospers,' said the Lady. Then we reached the hall, which was crowded with courtiers; and before such an audience they talked nothing but trivialities.

In 1063 the King lingered in London after the Pentecost crown-wearing. At Westminster his new buildings were taking shape, and he liked to spend long days watching the workmen and chatting with any monks who had the leisure to talk to him. He was now sixty years old, a very great age for a Cerdinga; in appearance and movements he was so ancient and venerable that a stranger might suppose him to be a survivor from the court of Charlemagne. He was as interested as ever in the technicalities of hunting and falconry (both highly technical pastimes which I do not profess to understand); but long hours in the saddle now tired him, and he was not always hankering after the forests of Cotswold.

Since he spent most of his waking hours at Westminster he might have become a distraction to the monks, who have very little time to spare for conversation; but he had chosen a worthy community, who would not neglect their spiritual office even to talk with Kings. When all the monks were busy he would stand or kneel for hours before the High Altar, sometimes reciting prayers, sometimes rapt in a meditation which shaded off into the reverie of an old man. The Londoners thought it very remarkable that a mighty King should pass so many hours alone with God when he might have been enjoying himself, and my lord began to be regarded as a saint. The Londoners happened to be right.

Late in October we were still in London, although that is the best part of the hunting season. The Lady had left us to go down to Wessex for a round of visits, a holiday at Wilton convent and an inspection of the hall at Winchester which would be her dower-house when she became a widow; but at the end of the month she came back to join us. Soon we must get ready for the long journey to Gloucester, where at Christmas the King would wear his crown. Since I came to court we had never stayed so long in one place, and I was already preparing for the awful business of the move. A great household collects useless rubbish every day, and the longer you have had it by you the harder it is to decide to throw it away.

One afternoon, as I was sorting out a pile of old mantles, the Lady came in. I was used to receiving suitors, for it was known that I spoke with the King when he was relaxed and in a good temper and likely to agree to any request; but never before had the Lady sought my meditation.

'Ah, there you are, Edgar,' she began with a charming smile. 'Can you spare me a moment? There's something I want from the King, something very absurd, I'm afraid. If I ask him at the wrong time he may tell me not to be silly. Yet I really want it, to please a great friend of mine. Do you know Godiva, the wife of Wulf?'

The Lady put her head on one side and looked appealing. She was in her middle thirties and her figure had lost its girlish slightness. But her face still showed an unflawed perfection of contour and texture, womanly enough but motherly and not at all sexually enticing; you see the same charm in many middle-aged nuns. I was anxious to please her, but I could not resist a pert answer. It was impossible to be afraid of the Lady unless you were planning something wicked.

'Godiva, the wife of Wulf? Madam, I know hundreds of them. Every Englishwoman who is not named Edith is named Godiva, and more than half the thanes of Wessex are called

Wulfstan or Wulfgar or Ethelwulf, Wulf for short. Which of this throng is the one who seeks a favour?'

'The one who was married not long ago, who lives in London and came to court yesterday. Her elder sister and I were schoolgirls together at Wilton.'

'Oh yes, madam, I know her – poor thing.'

'Poor thing indeed. That's what everyone says. It's horrid for a young bride to be so disfigured. That's what I want to see you about. She has tried everything for those nasty eruptions on her neck, and now a wise woman has told her that the King can cure them. But if we ask him clumsily he will say it's presumption and vainglory for him to try, and silly superstition for Godiva to expect a cure. You must ask him, Edgar, when you think he will consent.'

'Then we had better not mention the wise woman. Oh, I'm sure she hears Mass every day, and makes her confession once a month; they all do, or say they do, especially when they are suspected of uncanny traffic. But the King will say at once that he's not going to obey the instructions of a witch. By the way, what do the doctors call Godiva's affliction?'

'Some Latin word. What is it? Scrofula?'

'Ah, that makes it much easier. You may not know it, madam, but in Wessex we have an old tradition that scrofula can be cured by the touch of a King, even a King who is not himself holy. I can explain to my lord that in attempting this cure he does nothing more than his royal duty. He hates to be reminded that his subjects believe him to be more holy than the general run of his ancestors. I shall explain that the power derives from his kingly unction, not from his personal virtue. If I choose a good moment I am sure he will consent.'

But that evening, when I had explained the whole thing most tactfully to my lord, I ran into an unexpected difficulty. The King answered that he would gladly do all in his power to cure any of his male subjects.

' . . . but I won't caress the neck of a pretty young girl. Anyone who sees me doing it will misinterpret my motives; and in addition, Edgar, it's not so easy as some people suppose to keep a vow of complete continence. At the best I should be disturbed for hours afterwards. Perhaps this is a temptation sent by the Devil, a more subtle one than he usually employs. Godiva must endure her affliction. For all I know it may be a punishment sent down specially from Heaven.'

'If Heaven has decreed the punishment then the royal touch won't remove it,' I answered. 'But it seems to me lacking in charity to return a blank refusal. How would this do, my lord? Since the virtue resides in the kingly unction, not in yourself as a man, it must be something attached to your exterior. You need not lay hands on this young woman. Let me give her a bowl of the water in which the royal hands have been washed, and we can see if that will help her.'

'That's a little bit as though she regards me as a walking relic. I don't like it. It reeks of Pride.'

'Not personal pride, my lord. At your coronation you received this unction, which sets you apart from ordinary men. But you received it as the heir of the Cerdingas, not as the reward of your own merit.'

At length I was able to persuade the King by emphasising that the request was a tribute to his office, not to his personality. He washed his hands in scented water, which I presented to him in a fine silver bowl. The bowl had a cover. This I fastened with a silk cord, sealed with the private signet of the chamberlains. Even then I did not trust the bowl to a common servant, who would certainly have sold the royal water and replaced it from the nearest pump. I carried it myself to Godiva's lodging.

She offered me a purse of money, which I refused; I wished to avoid even the appearance of selling divine healing. But I accepted a silver arm-ring which the Lady afterwards pressed on me, for my tact in persuading the King deserved a reward.

Godiva washed her tettered neck in the King's water, and next day her skin showed unblemished. She was more beautiful than ever, and later became the mother of many fine sons.

When this was known there was no holding the Londoners. The whole city acclaimed King Edward as a saint, which greatly annoyed him. The road from the King's hall to Westminster, which he traversed every day, was thronged with cripples and beggars beseeching his aid. He got Bishop William to preach in St Paul's, explaining that Godiva's cure was due to the virtue of the kingly office, not to the merit of the King now reigning; but since Bishop William delivered his long sermon in Latin, with explanatory glosses in French, few of his congregation understood him. In the end we chamberlains arranged a lavish

163

distribution of alms at the eastern gate of the city whenever the King was due to ride west, the housecarles were a little more vigorous in clearing the way, and the beggars forsook the road to Westminster.

One man still persevered, a well-to-do burgess who did not seek alms but hoped that the holy King might restore his sight. Most of the blind men who beg outside churches have lost their eyes, put out forcibly by enemies or by pirates disappointed of a ransom. This man had eyes in his head, and they showed no sign of injury; but he could see nothing with them. He was devout, and had always lived uprightly, even when he could see; so the monks of Westminster were his friends. He had money, and could tip doorkeepers and housecarles. No one tried very hard to drive him away.

Eventually, because he would not take 'No' for an answer, he was admitted to the King's presence. For once my lord insisted on talking to him privately; even I, his cupbearer, could not hear what was said. But that evening, as usual, I heard all about it.

'This Wulf urges me to try to heal him. He says, quite truly, that if I fail he will be no worse than he is now. He won't understand that _I_ may be worse off, after I have yielded to a temptation inspired by Pride; or if he understands it he puts it aside as no concern of his. But Bishop William has told me that I will be lacking in charity if I continue to refuse. So tomorrow I shall do what I can.'

He stood in thought, staring at the lamp by his bedside. 'It must be terrible to be blind. If I were blind I would be ever more importunate in seeking a cure than this Wulf. All the same, it will be a very tricky business. At present his eyes are not utterly useless; he can distinguish day from night. So that whatever happens tomorrow he will go away saying that his sight has improved; he would be more than human if he admitted that bathing his eyes with water in which I have washed makes absolutely no difference. By tomorrow night half England will believe that with a touch of my finger I can raise the dead. So I have devised a most impressive religious ceremony, to be performed before a crowd of trustworthy witnesses.'

He paused to draw a deep breath and arrange in his mind what he wanted to say. King Edward was never very com

164

petent at marshalling a complicated succession of events, and this programme had cost him much thought.

'First of all we attend the conventual High Mass at Westminster. I shall sit in the throne they always give me, within the chancel, with the monks standing in their stalls all round me. When Mass is finished nobody leaves. Wulf is led up to my throne, and you present me with a basin of water. It will have to be a silver basin, since you set that unfortunate precedent with young Godiva. If I keep on doing these cures the silversmiths will ruin me. In the sight of the whole congregation I wash my face and hands. Then Wulf bathes his eyes in the water, and we all wait to see if it has done him any good. I suppose I shall lack charity if I hope it will fail; but a complete failure would spare me a great deal of annoyance. Why should I be granted the power to cure these unfortunate people? If I have the power, ought I to devote all my time to healing and do nothing else? I have my own work to do as King of the English, and when I am free I like to go hunting.'

I was able to console him, for the point had already engaged my attention. 'My lord,' I said, 'that need not trouble you. We have authority for the view that these cures should be performed sparingly. Long ago God Himself walked the earth, and by one act of will He might have cured all the ills in it. Yet how many healings of the blind are related in the Gospels? Ten? Twenty? There must have been some left in darkness, even among those who heard God speak with human lips.'

'Thank you, Edgar. You have put that very clearly. Even if I cure this Wulf I don't have to cure all the blind men in England. I wonder what will happen tomorrow? Well, I shall earnestly pray to God to cure him, and I can't do more than that.'

On the next day I stood by the King's throne through the very long and solemn High Mass of the Vigil of All Saints. At the end of it I held the basin for the King to wash, while the monks and the secular congregation in the nave stood on tiptoe to see what went on. Then Wulf, led up by a housecarle, plunged his face into the basin.

When he stood erect he moved his head clumsily, as though doing something he had almost forgotten how to do. I handed him one of the King's finest linen towels, and he rubbed his eyes with it. Then he threw back his head and shouted at the top of his voice: 'Praise be to God, I can see.'

'Can you now?' asked the King. 'What do you see?'

'I see the great church of St Peter at Westminster, and all the monks, and the King and his courtiers and housecarles, and a great crowd of Londoners.'

'Perhaps you do, but there's no proof of it. You knew when you were led here, blind, that these were all about you.' The King sounded positively cross. 'Now tell me, what's your name, Wulf, can you see what I am doing at this moment?' With his right hand the King stroked his beard, while his left tugged at the long white mane of hair at the back of his head.

'You have both hands to your head, my lord. One is at your beard, the other behind you.'

'Well, which is which? Is it the right hand at my beard?' As he spoke the King shifted his hands.

'Now your left is at your beard, my lord. You have just moved them.'

'This is amazing. The man can really see,' said the King, lying back in his throne as though exhausted. 'Lord God, I give thanks for Your grace. St Peter, I give thanks for your intercession. But, oh dear, why has this power been granted to *me*? Couldn't some little unimportant angel have found a proper holy man, a holy man who enjoys working miracles?'

We came out of the church in a long procession of triumph. Monks, burgesses, courtiers and housecarles all joined in the hymn of praise. Only the King wore on his face a sad, puzzled expression.

When he reached his bedchamber that night the King at once cast himself prone on the floor before his little image of St Peter. For more than an hour he prayed without moving. At last he raised himself and sat on the edge of his bed. He looked ruefully at me as I knelt before him.

'Get up, Edgar,' he said with a sigh. 'You kneel to God, and to the relics of the saints, not to an ordinary mortal man. But there – in future I shall have to put up with a lot of this nonsense. Any king of the English can cure scrofula, but it is no part of the heritage of the Cerdingas to heal the blind. That was something special, and quite unexpected. Already the loafers outside the gate shout that they have a saint to rule them. Can it be a trick of the Devil? I have always been proud and hot-tempered. If I were silly enough to believe that I am sure of Heaven I would be quite intolerable. No, the Devil does not restore sight to the blind. That was a true miracle, and I must endure it.'

After a pause he spoke again. 'This is a very heavy burden, but it has its consolations. If God has given me power to heal by my blessing, perhaps He has also given my cures power to blast the wicked. It's not very likely. In this world nothing ever harms the wicked – justice comes only after death. But if the people believe that my curse can blast, that will be nearly as effective as if it were really true. That's it, Edgar. Let's cheer up. I can stand up to Harold as much as I like. The idea lurks at the back of his mind that if need be he can dethrone me and put little Edgar Edwardsson in my place. He must forget it. If he harms a hair of my head the people will tear him in pieces. St Peter, forgive me! I recognise that your gift is a blessing after all. The English love the favourites of Heaven. They will support me against the ambitions of the Earls.'

'It won't make a great difference,' he continued in a lower tone. 'I shall permit Harold to go on ruling, because he rules better than I should. I haven't forgotten what a mess I made of things while the Godwinssons were in exile. But if I choose to put my foot down about something I really care about he will have to carry out my will.'

Finally, as he snuggled into the pillows, he spoke the last words he ever said about the healing of Wulf. 'There will be no more miracles,' he said firmly, 'unless God sends me an unmistakable command which I cannot disobey. Please, God, spare me the necessity. Edgar, if any more unfortunates come to court to seek my help, tell them to invoke St Peter before the High Altar of my new minster. If they pray there, God will do as much for them as if they had washed themselves all over in my bathwater.'

Nevertheless, though the King did not know it, he went on performing miracles for the rest of his life. Next day six blind men arrived at his hall. They were undoubtedly and most horribly blind, for their eyes had been put out by the vikings whom Harold led into Somerset more than ten years before; the pirates were hungry, and these west-country peasants would not tell where their pigs were hidden.

They did not even ask to see the King. They were humble men, and all they wanted was a basin of the water in which he had washed. They offered me a bag of silver, and I took the money because if I had refused it they would never have believed that the water I gave them was the genuine article. They bathed their faces, and they saw again. There is nothing more to be said, except that when I knew they enjoyed God's favour I gave them back their money and they offered it to St Peter.

After that many cures were wrought by means of the King's washing water. We did not tell the King about these things, though in a general way he was aware of them. But we knew that we served one of God's chosen saints. Any chamberlain will agree that such knowledge brings with it a most disquieting tremor of fear, as well as a sense of holy awe.

CHAPTER IX

Earl Harold's Oath

The King was very old and very frail, and considered by all
his subjects to be a saint. In his own mind he had very nearly
left this earth. The business of ruling England scarcely occupied
him, since Earl Harold did all the work. He prayed for most
of the night, and passed the morning in visiting some church.
His only recreation was a gentle hunt on fine afternoons, his
only secular duty attendance at the long dinners and suppers
of the Council at the time of the three annual crownwearings.
On these occasions he would lean back in his chair with closed
eyes, his long white beard flowing down to the board. Harold,
seated on his left, would talk across him to Stigand on his right;
then the decision of the Council, that is the decision of Earl
Harold, would be laid before the King for his formal assent.
Wearily the King would agree to whatever was proposed,
anxious only to end the feast so that he might get back to his
prayers in his chamber.

What Harold proposed was always wise, and usually as
equitable as decisions of statecraft can be in a fallen world;
for Harold was just unless the interests of the Godwinssons
were concerned. Besides, if he had proposed anything obviously wicked the King would have forbidden it. The King's
assent was very nearly a form; but was still a neccessary form,
and it set limits which even Harold dared not pass.

The King hunted, I believe, chiefly from habit. For more
than twenty years, ever since he had become King of the
English, hunting had been his pleasure, the only pleasure befitting his rank which carried with it no hint of sin; a virgin
who was not interested in food or drink could find no more
innocent pastime. In his active maturity he had enjoyed the

chase; and now that old age and infirmity forbad him to gallop through thick woodland he still held in his mind a picture of hunting as something supremely enjoyable. Those who understand the pastime, as I do not, tell me that there can be great pleasure in planning the drawing of a covert, and in arranging all the complicated sequence of a long day among the muddy thorntrees. The King would gossip happily by the hour with his huntsmen and foresters. If he was feeling tired he would potter out to some hill above the open plain, to watch his hawks chase birds through the sky; he could follow them with his eyes while his horse stood still. I have never been able to see the attraction of hawking, which seems to me a passive sport. But I know that it can delight even intelligent and active men; Earl Harold, for example, usually rode with a hawk on his wrist. So perhaps it was not really odd that the King should take pleasure in it.

In that spring of 1064 the King was more than sixty years old, and only settled fine weather could tempt him into the open. But Earl Harold still believed that the most acceptable present he could give to his lord would be a hunting-box in fresh country. He sent men to build a hall near the mouth of the river Usk, in the forest which had been conquered from the unfortunate King Griffith. My lord was delighted to hear of this, and talked eagerly of exploring the new coverts next season.

For the Easter crownwearing the court moved as usual to Winchester, and at the solemn High Mass of Easter Day in the Old Minster my lord was granted another vision. By this time I could recognise the symptoms. When the King knelt unmoving, his eyes blank, I knew that he was not distracted by secular thoughts but rather looking into Heaven. When Mass was finished all the courtiers waited patiently until presently the King came to himself with a start. But he did not then kneel down to give thanks, as we had expected. Instead he summoned his housecarles with a curt nod, and swept out of the minster as though urgent business awaited him.

Arrived in his hall he went straight to his chair at the high table; though it was early to begin dinner, and the Earls had expected to be summoned for a private meeting of the chief Councillors before the public feast. But when the King takes his place dinner must of course be served, and the great men took their places also. As soon as the hall was full the King

170

commanded silence; then he rose to address the meeting. After a few words he found the effort too much for his feeble strength. He lay back in his chair and whispered to a stalwart housecarle, who shouted the royal speech sentence by sentence.

'The King has seen a portent, prophesying calamity to all Christendom,' he began. At once there were cries of dismay. 'The calamity will not affect the English in particular,' he went on, and everyone felt more cheerful. If all Christendom were involved we would have companions in misfortune, and perhaps our remote corner of the world might escape altogether. 'During Mass the King saw a vision of something which has happened very far off, almost at the other end of the inhabited world. Beyond the middle sea, in Greekland, lies the city of Ephesus. In Ephesus, in Greekland, the Seven Sleepers have turned over from their right sides to their left.' The King waved his hand to show he had finished, and with a bow the housecarle went back to his seat at a lower table.

Everyone burst out talking at once, though that was a breach of the etiquette proper to these solemn crownwearings. I know where Greekland lies. If you take the easiest road to Jerusalem, through Hungary, you traverse Greekland from end to end; Sweyn Godwinsson had died in that land, and the best jewels and silk come from its great cities. I had heard mention of the Seven Sleepers, though I did not know their story. Most of the thanes and housecarles at the lower tables knew even less than I did.

Seeing everyone look puzzled, Bishop William got up to explain.

'The Seven Sleepers are holy men who have been permitted to remain on earth until the Day of Judgement,' he said. 'Eight hundred years ago and more, when the wicked Emperor Diocletian had decreed death for all Christians, they hid in a cave to escape martyrdom. In the cave they fell asleep, and there they have remained ever since; asleep, without food or drink, their lives preserved by miracle. Six hundred years ago the men of Ephesus found them. Their cave is known, though seldom visited.' He spoke in clear English, with only a slight French accent; he had taken trouble to learn the language of his flock.

Stigand hoisted himself right off the bench to whisper in

William's ear across several other Councillors; in this posture he presented his enormous rump to the King, but Stigand never bothered to show courtesy to those he did not fear. 'You know all about these Sleepers,' he said in a tone that was technically a whisper, though he made no real effort to speak quietly. 'Tell me, had you ever heard that when they turn over it means calamity?'

'Well, no, I hadn't,' answered Bishop William with a worried frown. 'But it seems reasonable on the face of it; and the King ought to know what his own vision forebodes.'

'Why should he? Does he know anything else? Would you follow his advice on any secular matter? This is the Council of the English, not a parcel of monks at recreation,' Stigand answered impatiently.

Then he rose, to address the gathering in due form.

'This is a matter of such gravity that the whole Council should inquire into it. The King saw a vision. But the interpretation of what he saw is not immediately apparent; and we must not forget that a vision, even a vision seen in my minster during the High Mass of Easter, might conceivably be a snare of the Devil. News of this portent will cause great alarm; we shall be to blame if the alarm is needless. Luckily, it is easy to confirm what the King saw, or is persuaded that he saw. Ephesus lies a long way off, but it is a known place that can be visited. Let us send an embassy to the King of the Greeks, asking him to inquire from the Bishop of Ephesus. When we know for a fact that the Sleepers have turned over to the left side, the unlucky side, we may take measures to prepare for this calamity.'

The King remained silent, leaning back in his chair. When Stigand's proposal had been carried he gave his assent with an absent wave of the hand. The Council had agreed formally to inquire into something the King had told them as truth. I think that if any of our veteran housecarles had understood the insult implied he would have taken Stigand's head then and there, in the King's hall; but housecarles never listen to any discussion in Council unless it is concerned with their pay. Only I, and a few other courtiers, realised the full insolence of Stigand's proposal.

A few days later a group of clerks duly set off from Winchester; though they never saw the Seven Sleepers with their own eyes, in Constantinople they had audience with the King

172

of the Greeks, and he told them that the vision was true. The Sleepers had in fact turned over, and all the East was dismayed. The calamity thus portended can now be recognised; within ten years the infidel Turks had overrun all Christian Asia, until now it is impossible for a pilgrim to reach Jerusalem unless he pays them heavy blackmail.

In those days the Kingdom of the Greeks still stood in all its glory. About the end of the year the envoys returned, bringing confirmation of what loyal men had never doubted: that the King's vision was true. During the summer of their absence we waited anxiously for the unknown calamity to afflict Christendom.

The King worried more about the future than any of his subjects. He worried so much that he broke off his hunting on Cotswold and came to London to confer with Earl Harold. London held other attractions for him, since the new buildings at Westminster were nearly complete; but the real reason for the journey, an unusual reason to fetch the King from his hunting, was concern for the welfare of his realm.

On his first evening in London he explained it to the Lady, while we were both putting him to bed after his long ride.

'I don't usually worry about the future,' he said, as though puzzled by his own state of mind. 'We know that the Day of Judgement will bring the world to an end. Perhaps the Last Trump will sound tonight, and then anyone who is found worrying about the future will look very silly. They tell me some Kings never stop worrying; I have found it quite easy to be a carefree King. Just remind yourself that the English are no more important than any other nation, and that what matters to individual Englishmen is whether they end in Heaven, not whether they live in prosperity and die in their beds. When you have recognised statecraft as unimportant you won't find it difficult as well. Only once have I been seriously uncertain about my duty; when I found out that I could sometimes heal the blind, and wondered whether I ought to devote my life to doing nothing else. But Edgar here explained it all very sensibly; and anyway the blind are healed by the water I have washed in, and I would wash myself whether washing helped the blind or not. So the problem proved quite a simple one after all. Oh dear, I wish God and St Peter would not grant miraculous cures at my intercession! But they do, and I must adjust my life

173

to it. What was I talking about?'

'About the wisdom of allowing the future to take care of itself,' answered the Lady patiently. 'But though you think it foolish to worry about the future, and indeed I agree with you, you are now worrying about it. Tell me your worry, and perhaps I can help you.'

'Oh yes, that was my worry, the future, wasn't it? The future of this Kingdom, of course. Not that I can do anything to help my people after I am gone, except to give them a competent successor. That was it. And then of course there is the matter of my promise. A King is shamed if he does not keep his pledged word.'

'Please, my lord, I still do not know what worries you.'

The Lady spoke sharply. It was never easy to keep the King to one point, and especially difficult when he was tired after a long ride.

'Oh didn't I tell you? I am worrying about the succession. As you know, I promised Duke William that he should be the next King of the English; and in those days, when I had more energy than I have now, I took quite a lot of trouble to smooth his path. I persuaded everyone who mattered, nearly all the Council, to swear that they would support him. And now it has just occurred to me that all those great men are dead, and here I am still King of the English. All that work has been wasted, and I feel too tired to begin again from the beginning.'

'Are they all dead? Who were they?' asked the Lady; and bit her lip in exasperation when the King waved his hand airily to indicate that he could not remember.

'Perhaps I can help you, madam,' I said, looking up from the little brazier where I was warming the King's nightcap. 'I remained at court while you, madam, revisited Wilton. I think I can recall the chief events of those times.'

I had no power and no money; but I was in a sense the King's most intimate friend. I was as secure in my position as any servant of a King can be. Perhaps a concerted complaint from the whole Council might have dislodged me, but I was too firm in the royal favour to fear the Lady. I am ashamed to say that sometimes I took pleasure in reminding her that when the King turned against her, in the year of Earl Godwin's exile, I had remained a familiar servant of the bedchamber.

'Very well, Edgar,' said the Lady coldly. 'You know my lord's policies, and it seems that I do not. Search your memory, and tell me whether any of the great men now ruling the English have sworn loyalty to Duke William.'

I thought for a few minutes, out of politeness; though I was already sure of my answer.

'Madam, your father swore, and he is dead. Others who swore were the Earls Leofgar and Siward. It was more than ten years ago. The only Councillor still bound to Duke William is Bishop Stigand, who governs the church of Canterbury.'

'Stigand, of course. I knew one of them still lives,' said the King absently.

The Lady answered with more determination. 'I'm glad you don't style him Archbishop of Canterbury. He isn't that, for all that he enjoys its revenues. What an absurdity, that the succession to the Kingdom of the English should depend on the oath of Bishop Stigand, who would swear anything for twopence and break his oath for threepence.'

Then she turned to the King with a forced smile, as though making allowances for a fractious invalid. 'I see your worry, my lord. You want my brother Harold to take this oath, and you fear that if you command him to do so he will refuse. Why is that? Do you suspect that he will try to make himself King when you are dead?'

'Of course not, my dear,' said the King quite briskly, coming out of his dream because at last he was really interested. 'How could Harold make himself King? Nobody wants him to be King. He is the leader of the Anglo-Danes, I grant you. But the King they want is the other Harold, Hardrada of the Norwegians. The true English would never accept your brother, precisely because he is the leader of the Anglo-Danes. No, Harold can't be King. But he may rout out some insignificant atheling of the true Cerdinga line from a foreign land, as he routed out my unfortunate nephew Edward. He wants a King who doesn't matter, a King ignorant of the country, so that he may continue as the greatest Earl in England. He won't want to set up my cousin William, because William will be a strong King and there will be no room for a chief minister under him. That's why Harold must swear allegiance to William while I still live. And I can't think how I am to force him to swear against his will.'

'If that's your only trouble it is easily solved,' the Lady

answered at once. 'You have forgotten my other brother, Tostig. You are always forgetting him, and I wish you wouldn't. He will be in London next week, not on any official business but just to pay a visit to his sister. He has the Northumbrians behind him, and behind Northumbria all the levies of his blood-brother the King of the Scots. If he threatens Harold he will have the support of young Edwin of the Mercians, for what that's worth; and very likely my other brothers will stand neutral. If you take the opportunity while Tostig is at court you can compel Harold to obey you, or threaten him with exile.'

'Thank you, my dear. I never thought of that. It only shows that being a King is quite easy after all. Just do what you think is right, even against the will of a powerful subject; and when you need help it will be forthcoming.' The King settled himself into bed with a placid yawn.

A few days later the King rode hawking in the Essex marshes with the Earls Harold and Tostig. A falconer told me that the three lords rode together, apart from their followers, and seemed more intent on private discussion than on sport. The King came home cheerful.

But a great Kingdom cannot be governed by secret agreements. Such agreements will not be kept unless all men are aware of them. Between East and Pentecost the King spoke with Earl Harold publicly in his great hall, in the hearing of all the housecarles and courtiers. In set terms he ordered Harold to proceed to Duke William in Normandy and there swear in public to be his man and help him to the throne of England. The King sat on his throne as he gave these commands, and Earl Harold stood before him with uncovered head. I do not know why these orders were given so publicly, with Harold standing meekly to receive them. The King would not publicly humiliate an Earl, merely to show that he was his master. It seems to me likely that Harold himself suggested this formal procedure; wishing to prove to all England, and indeed to all Normandy, that he went to Duke William unwilling, against his better judgement.

But he went, which was the great thing; and we all breathed more easily after he was gone. In spite of the Lady's brave words it is not at all certain that he could have been compelled to go. Earl Tostig would have supported the King against his brother;

Tostig was loyal, and also jealous of Harold. But perhaps the Northumbrians would not have followed their Earl in what might seem a mere private quarrel between two of the unruly Godwinssons.

Earl Harold set out from Bosham, taking with him his youngest brother, little Wulfnoth, who was not yet of an age to bear arms. That proved that he went in good faith, for the youth must be intended to remain as a hostage at William's court, a guarantee of Harold's loyalty. They carried also a sealed letter from the King, in which I believe he advised Duke William to offer the warleader of the English a high post under the new government. The King was very proud of that letter, which he had drafted himself with the help of Bishop William; but though he talked of it often I never learned its exact contents.

Then we heard that Earl Harold had been lost at sea with all his company. For a few days the whole court was absorbed in delicious speculations; busy careerists threw over their friends and made friends with their enemies to secure a share in the great Earldom of Wessex.

Before we had got very far with this, a pastime which delights me all the more because I can watch it from the outside at no risk to my own neck, we heard that Wessex still had a thriving Earl. Harold's ship had not been sunk. Instead a storm had driven it off course, and he had come ashore in some land which bordered Normandy. The ruler of those parts threw him into prison, hoping to extort a fat ransom; but Duke William heard of it, and rode to rescue his guest. All the rulers of northern France feared Duke William, and Harold was soon safely lodged in Rouen.

Before Michaelmas he was back in England, though little Wulfnoth had been left behind; which suggested that all had gone according to plan. But Harold was very angry, and so were his companions.

As soon as he arrived at court he delivered a formal speech in hall, saying that he had done all that had been commanded and that Duke William held his oath. But that evening he came to the King's bedchamber and demanded a private interview.

The King sat on the edge of his bed; he was impatient to begin his evening prayers, as I knew but Harold did not. Of course the great Earl took his time, thinking that no one would be anxious to end such an important conference; which put the King in a bad temper. All the same, Harold quickly came to the point.

'My lord, your cousin Duke William is a cheat and a scoundrel,' he said fiercely.

'They speak of him as an honest man. You have been in his power, and here you are safe,' the King answered with a frown.

'Yes, safe. But I am his sworn vassal, and my brother is his hostage.'

'Isn't that exactly what we arranged before you left England? You went to swear allegiance, and you took Wulfnoth to leave him as a hostage.'

'He made me swear more than I had intended, and he stole my oath by trickery. Oh, to begin with he got me out of a tight place. He took me to his court and gave me splendid presents. But I'm not at all sure it wasn't a put-up job from the beginning. The little French Count who imprisoned me is one of William's vassals, and may have acted on William's orders. I was rescued just to make me grateful.'

'Did William raise the storm that drove your ship off its course?' asked the King with sarcasm.

'Very likely he did. He's probably a wizard as well as a cheat. But I must tell you the whole story. First I was imprisoned, as you know. That's a vile law they have in France, that all shipwrecks are the booty of the lord of the shore. It proves that the French are not fit to govern themselves. A Frenchman should not aspire to govern the English.'

'In England it isn't the law, but you know as well as I do that it happens. If one of your ships were wrecked anywhere in England, how much of the cargo would you see again?'

'My lord, let me tell this story in my own way. In England we have plenty of thieves, but they can't quote the law to justify themselves. . . . Well, after Duke William had rescued me from prison he treated me with all honour. He gave me one of those long mailshirts they wear in France, and showed me how to fight on horseback. It's not so difficult as it looks, when the horse knows his job; how they train the horses in the first place beats me. On the Duke's horse I managed quite well, but I shall never try it on an ordinary English hunter. When I could wield my lance in the saddle without falling off the Duke said I must see a little of the genuine thing. So he took me with him on a

178

campaign against his neighbours in Brittany. Certainly those Bretons are afraid of him. We had no real fighting. When they met us in the open they ran away, and when we reached any of those famous French castles the defenders at once opened their gates. All the same, those castles are useful things, my lord; you were quite right there. With your permission I shall build one in my town of Dover, on that hill where the old Roman fort stands. . . . So in this war we had no fighting. The only time we lost a few men was when the tide caught us fording a river. Even then I was able to rescue some of them, while the Frenchmen panicked and waved their arms in the air. They don't understand the sea like Danes and Englishmen. The Duke was pleased that I had rescued his followers, and he gave me armour and weapons to take home, beside the outfit he had lent me for this campaign.'

'That was more than a present,' said the King, interrupting. 'According to French ideas when he gave you weapons like that on campaign he adopted you as his chosen war-companion. I hope you thanked him properly.'

'Oh, they made quite a ceremony of it. I saw it was important, and I don't think anyone could have complained of my manners. When we got back from Brittany we were all very good friends. Then the Duke held a great feast and suggested that with all his followers looking on now was a good time for me to swear my oath of friendship. Well, as I say, we were friends, and anyway you had commanded me to take this oath. So I agreed, and he asked me to lay my hand on a little table as I swore. I thought it was just another queer French custom, so I did as he suggested. Then after I had sworn they whipped the cloth off the table, and underneath was a whole nest of relics. One of them was a great round ball of crystal that they call the Bull's Eye. It's got a piece of the True Cross inside it, or something equally grand. That's what I mean by trickery. An ordinary polite promise of friendship, which I couldn't refuse unless I was willing to insult my host under his own roof; and he turns it into an oath that will bind my soul to the Day of Judgement and after.'

'But you were willing to promise without relics,' the King objected. 'You are no worse off, unless indeed you had made up your mind that you would break the promise, even before you gave it.'

179

'Well, my lord,' said Harold sulkily, 'a promise is a promise, of course. No honest man makes a promise intending to break it. But no one can foretell the future. We are trying to plan a peaceful succession to the throne of the English after you are dead. When will that be? A long time hence, I hope; but we don't know. We can't be sure that I shall outlive you. Circumstances may change so that the promise is obviously incapable of fulfilment. But this oath which I took unawares! It binds me to make King William King of the English, even though I may then be the only living Englishman willing to submit to his rule.'

'And if you are you can still make him King. You are the warleader of the English, and the greatest man in the land. That is chiefly due to your own prowess, I grant you.' The King spoke firmly. 'But you cannot keep your power unless you are willing to work with me. I have commanded you to serve Duke William after I am gone. You have promised obedience. All will work out in the end, and perhaps the English will have peace when the rest of Christendom is afflicted by the calamity foretold by the Seven Sleepers.'

'When Duke William reigns I shall not be warleader. He is a warrior, and younger than I.'

'That is true, and of course it bothers you. But that's only because you cannot imagine yourself an old man. Hardly anyone really believes that one day he will be too old to enjoy battle. All the same, a time will come when you will be glad to lay aside your arms. Surely when you gave your oath the Duke made promises in return? I wrote to him, asking him to recognise the great position you have earned by your gallant service against the Welsh.'

'Oh yes, my lord, the Duke made splendid promises, I am to be his representative and agent among the English while you reign. He will send experts to build my castle at Dover, and I shall hold it for life as his vassal. When he is King I shall still be the greatest Earl in the land, and I shall rule as his deputy whenever he visits Normandy. All that was definitely agreed. To make our friendship more secure he suggested that I should marry his sister. I didn't actually refuse the offer, though we did not fix a date for the wedding. If I decide to go through with it I can easily get an annulment of my existing marriage. I can persuade the court of Rome that Edith Algarsdaughter never gave her free consent.'

180

'You have no difficulty there. It is not a business I care to discuss. If you repudiate that unfortunate young woman you must of course give her a sufficient maintenance.'

'I am rich enough to be generous, my lord.'

'Then there is nothing more to be said. You complain that Duke William tricked you with his hidden relics; but unless you were planning to trick him no harm was done. He has offered you the high position you hold under me; and the hand of his sister, which is more than I have given you. Everything has worked out as I had planned it. Now go away and serve me loyally, and under the next King of the English you will prosper.'

'Under the next King of the English I shall prosper indeed,' answered Harold with a ring of menace in his voice. 'I thought you would agree that Duke William has tricked me. But if what he did was in accordance with your will I waste my time, and yours, in complaining. Duke William is your chosen heir, I am his chosen minister. Perhaps, when the time comes, all will go peacefully.'

He took his leave with a courteous smile. It had been an odd, inconclusive interview, and I could not see what Harold had hoped to gain by it. But Harold, like his father, always tried the easy way first. He tried to persuade, and when he failed he would agree with his adversary, in words. But his agreement never proceeded genuinely from the heart; he would say anything for the sake of gaining a few more days of peace.

During that autumn the King was happy and tranquil. All the world knew that Harold was committed to Duke William and, what was more important, Tostig was a genuine supporter of the King's chosen heir. My lord was failing, and knew that soon he must leave this world. But he was secure in his hope of Heaven, and if he lived also to see the consecration of Westminster he would die happy, knowing that he had provided for the good government of his people after he was gone.

181

CHAPTER X

The Fall of Earl Tostig

In 1064 the court kept Christmas at Gloucester, as usual. All the Bishops and Earls came to the Council, and there was the usual crowd of thanes and burgesses with petitions and complaints. In fact there was rather more than the usual crowd; half the noble houses of Northumbria sent deputations to complain against Tostig.

It is impossible for a West Saxon to find out the rights of a Northumbrian quarrel. The north is the home of the blood-feud, and some of these private wars have been handed down from father to son for more than two centuries. The Northumbrians, like the other dwellers in the Danelaw, may be divided into English and Anglo-Danes. But in addition the English among them are divided into Bernicians and Deirans, the followers of two ancient royal houses now extinct; what makes it worse is that a great many hereditary adherents of the house of Deira live in Bernicia, and the other way round, so that you cannot even guess a man's political prejudice from the name of his home. In those days some Englishmen revered the memory of Earl Siward the Dane, and some Danes hated his kindred. When a Northumbrian lays an accusation, and backs it with a solemn oath, you can be pretty sure it is a move in some ancestral feud. But you cannot divide the complainants neatly into factions, Danes, Bernicians, Deirans and so on; all you know is that everyone is lying.

So the Council did not pay very much attention to the numerous accusations against Earl Tostig. Even what sounded like very grave charges evaporated under investigation. Men took oath that Tostig had summoned two thanes to his court at York, and there murdered them. Then it appeared that these young men had indeed been murdered while they were in attendance on the Earl; there could be no doubt of the fact, for one morning their headless bodies had been discovered on the dungheap behind his hall. But there was no evidence that Earl Tostig had procured their murder; such men would have plenty of enemies who would kill them by treachery at the first opportunity. In short, the killings had been a very grave breach of the special peace which dwells in the hall of every ruler; but that is the kind of behaviour you expect from Northumbrians.

A young thane named Cospatric was especially ardent in his accusations against Tostig; his oath would weigh heavily, for he was heir to the ancient royal house of Bernicia. But he never made his formal charge. On the fourth day after Christmas, the day appointed for him to take oath, his headless corpse was found lying on the King's own dungheap.

There was a frightful to-do. Such an insult to the special peace of the King's hall had not been known since the bad old days of the heathen King Sweyn. All the chiefs of the household inquired into the mystery, and I myself examined the lesser chamberlains.

It was not difficult to exonerate them, for chamberlains do not carry axes; if one of my men wanted to murder an enemy, and some of them were capable of it, he would poison him, or stick a knife into his ribs. Cospatric had been killed by one blow, struck from behind. Only a housecarle could have cut off his head.

With so many visitors at court we had many strange housecarles staying with us; and there is a fellow-feeling among housecarles which makes them reluctant to incriminate even a stranger who follows the same calling. During the formal Council of Christmas sentries were posted all over the place; among them they ought to have seen everything, but they swore they had seen nothing. After a long day of inquiry evening found us all depressed and miserable.

At bedtime the Lady burst into the King's chamber unannounced. She was too agitated to notice me, and the King could never remember whether I was there or not unless I was actually touching him; so nobody ordered me to withdraw, and I heard everything.

'I know who killed Cospatric,' the Lady began, 'but I shall not tell you his name. He thought he was doing his duty, by the

183

rules of those savage northern bloodfeuds. He has gone into exile, and he will never again trouble the court.'

'His honour may have guided him to kill the thane Cospatric,' the King said crossly, 'it could not guide him to break the special peace of the King's hall. It's not fair to me. When my guest is murdered I am sure to be blamed; it may even be supposed that I killed him myself. If the murderer has fled, and he is a friend of yours, we need not try very hard to catch him. But it's only right that his guilt should be made known, to clear other suspects. Who is he?'

'No, my lord, I promised not to tell you. It was an honest killing, for vengeance, not for gain. That is all you need know.'

'Very well, my dear, if you say so. Of course the murderer is one of your Danish housecarles, but you say he has fled and will never return. I presume that sooner or later he himself will be murdered in the course of this bloodfeud. Since I can't hang him, that will be the most satisfactory end to the affair. But have you understood that anyone now at court may be blamed for the murder unless we name the murderer?'

The Lady agreed that blame might be attributed unjustly; but still she would not name the criminal. In the end the King paid full compensation to Cospatric's kin, since he was at fault for not guarding his guest more carefully; and any magnate who chose to do so was allowed to swear publicly that he was innocent. That was the best that could be done to close the case.

I believe even the Lady was dismayed when she discovered that rumour laid the murder at her door. It was whispered that she had procured the killing of Cospatric because he was a dangerous foe to her beloved Tostig. Now I come to think of it perhaps that was the truth. The Lady was not in general an assassin, but there is very little she would not have done to help Tostig.

It did not help Tostig. Even those who did not blame the Lady believed the thane had been killed to please the Earl of the Northumbrians; it proved that his subjects were never safe from his unlawful vengeance, even when they took refuge at the court of King Edward. In Northumbria the discontent was greater than ever.

One day in the high summer of 1065 the court rode across Cotswold, on the move from one hunting lodge to another. On these journeys the King rode with his huntsmen and falconers; while the chamberlains were placed at the head of the column, so that we could begin to unpack his baggage before he dismounted. I disliked these moves, partly because riding makes me sore; but even more because it was difficult and chancy work to make the King comfortable in a chamber that had stood empty only a few hours ago. By his bed every little knickknack had to be in its accustomed place, and if anything got lost during the move I would be blamed.

I was in a bad temper as I rode through the customary midsummer rain, and when a little group of beggars cried out from the roadside I pushed my horse into them to chase them away. If they reached the King he would give them his purse; and then I would have a tiresome interview with the treasurer, who suspected me of peculation whenever I asked him for more pocket-money for my lord. It was a wearing business to get rid of beggars, for the King would be angry if he saw them roughly treated; but a faithful servant must be rough with them if the King was ever to have an hour's peace or a penny in his purse.

One beggar shouted that he had a message for the King's private ear, and that he carried a token to prove it. But beggars will shout anything when they are struggling to get near a generous lord. Then this beggar, capering beside my restless horse, waved a ring at me. I reined in and looked more closely. It was a valuable ring, and one I had known.

I called up a housecarle. Together we put a halter round the beggar's neck, and led him before the King. I had recognised the ring as one the King himself had lost in a crowd earlier in the year. It was a very fine ring, an ancient cameo carved with an image of St John. I thought the King would be pleased to recover it, and would order the thief to be strung up then and there by the roadside.

I had an unpleasant surprise. The bound beggar spoke with the King, who then ordered the whole column to halt. 'I want to talk with this man at leisure,' he said, 'and I find it awkward to bend down to hear him. He must be put on a horse, to ride beside me. Edgar, give him your horse. It's sure to be quiet enough for him to ride, and a little walking exercise will be good for your figure – and your pride. When you recall this walk you will be more polite to the next holy pilgrim you meet. Perhaps I ought to put a halter round your neck, as you put one round his. I shall spare you that, on condition you really walk for at least five miles. No getting a lift on someone's crupper, mind. Fair walking, as fast as we travel. And tell me in the evening if you don't feel the better for it.'

For a full hour the King conversed with this tiresome beggar.

That evening in the bedchamber I was very distant with my lord. As senior chamberlain I was entitled to ride a fine horse whenever the court travelled. Perhaps I was a little stout. But then my work was to look after fine clothes and valuable jewellery under a roof; if I had kept myself fit by going for long rides every day I would have been neglecting my duty. The King himself was as thin as a pole, because he was always fasting and praying even on days not commanded by the Church; and he was in the saddle every day for as long as his strength would permit. It amused him to make fun of any of his household who happened to grow a bit fat; but I had been unfairly treated, in front of a lot of unmannerly housecarles. I sulked, and I still think my sulking was justified.

Of course the King noticed it at once, and tried to coax me into a more cheerful temper; perhaps he was a little bit ashamed of the way he had treated me during the journey. King Edward was proud of his sense of humour, which he considered to be an attribute of every true Englishman; but he did not think as most of his subjects thought (for a saint does not think as other men) and his jokes often fell flat.

'This afternoon you made a sad mistake, my dear Edgar,' he said with a smile, 'but it was a natural mistake. In every holy book we read that the most honest men can fail to recognise a messenger from Heaven. But even if there had been no smell of a miracle you should not have arrested a pious pilgrim, to carry him bound before me as though he were a common thief.'

'What's this about a miracle, my lord?' I asked eagerly. My curiosity is always stronger even than the bad temper induced by a grave grievance. 'I saw the man was a begging pilgrim, but I did not suppose he would be witty enough to entertain the King of the English throughout a long ride.'

'He carried important news, Edgar. It's good news, and I believe it to be true. As soon as I spoke to him he told me that within six months I shall see God in Heaven. We can none of us feel at home until we get there; because we were made to inhabit Heaven, not to inhabit this world. When he had given me this

186

news he acted like a sensible messenger and displayed his credentials. Didn't you recognise that ring he waved before your eyes?'

'I recognised it as yours, my lord. Last year you wore it at the consecration of some church in Winchester, and told me afterwards that you had lost it in the crowd.'

'Did I say that? Oh dear, it never pays to conceal the truth. At that consecration I got excited, and then I was afraid to confess what I had done. You scold me so when I give away valuable jewellery.'

'The treasurer scolds me if I fail to return it. My lord, you are the King, and you may do what you wish with your own. But the treasurer and I are responsible for seeing that the King shall look regal, and for that we must have rings and other jewels.'

'Of course that's true. But I have so many rings. And now I have one more than I had expected. Last year I gave it in alms to a beggar. In the crowd at that consecration I could not get near my almoner. In my robes of state I carry no money, and I could not send a beggar empty away. It's just as well I was generous. Of course he was no ordinary beggar. Can you remember which saint we honoured in the dedication of that church?'

'No, my lord. We see so many churches consecrated.'

'That's so, and a good thing too. We can't have too many churches, if Englishmen are to keep on the road to Heaven. It was dedicated to St John the Apostle, and St John himself came to the consecration. St John was the beggar. St John had my ring.'

'Did I put a halter round the neck of St John?' I exclaimed in alarm.

'Not as bad as that. The man who came to me today is a pilgrim just returned from the Holy Land. There he and his companions were lost in the desert, until St John appeared and led them to shelter. Then he gave that man my ring. He told him to deliver it to the King of the English, with the message about a peaceful death within six months. Isn't it lucky that I have made Harold swear allegiance to Duke William? When I die, some time this winter, the new King will come in peacefully.'

I did not suggest to my lord that he might live longer. His mind was made up, and already he was homesick for Heaven.

The King waited quietly for his promised release. But during that autumn his realm was continually troubled. In August the Welsh made an incursion, for the first time since Earl Harold had taken the head of King Griffith. It was a raid, not a serious campaign; but as a raid it was insulting, not to say impudent. The raiders, bursting out from the inner hills of Gwent, burned the new hunting lodge which Harold had commanded to be built as a present for the King. My lord had intended to visit this new forest after Michaelmas, but now he told Harold to abandon the project. The lodge could not be finished until next spring, and by next spring there would be another King of the English.

Earl Harold began to muster an army to take vengeance on the Welsh. But he never again had time for an invasion of Wales; as far as I know these raiders still keep their plunder unpunished. At the beginning of October came news of the far more serious trouble in Northumbria.

Earl Tostig happened to be staying with us; or rather, he was visiting his sister, the Lady. The two of them had been drawn together by the scandal attending Cospatric's murder; it may even be true that the Lady had instigated the killing to serve her brother, or at least Tostig may have believed so. Brother and sister were in the garden outside the little hunting lodge at Britford in Wiltshire, while the King took advantage of the fine autumn day to ride out hunting; it was his last day of pleasure in the woods.

At sunset a bedraggled courier rode in. He was one of Tostig's housecarles from York, and he had barely escaped with his life. He told us that the thanes of Northumbria had risen in arms, plundered the Earl's hall, and killed as many of his followers as they could catch. All the north was in rebellion; but the revolt was not directed against the authority of King Edward. The cry of the rebels was for another Earl, not for an independent Kingdom of Northumbrians.

As soon as my lord got back from his hunting he consulted those of his Councillors who happened to be at court; that is to say, Earl Tostig and a few Bishops. Harold was mustering his army at Gloucester, and at that season of the year the other Earls were in their governments. It was agreed that nothing should be done until Harold had marched his army into the midlands.

It quickly became apparent that this was not a spontaneous revolt, but the outcome of a conspiracy plotted by many great magnates. The Northumbrians marched south, wasting Danish Mercia as though they were vikings; but when they reached Northampton they were joined by Earl Edwin with the levy of English Mercia and a strong contingent of allied Welshmen. In gratitude the Northumbrians chose Edwin's young brother, Morcar, to be their Earl. The main body of the rebels halted at Northampton, sending out foragers to pillage far and wide; but their leaders seized Oxford, on the very border of Wessex, and from this strongly fortified base sent envoys to treat with the King.

Tostig and the Lady were in despair. The combined armies of Northumbria, Mercia and north Wales were stronger than any force that could be raised in Wessex; and Harold was not even trying to muster the whole levy of Wessex. He said that the troops gathered in Gloucester would be enough to guard the courts while he negotiated. On the Lady's advice the King named young Waltheof Siwardsson Earl in the central Danelaw, including the shire of Northampton. Waltheof was young for such great promotion, and not especially bright; but it was hoped that a leader of his ancestry would draw some Northumbrians to the King's side. The scheme failed; the rebels would not allow Waltheof even to enter Northampton.

The King was eager for war. But he was himself too old and sick to lead an army, and his chosen warleader would not fight. Harold said frankly that the rebels were too strong for him, and that anyway they had a good deal of right on their side. I remember a very stormy meeting of the inner Council, after supper in Britford hall. I stood behind the King as cupbearer; but the housecarles and servants had been sent outside so that the great men might lay their plans in private.

Stigand was the only clerk present, for this was a council of war. But it was also a meeting of the Godwinsson faction, so the Lady came over from the women's table to sit among her brothers. When serious issues were at stake the Godwinssons cared nothing for convention; they would welcome a woman to their councils if they thought she could offer practical advice.

Stigand sat on the King's right, taking the precedence of an Archbishop of Canterbury; on his right sat Harold, and beyond Harold the younger Godwinssons, Gyrth and Leofwin. On the

King's left sat the Lady, with Earl Tostig beyond her. Thus the two parties at court were neatly divided; Harold and his supporters on the right, the two loyal followers of the King on his left.

The King opened the Council with a warlike speech.

'Tomorrow I shall ride against these rebels, at the head of my housecarles and any other honest men who will follow me. When the battle begins no true Englishman would cut down a Cerdinga, and if some Dane takes my head it doesn't matter. I have only a few months to live, at best, and I shall die King of the English.'

'Spoken like a King,' said Harold courteously. 'But you have not faced what will really happen when you reach Northampton. No one will raise a hand against you, my lord. But the rebels will kill your followers, and then make you their prisoner. Are you willing to be in name King of the English, when Edwin and Morcar and the Danes of the north rule as your ministers?'

'Besides,' said the Lady, 'you cannot ride so far; you are not strong enough. Before you reach Northampton you would fall from your saddle and die of exhaustion by the roadside.'

'Then I shall be carried, slowly, in a litter,' the King answered stoutly. 'That will allow time for all the West Saxons to join my banner.'

'My lord, the West Saxons will not march against all Mercia and Northumbria,' Harold objected. 'My brothers will bear me out; the thanes fear civil war. They guard their homes, knowing that the King of the Danes will invade us if we kill one another in heaps. In Gloucester I have my housecarles, and a few other faithful followers. But I cannot muster all Wessex, even to fight the Welsh.'

'All the Northumbrians marched south,' said the King.

'Exactly, because they are in arms against a foe whom they hate more than they hate the Danes,' answered Harold triumphantly.

'I gave them justice. Is that so intolerable?' Tostig exclaimed in anger.

'Perhaps it is, to Northumbrians,' said young Gyrth with a snigger. 'Besides, you murder their chief men when they come to your court. You can't expect anyone to like that.'

'That's a foolish slander,' said the King.

'It is,' Harold agreed with a smile. 'Whoever murdered young

190

Cospatric it wasn't Tostig. But that's what those Northumbrians believe, and if we investigate too thoroughly we may find the truth unwelcome.' He grinned unpleasantly at his sister.

'Never mind the reason why they hate Tostig,' said the Lady hurriedly; the death of Cospatric was a dangerous topic. 'These men have made war on their rightful Earl. Are we to submit to their rebellion?'

'We must submit. That's what I keep on telling you,' cried Harold in exasperation. 'I would fight for Tostig's Earldom if we had the slightest chance of winning. But if we fight we shall be beaten, and then we shall lose everything. Whereas if we make peace Gyrth and Leofwin keep their lands, and I remain warleader of the English.'

'A warleader whose men will not follow him to war,' said the King. 'If that contents you we also must submit. Without you we can't fight. Very well. Then I suppose Tostig must go oversea?'

'That seems to be the wisest course.' Harold was now the elder statesman, heavy with responsibility. 'Look here,' he added with a smile, as though offering a great concession, 'how would it be if I myself see these rebels in Oxford, and fix up terms of peace? Remember, they have gone out of their way to proclaim their loyalty to the King of the English. If you allow them to keep Morcar as their Earl they will serve you faithfully.'

'I give in. Do as you wish,' said the King in a pet. 'It's no good trying to rule such beastly people. I shall go to bed.'

As I had expected, both Earl Tostig and the Lady came to see the King privately in his chamber that same night. Both were bitterly angry, and both suspected Harold of double dealing.

'I helped him against King Griffith,' said Tostig mournfully. 'The Welsh would have overwhelmed him if I had not ridden with my Northumbrians along the dangerous path by the coast. Now he can't be bothered to help me; or rather, he won't run the slightest risk to help me. Perhaps the Mercians might beat us in a pitched battle, though with Waltheof in our ranks we should find the Northumbrians divided.'

'He never intended to fight,' cried the Lady. 'Don't you see? The rebellion is his work. Harold is warleader, the greatest man in the land. There are other Earls, but which Earl can rival Harold? Not Edwin, who does not care what happens outside

191

Mercia. Not Morcar, clinging to power that is not rightly his. Not Waltheof, child of a famous father, himself so insignificant that his father's old vassals will not follow him. In all England there was only one man to rival Harold. So now Tostig is driven into exile.'

'Is that how you see it?' asked the King in surprise.

'It is how everyone will see it when they have had time to think it over,' answered the Lady. 'Harold plotted to remove Tostig, so that he may reign without a rival. Suppose Harold should snatch at your crown after you are gone? Who would oppose him? Tostig alone.'

'And I *shall* oppose him, even from exile,' shouted Tostig. 'Tomorrow I start for Flanders, because that is Judith's home. But from Bruges I shall get in touch with Duke William. I still have friends among the Northumbrians. When Duke William wants me I shall return to the north.'

'I wish I might live a little longer, to see how all this will turn out,' said the King, with such candid simplicity that the words did not sound at all odd. 'But I have been granted many visions, and all of them proved true. I must believe that pilgrim also saw true. Within six months from last July I shall be with God in Heaven.'

'In Heaven you will see what comes to the English, and your prayers will help us,' said the Lady gently.

Next morning the King stayed in his bed, complaining of weakness. Until the end of the month Harold rode between Britford and Oxford, negotiating with the rebels. In the end the Northumbrians got all they desired, as of course must happen when Harold refused to fight them. On the 1st of November Tostig embarked for Flanders; and on the same day the King began a slow journey to London, sometimes carried in a litter when he felt too feeble to ride.

CHAPTER XI

The End and the Beginning

On Christmas Day the King feasted in state, his crown on his head. It was the first time he had kept Christmas in London, but in other respects the ritual of the feast was as usual. Yet he was a very sick man, and he sat in silence while the Councillors gossiped together and discussed the future.

Only Harold's faction had come to the crownwearing; for the Earls Edwin and Morcar were too shy to attend so soon after they had borne arms against the King. Gyrth and Leofwin were there, of course, and Stigand of Canterbury. Earl Waltheof came also, a timid and awkward young man. He recognised that his family was in decline since he was not Earl of the Northumbrians as his father had been; he was rather too obviously looking for allies, and made clumsy overtures to Aldred, Archbishop of York.

After dinner the King looked so feeble that the Lady left her place at the women's table to come over and stand beside him. Earl Harold courteously moved along the bench to make room for his sister until she could sit beside her lord. I felt it strange to be pouring wine for a female at the Councillors' table; in those days, when our rulers were English, women were not supposed to take any part in politics.

But Harold said cheerfully: 'Here is a seat for you, Edith. That is as it should be. The Godwinssons sit at the right hand of the King, united to strengthen his rule.'

The Lady answered sharply: 'The Godwinssons are not united. Wulfnoth is a hostage in Normandy, and Tostig is in exile because his brothers would not save him.'

'Well, my dear, I'm sorry about young Wolfnoth, but it's not my fault. I left him with the Duke because the King so commanded me. Tostig is in exile because the Northumbrians can't abide him, and anyway he was never very loyal to his kin.'

'He was loyal to his lord. I hope you also will be loyal to your King. That is his bread you eat.'

'And the King's bread can be dangerous to men of our house, eh, Edith? Well, so far it hasn't choked me, so I can't be plotting treason. Even if we don't agree on everything let us keep on good terms. Remember, when Duke William is King he has promised to keep me as his chief minister. My position will be awkward if the Old Lady distrusts me.'

'Don't talk about the next reign as though the King were already dead. These messages from Heaven are sometimes hard to interpret. He may live for many years.'

'No, Edith, look at him. It's all right, he can't hear what we say, he is already listening to the songs of the angels. Surely you can see death in his face? What's the good of having a Danish spaewife for a mother if you can't see his doom fluttering round the head of a dying warrior?'

'Ah, you call him a warrior?' said the Lady, pleased.

'Of course he is a warrior, and a stark one. What does it matter that his axe has never tasted blood? Long ago he commended himself to God, and he has served his lord faithfully. That has been a long, hard fight.'

'You know him, and you recognise his worth. Harold, will you be loyal to his commands after he is dead?'

'I am loyal to him now. Since my father died I have served him loyally. But the commands of a dead King do not bind the living. The magnates will choose the next King of the English.'

'God has already chosen the next King of the English. That was revealed to Bishop Britwold many years ago,' said a piping voice.

Everyone started. Since the Council began the King had leaned back in his chair, his eyes closed; he had said nothing, and it seemed that he paid no attention to anything said beside him. Now, still with his eyes closed, he spoke clearly and distinctly. For a moment the high table was hushed.

'If God should impose the King of His choice by an undoubted miracle, I shall not oppose God's elect,' said Harold easily. 'But in these matters God often works through human agency. In the Kingdom of the English as it exists at present it would be reasonable that God should work through my agency, since I am warleader and the most powerful of the Earls.'

'My lord, do not tire yourself,' said the Lady, laying her hand on the King's shoulder. 'There is no need to make speeches to your Councillors. We know that you have chosen Duke William to succeed you, we know that Harold has sworn to serve Duke William. All has been done as you commanded. The Council knows your will, and obeys. Do not persuade the obedient.'

The King sighed, and his next words came in a faint whisper.

'Since you know my wishes and have sworn to obey them, I shall go to bed. Make what appointments are needed, settle the details of the taxes. This has been my last crownwearing, and for me it is already finished.'

He struggled to rise from his chair. The Lady took his right arm and I supported him on the left. Together we helped him to walk to his bedchamber, for the last time.

On the Feast of the Holy Innocents, three days after Christmas, the great church at Westminster was finished and consecrated. For twenty years the King had planned this great construction, and now he could not come to see the end of all his labours. At the hallowing of the most splendid church in England he was represented by the Lady; behind the High Altar masons were already preparing the tomb of the founder.

I also had greatly desired to see the consecration; but the King asked me to wait in his chamber beside him. From a little window beside his bed there was a clear view westward to the roof of the tall minster; I stood on a stool to peer out, and presently saw a mason climb a ladder to place a gleaming golden weathercock on the apex of the squat tower. That was the finishing touch to the building, by custom added at the moment of consecration. I told the King, and I think he understood what I said.

The King was not yet sixty-five, but he was dying of old age. That is not so extraordinary as it sounds, for he had surpassed by more than twenty years the greatest age attained by any other Cerdinga. Perhaps disappointment and vexation added something to his weakness. It was just ten weeks since, yielding to the Northumbrian rebels, he had acquiesced in the outlawry of Tostig.

The King knew that he was dying, and so did all his court. It was not an occasion for sorrow; he was going to Heaven, going home. He showed no fear of death, but he was distressed for the future of the country he was leaving. All through these last days he talked, in a high weak wandering voice; sometimes he recalled his youth, sometimes he spoke to imaginary companions, sometimes he told of what is hidden from ordinary sinners; and sometimes he warned us, as God had warned him.

During the first days of his sickness the Council met every afternoon in the hall beyond his bedchamber; but the trampling of horses and the clang of arms as bodyguards waited for their lords reminded the King of war and deepened his distress. The Lady asked the Council to meet in some other place, and perhaps this was a mistake; for then they met in Harold's hall, the great hall in Southwark from which Godwin had conducted civil war when he returned from exile. Harold was already war-leader, and in the King's absence he presided over the Council; when the magnates met in his hall he had in addition all the authority of the host.

So it went on, day after day, until the Tewlve Days of Christmas were nearly ended. The Lady was worn out with watching, and I myself wandered from chamber to hall to kitchen in a daze of exhaustion. The King would eat nothing. He hovered perpetually between sleeping and waking, neither utterly unconscious nor really aware of us beside him. But what chiefly troubled me, and kept me running to the kitchen for linen cloths soaked in hot water, was that he always complained of the cold.

The weather was frosty; and the chamber lacked a chimney, so we could not make a great fire. I placed braziers of charcoal under every window, for the foul air from charcoal must have an outlet; and the Lady piled coverlets and furs on the sufferer's bed. Still the King cried that he was cold. Once he thought himself back into his childhood, in the days of the Danish devastation; shivering, he pulled the blankets closer and whimpered that the heir of the Cerdingas had but one rug while Sweyn the pirate had the fleece of all the sheep in England.

At dawn on the Vigil of the Epiphany we saw that he could not last until sunset. When Earl Harold crossed over from Southwark he was asked to wait for the end, in the King's chamber. Stigand had sent to inquire, and he also was sum-

moned to the chamber. When there is no King in England the
Archbishop of Canterbury is trustee for the people. If Stigand
had been truly Archbishop he would have taken precedence
even of Harold; in his equivocal position he was at least entitled
to be present at the deathbed of the King.

Still my lord complained of the cold. In desperation the
Lady lifted the coverlets and sat at the end of the bed with
her husband's feet in her bosom. Looking down, the King,
thanked her with a smile. Stigand knelt before a little desk,
reciting the prayers for the dying. Harold stood by the head
of the bed. I knelt by the door; but I took care to recite the
psalm that Stigand had just finished, lest by inadvertence I
should mingle my prayers with those of a schismatic.

In a wandering voice the King chatted with St Peter, St
John, and Robert, his Norman falconer. Robert was far away
in Wiltshire, but I am inclined to think the others were present
in the chamber. Sometimes he spoke in the French of his exile,
then for a time he went back to the old-fashioned language of
his father's court, in which gentlemen spoke pure English
without any admixture of Danish. Harold and the Lady listened
with puzzled frowns; but to me, a Saxon of Winchester, that
seemed how the King of the English should speak.

Suddenly he came to himself and knew where he was. He
tried to sit up, and by the time he sank back he was talking
quite rationally to the chiefs of the English gathered round
his bed: Harold the warleader, the Lady, and the head of the
clerks in England who might just possibly be Archbishop of
Canterbury.

'I have spoken with two friends of my youth,' he said,
'Norman monks who comforted my exile. They are dead, but
they have come to me to help my passing. They have warned
me of the evils that will afflict the English after I am gone. Woe
to England! Because the Earls and the Bishops and the clergy
are not what they should be, but rather servants of the Devil,
the whole land will be given over to Satan for a year and a
day.'

'Not if we repent,' said Stigand without hesitation. He was
accustomed to quelling visionaries who threatened him with
the wrath of God.

'You will not repent. I asked these old monks, the friends
of my youth, and that is what they told me,' answered the

197

King. The Lady shuddered, and I felt even more worried than before. These were not the babblings of a dying man; the King understood what was said to him and replied to it.

'Well, what can we do to avert this calamity?' asked Harold.

'You can do nothing. Perhaps God will spare you, just as perhaps by His grace a tree that has been cut down and dragged three furlongs from its stump might send down fresh roots and grow again. The one is as likely as the other.'

Stigand shrugged his shoulders.

'The King is a very holy man. Very holy men are shocked by the human weakness of their neighbours,' he said lightly. 'Besides, he is dying and his mind wanders. We should not let him see that we think he talks nonsense, for that would distress him; but we need not worry unduly.'

'And I say that the King knows the will of God, and speaks true prophecies,' said the Lady fiercely.

Meanwhile the King continued to foretell evil for his people. At times he spoke vehemently, and even I would wonder whether he was raving; then he would recollect himself, and address us by name to show that he knew what he was doing. About midday he fell silent. Two hours later, while the exhausted Lady still strove to warm his feet in her bosom, she felt the chill that meant that he had died in silence.

We sent to warn the Abbot of Westminster to prepare for the funeral next day, immediately after the High Mass of Epiphany. Then Stigand walked across to St Paul's, to arrange with Bishop William about Requiem Masses. Earl Harold and his strong escort of housecarles rode off to Southwark, where the Council would meet in the evening. The Lady and I, with the treasurer and other chiefs of the household, arrayed the dead King in his robes of state and laid him in his coffin. As soon as the chaplains and the clerks of the chancery had taken up their watch, kneeling by the bier, I went to the wardrobe. Now I was merely a chamberlain among many chamberlains; there was no longer a King's bedchamber in which I was his trusted companion.

Even in this house of mourning the living must eat. The Lady called for bread and wine in her chamber, unwilling to face the throng in the great hall. I was gratified, but not really surprised, when one of her women told me that the Lady wished me to pour her wine.

198

Normally I am ill at ease in the company of females; but it was easy to forget that the Lady was a woman. In middle age her sexless beauty made her look merely a commanding figure, apparently without bodily functions. She lay back on a pile of cushions, very tired after her long watching. Soon she was chatting with me easily, as though we had long been colleagues in the management of court ceremonial.

'No one has been taken by surprise,' she said. 'The monks of Westminster will have practised the funeral psalms, and the tomb will be ready. My lord shall be buried on the great feast of Ephiphany, in the minster he founded. That is as it should be. The funeral will be worthy of a great King. When the tomb has been closed I shall gather my household and pack my gear. There is nothing to keep me in London, and the Council will be glad to see me go. No woman should give advice on such a great matter as the succession to the crown of the English; and yet so long as I remain in the King's hall the magnates will feel awkward if they ignore me. Will you come with me, Edgar, and be my chamberlain in Winchester? The new King will have Norman chamberlains about him, even though he has promised to rule with the advice of the English Council.'

'I suppose the new King *will* be Duke William, madam?' I said doubtfully. 'Edgar Edwardsson, the young atheling, is in London, and the burgesses may cheer for him.'

'But luckily the Council meets in Southwark, and cannot hear the cheers of the London burgesses. Perhaps the absence of Edwin and Morcar is another piece of luck, or rather a mark of God's special favour. At Southwark Harold will be the only great secular magnate, and it is less than two years since he commended himself to William. He holds his new castle at Dover on purpose to ensure William's peaceful entry into England. Tomorrow, after the funeral, King William will be proclaimed in his absence. Within ten days he will be here for his crowning. I want to be in Winchester before he arrives, so that I do not embarrass him.'

'Then, I suppose,' she went on, 'trouble will come in the north. My lord spoke of war and rapine for a year and a day, and I am sure he prophesied truly. That must be it. Edwin and Morcar will proclaim themselves independent, and perhaps King Harold Hardrada may attempt to revive the realm of

King Canute. But Duke William will overcome them. Best of all, he will bring with him my brother Tostig, his faithful vassal.'

'Perhaps it would be well to make sure that Earl Harold has sent the news to Normandy. Tonight he is supreme in England, and he may be tempted to prolong his power by delaying the message. Unless Duke William is proclaimed tomorrow the atheling Edgar is sure to put forward his claim.'

'Very well, Edgar. Go out and send a reminder to Southwark. I know you feel you ought to be doing something. In a crisis like this it's hard, isn't it, to sit still and do nothing? But you and I must learn to do nothing. Our lives ended today, though we may have to wait many years for death.'

But when I went to the outer gate to find a messenger I saw a messenger just arriving.

He was a smart young housecarle of Earl Harold's bodyguard, fully armed and well mounted; though Harold's hall, just across London Bridge, was so near that it would be quicker to walk than to saddle a horse for the journey. Nobody barred his way, since we were all busy and a little disorganised; but he sat his horse by the gate and called for the captain of King Edward's bodyguard as formally as if he had come to introduce a foreign embassy.

'That's all right, my man,' I said easily. 'Come in, if you have something to say. All our housecarles are guarding the treasury, in case the burgesses try to plunder it while there is no King of the English. We don't get back to the proper ceremonial until Duke William arrives to take up his inheritance.'

'I have a message for the commander of the royal housecarles,' he answered stiffly, 'but perhaps you can deliver it for me. You are the chief of the chamberlains, aren't you? You should tell the Lady as well, for the news concerns her. Here is the message. The magnates of the English, both Bishops and Earls, assembled in Council at Southwark, have offered the crown of the English to Harold Godwinsson, Earl of the West Saxons. He has accepted. Since the Council is gathered, and the Archbishop of Canterbury present in London, there is no need for delay. In Westminster tomorrow King Harold will be crowned, immediately after the funeral of the late King Edward.'

I stood silent in amazement. Then I glanced anxiously at

the axe which hung at the messenger's saddlebow. But the housecarle sat erect, glaring down at me. This message was a formal defiance, not the opening move in a bloody massacre.

'I shall deliver your message to the housecarles and to the Lady,' I said stiffly. 'If your captain questions you say that Edgar the chamberlain makes himself responsible for its delivery. Say also that at dawn King Edward's body will be taken out for burial. It will be laid in the tomb at Westminster immediately after the High Mass of the Epiphany.'

Then I ran to tell the Lady.

It still seemed strange to be in a bower, surrounded by females. The waiting women wailed in the conventional cries of mourning that must be kept up between the death of a great lord and his burial. The Lady herself sat praying with a Norman chaplain, and occasionally did her duty by throwing back her head and joining in the screams. But when she had heard my news she sent off her attendants to wail in the great hall, and kept only one maid to help her pack her jewels. We stood by a brazier, for it was bitter cold through all that grim Christmas. The Lady looked calm and composed, and she made her plans with all the political sense and acceptance of unwelcome facts that showed her to be a true daughter of the great Earl Godwin.

'Harold is my brother,' she said with a frown, 'but he has broken the oath he swore to Duke William. That makes him worthless, nithing; as my brother Sweyn was nithing. He is no longer my kinsman, for I have kept my honour. Yet not all the Godwinssons are nithing. Tostig is true; and I, the Old Lady of England, will strive to carry out the commands of my dead lord. Therefore Harold is my enemy, as I suppose, Edgar, he is yours. Very well. What shall we do, now, tonight?'

'Tell Duke William to claim his inheritance,' I answered.

'If Harold catches us sending a messenger to Normandy we shall lose our heads. It's too dangerous. But even if Harold keeps the news from France it will reach Flanders; every day the fishermen of Kent meet the fishermen of Bruges in the Channel. So we must send the news secretly to Tostig in Flanders. I know he will work for Duke William. Who else will support us? Who are the magnates who follow Harold the forsworn usurper?'

'Ah, that's not so bad as it seems, madam.' I had been reckoning up Harold's power. 'Even if it's true that every magnate in London declared for him some may have been reluctant; and the Council that met tonight does not represent all England. Edwin and Morcar are in their governments; they will not willingly serve a Godwinsson. Earl Waltheof will be loyal to no one until he has received his father's Earldom in Northumbria. Apart from Waltheof there is no one in London who carries any weight north of Trent, unless you count the Archbishop of York.'

'Aldred is a good man, and a true Archbishop. But I can't see armies following his lead,' said the Lady with a wan smile. 'So the thanes north of Trent are not committed to Harold. I shall advise Tostig to land in the north.'

'And meanwhile we must get down to Winchester immediately after the funeral,' I reminded her. 'It will be difficult to remain in London without giving open support to this usurping King.'

'I can't understand why the Council made him King, even with that scoundrel Stigand to lead them,' said the Lady. 'All England knows that Harold has commended himself to William; he took oath on the greatest relics in Normandy. Do the English *want* to be ruled by a perjurer?'

'Stigand and Gyrth and Leofwin want to be ruled by a Godwinsson. I suppose the others were taken by surprise, and did as they were told.' I spoke doubtfully. It was a disgraceful business, and I felt as sad and distressed as the Lady.

'When they have thought it over they will acknowledge their shame,' she said stoutly. 'Meanwhile we shall go quietly to Winchester, and hold ourselves ready to join any resistance that shows its head. At least, I suppose you will come with me, Edgar?'

'Madam, I am grateful. I have been trained as a chamberlain, and it is the only trade I know. I cannot serve this usurper, and when the Duke comes into his own he will have Normans about him. Your hall will be my home, as King Edward's hall was my home while my lord lived.'

On the next morning the holy King Edward was buried among the lamentations of his people. We lamented because he had been taken from us, not because we feared for him. He was with God, and we knew it. He had gone home.

The Lady dared not walk out of the minster before the

coronation. I saw the usurper in all his glory, the vassals of the Godwinssons crowding round to commend themselves to him. At the climax of the ceremony Stigand picked up the crown of the English to place it on the false King's head; but Harold roughly pushed him aside, and beckoned for Aldred of York to perform the rite. For all his double-dealing and treachery Stigand could not win recognition even from his accomplice in crime. When the time came for the household of the late King to swear allegiance I fell on my knees and appeared to be absorbed in prayer. Everyone knew that I had been the loved companion of King Edward, and even the Godwinsson housecarles respected my grief. So I managed to avoid the oath. I believe the Lady thought it prudent to bend the knee before Harold and wish him prosperity; but in those days an oath of allegiance was never demanded from a woman.

In the evening we left London for Winchester.

King Edward's prophecy was abundantly fulfilled. Within a year and a day all England had been ravaged by armies, and of the house of Godwin only Wulfnoth remained, the youth who had never borne arms and who still lives as a prisoner in Normandy.

The first to fall was the gallant reckless Tostig. As soon as he heard of King Edward's death he left Flanders with a few shiploads of vikings and attempted to land among the East Angles. Beaten off, he tried again farther north, until after repeated failures he found himself off the Scottish coast. There he fell in with a great fleet of Norwegians, whom Harold Hardrada was leading to the invasion of England. He joined them, I suppose because any foe of King Harold his brother was his friend. But Harold killed him on the field of Stamford Bridge.

Harold himself, Gyrth, Leofwin, and all the housecarles of the Godwinssons died gallantly at Hastings. They were brave men, who fought well and died with their wounds in front; but they had gone into battle perjured and forsworn.

After the house of Godwin had fallen a few hot-headed magnates tried to set up the child atheling, Edgar Edwardsson. But since Duke William took London no other man has called himself King of the English. There were those who tried to abolish the Kingdom altogether. It was suggested that William might keep the south-east, while the west and the north went their separate ways. But in this matter the Old Lady was able to help the rightful heir of her lord. She persuaded the men of Exeter to yield, though they had rallied round Gytha the mother of Harold. Earlier she had arranged the peaceful submission of Winchester, after the burgesses had stayed neutral during the brief war. For Harold had not dared to enter as King the old city of the Cerdingas whose crown he had usurped. Under the rule of King William the Old Lady lived peacefully in Winchester, until in the year 1075 God called her to join her husband. Her household was dispersed, and I went to be head chamberlain to the Norman Count of Winchester.

I BOUGHT A MOUNTAIN

by Thomas Firbank

This is the spellbinding story of life on a sheep farm in
the Snowdon district of Wales. Of the fight to build it
into prosperity, against every hazard of blizzard and
misadventure.

It is also a story of high adventure and climbing, including
the record-breaking race over fourteen mountains . . .

This book has been one of the biggest post-war
successes, with sales running into hundreds of
thousands. It is brilliant, enthralling, a story to delight
even the most blasé reader.

'A delightful book'   **DAILY TELEGRAPH**

NEW ENGLISH LIBRARY

THE CRUSADER'S TOMB

by A. J. Cronin

Stephen Desmonde, a graduate of Oxford, has been brought up to follow in his father's footsteps and, eventually, to succeed him as rector of Stillwater. But instead, despite all entreaties to prevent him, he chooses to become an artist in Paris.

In the face of life's despairs, privations, ostracisation and humiliation, his struggle for recognition never wavers.

A remarkable, gripping, often tender novel in the mould of A. J. Cronin's classic bestsellers.

THE NEW ENGLISH LIBRARY

NEL BESTSELLERS

T011 682	ESCAPE ON VENUS	*Edgar Rice Burroughs*	40p
T013 537	WIZARD OF VENUS	*Edgar Rice Burroughs*	30p
T009 696	GLORY ROAD	*Robert Heinlein*	40p
T010 856	THE DAY AFTER TOMORROW	*Robert Heinlein*	30p
T016 900	STRANGER IN A STRANGE LAND	*Robert Heinlein*	75p
T011 844	DUNE	*Frank Herbert*	75p
T012 298	DUNE MESSIAH	*Frank Herbert*	40p
T015 211	THE GREEN BRAIN	*Frank Herbert*	30p

War

T013 367	DEVIL'S GUARD	*Robert Elford*	50p
T013 901	THE GOOD SHEPHERD	*C. S. Forester*	35p
T011 755	TRAWLERS GO TO WAR	*Lund & Ludlam*	40p
T015 505	THE LAST VOYAGE OF GRAF SPEE	*Michael Powell*	30p
T015 661	JACKALS OF THE REICH	*Ronald Seth*	30p
T012 263	FLEET WITHOUT A FRIEND	*John Vader*	30p

Western

T016 994	No. 1 EDGE – THE LONER	*George G. Gilman*	30p
T016 986	No. 2 EDGE – TEN THOUSAND DOLLARS AMERICAN		
		George G. Gilman	30p
T017 613	No. 3 EDGE – APACHE DEATH	*George G. Gilman*	30p
T017 001	No. 4 EDGE – KILLER'S BREED	*George G. Gilman*	30p
T016 536	No. 5 EDGE – BLOOD ON SILVER	*George G. Gilman*	30p
T017 621	No. 6 EDGE – THE BLUE, THE GREY AND THE RED		
		George G. Gilman	30p
T014 479	No. 7 EDGE – CALIFORNIA KILLING	*George G. Gilman*	30p
T015 254	No. 8 EDGE – SEVEN OUT OF HELL	*George G. Gilman*	30p
T015 475	No. 9 EDGE – BLOODY SUMMER	*George G. Gilman*	30p
T015 769	No. 10 EDGE – VENGEANCE IS BLACK	*George G. Gilman*	30p

General

T011 763	SEX MANNERS FOR MEN	*Robert Chartham*	30p
W002 531	SEX MANNERS FOR ADVANCED LOVERS	*Robert Chartham*	25p
W002 835	SEX AND THE OVER FORTIES	*Robert Chartham*	30p
T010 732	THE SENSUOUS COUPLE	*Dr. 'C'*	25p

Mad

S004 708	VIVA MAD!	30p
S004 676	MAD'S DON MARTIN COMES ON STRONG	30p
S004 816	MAD'S DAVE BERG LOOKS AT SICK WORLD	30p
S005 078	MADVERTISING	30p
S004 987	MAD SNAPPY ANSWERS TO STUPID QUESTIONS	30p

NEL P.O. BOX 11, FALMOUTH, TR10 9EN, CORNWALL

Please send cheque or postal order. Allow 10p to cover postage and packing on one book plus 4p for each additional book.

Name ....

Address...

....

Title ....
(SEPTEMBER)